Music Love Drugs War

Music Love Drugs War

GERALDINE QUIGLEY

FIG TREE
an imprint of
PENGUIN BOOKS

FIG TREE

UK | USA | Canada | Ireland | Australia
India | New Zealand | South Africa

Fig Tree is part of the Penguin Random House group of companies
whose addresses can be found at global.penguinrandomhouse.com.

First published in Fig Tree 2019
001

Lyrics on p. 68 taken from 'Five Nights of Bleeding' by Dread Beat an' Blood,
by kind permission of Linton Kwesi Johnson.

The moral right of the author has been asserted

Set in 12/14.75 pt Dante MT Std
Typeset by Jouve (UK), Milton Keynes
Printed and bound in Great Britain by Clays Ltd, Elcograf S.p.A.

A CIP catalogue record for this book is available from the British Library

ISBN: 978-0-241-35413-1

www.greenpenguin.co.uk

For Thomas 'Mutts' McDermott,
our friend

There was a bar and a home and streets full of people, friends and enemies and music.

That's how she remembers it.

Everything, each drop of life, layered with a thrilling fear, a razor-edged excitement.

Yes, she thought. That's how it was.

1981

I

The Cave was invisible to outsiders. It was grubby and obscure. A passing parent might give its door a sideways glance but they never warned their teenagers away. It was off their radar.

Once a grown-up wine bar for discerning couples, it had quickly degenerated until its design as a Mexican cantina – white stucco walls and moulded vine leaves – was the only indication of that original intention. The Cave was dirty, rough, bathed inside by a dim orange light, the haunt of bikers, rockers, hippies, punks, hookers, and the occasional gay man seeking a safe place; somewhere no questions were asked. Anyone entering the bar for the first time could be forgiven for thinking they were the cleanest thing in the place. They probably were.

It was St Patrick's night and a haze of smoke clung to the ceiling. 'Hey Joe' blasted from the jukebox at the back of the room and Paddy McLaughlin sat, trapped, his big frame squeezed between the table and the wall behind. His younger sister, Elizabeth, ignored him from the other side of the table, her conversation moving between her boyfriend, Kevin Thompson, and her friend Orla. Paddy twisted painfully in his seat and shouted across the table.

'Swap seats with me, Liz.'

'Stop asking,' she said, without turning her head. 'It's not goin' to happen.'

Orla sipped demurely at a half-pint of beer, nodding as Liz continued describing the coat she was trying to persuade her mother to buy her.

'It's got these metal buttons running down the front, and big lapels.'

But Paddy wasn't done.

'It's my birthday,' he said. 'And you're smaller than me.' Shifting heavily, he shoved the table, jolting it forward an inch. The glasses on top juddered.

'Hey!' said Kevin, quickly lifting his.

At the other end of the table, Christy Meehan was drunk and lecturing on his pet subject, Vietnam. He had stolen a book from a local shop where the staff were too 'right on' to complain, and it offered new insights on the war, insights beyond the tales of experimental drug-taking he revelled in.

He stabbed at the table with his finger.

'The Vietnamese were organised, you see? But the Yanks – them boys didn't give a fuck. They only wanted to get home alive. See in Vietnam? There are tunnels everywhere.'

He swung his arm above the table, inviting them to visualise swathes of jungle and endangering the glasses that had survived Paddy's ill temper.

'The Viet Cong used them to move around the country. There's this part, about Khe Sanh, the Tet Offensive – crazy stuff. You have to read the book, Noel – Coppola based *Apocalypse Now* on it.' He paused to take a drink.

'*Heart of Darkness*,' said Noel, raising his voice over the noise. 'That's what the film's based on.' He leaned back in his chair, the loose neck of his washed-out shirt gaping around skeletal collarbones. 'Joseph Conrad – I read it at university. I didn't like it much.'

There was nothing as pleasant as using your degree to impress your less educated friends, and Noel Baxter made use of it as often as he could. But his languid, bohemian image fell apart when he opened his mouth, a broad country accent betraying his Protestant farming background.

6

Christy ignored the correction. Baxter might be older than him, he might have his own flat, but he was still a bit of a wanker sometimes.

'The Vietnamese definitely produced a better class of war,' he said, checking out the room over the top of his glass as he took another drink.

'Looks like you stole the wrong book, Meehan,' said Kevin. 'Hi, "Charlie don't surf . . ."!'

Christy laughed. '"I love the smell of napalm in the morning . . . Smells like . . . victory."'

Both could spool off a dozen lines like this: between them they had seen *Apocalypse Now* five times.

'"The horror . . . the horror . . ."' mouthed Kevin softly.

'"How you feelin', Jimmy?"' shouted Christy.

'"Like a mean motherfucker, sir!"' replied Kevin.

Suddenly, Liz stood up. 'I'm going to the toilet.' She pointed to her brother. 'Don't let him take my seat.'

'I'm coming too,' said Orla.

Moving chairs and squeezing past bodies, they made it to the girls' toilet and pushed at the door. It was held firmly closed by someone leaning against it on the other side – there was a queue.

Liz stood against the jukebox, cupping her hands over her eyes. 'They're really burning,' she said. 'I don't want to rub them.'

'Put your glass over your eye – the moisture will help,' said Orla.

'I'm not doing that,' said Liz. 'It's disgusting. This bloody mascara's running.'

She took her hands away to wipe under her eyes, then looked across the bar to the corner where their friend Sinéad was involved in a passionate session with a large biker.

'Do you think we should rescue her?' she said.

They could just about make out Sinéad's blonde curls behind his leather jacket, ponytail and muscular neck.

Orla stuck her head around the corner to have a look. 'I can't believe that – he's minging,' she said. 'Leave her.'

As several girls came out, they pushed through the open door and took their place in the dingy toilet, where someone had been sick in the sink.

There were two cubicles, both occupied, with no locks on the doors. Another girl had her hand on top of one, holding it closed for her friend inside. The cubicle beside her opened and two large biker girls came out, big-chested, in too-tight jeans. Everyone shuffled around to let them out and Orla and Liz found themselves with their backs to the sink. Liz ran the tap to clear the vomit.

'Do you have your lipstick?' she said, checking herself in the mirror. Orla reached into her handbag and handed her the plastic tube.

'I love this colour,' said Liz, smearing the scarlet cream on her lips.

When the door opened again, Sinéad bounced in, sporting a grubby denim waistcoat.

'What?' she said, as her friends rolled their eyes. 'Dave let me wear it.'

As she swung around to display the eagle, wings outstretched, sewn onto the back, she banged her elbow on the edge of the door. Liz and Orla winced, but nothing registered on Sinéad's face.

'What do you think?' she said.

'You'll probably catch something off it?' said Orla.

One of the cubicles emptied and they were next. Sinéad was too fast for them.

'I'm really busting,' she said, running into the toilet. 'Hold the door for me, Liz.'

She slammed it behind her. Obediently, Liz stood guard, her foot hooked under the door.

'Do any of yous have a tissue?' called Sinéad.

'No,' said Liz abruptly. 'You'll have to drip-dry.'

Liz read the graffitied door while she waited for Sinéad to finish, her arms folded, reviewing the scrawled genitals and biro'd phone numbers. There was a hole put through one door, stuffed with paper to keep out peering eyes. Inside, neither toilet had an actual seat, just the rusted remains of the two hinges, and only the bravest customer would consider sitting down. Most people hovered – not easy when sober and near impossible when drunk.

'You and Kevin are going with each other three months this week,' said Orla, retouching her own lips.

'How do you know that?' said Liz.

'I remember the night,' said Orla. 'It was icy. Noel slipped on the road and fell.'

'Was that three months ago?'

'Nearly to the day,' said Orla.

'Ooh, going steady,' said Sinéad sarcastically from behind the door. 'Hope you're on the pill, Liz.'

'Jesus, Sinéad, shut up!' shouted Liz. She pulled her foot away and the door swung open.

'Hi!' shouted Sinéad, pulling up her knickers and jeans. She came out, still doing up her zip. 'I was done anyway,' she said.

Liz rushed in to pee and this time it was Orla's turn to hold the door.

'Have you thought about it?' she said to Sinéad who was admiring herself in Dave's waistcoat, twisting to see the artwork on the back.

'Thought about what – the pill?'

Liz came out. 'I wouldn't even know where to get it from,' she said. 'I couldn't go to the doctor, not in our house.'

'You go to the Family Planning,' said Orla casually. Sinéad and Liz both looked at her. Sometimes Orla was full of surprises.

'How do you know that?' said Liz, but Orla only shrugged her shoulders.

'I heard it somewhere,' she said, pulling the door open to leave.

'Do you not have to go?' said Liz.

'Naw,' said Orla. 'I only came in to keep you company.'

Outside, the crowd at the table was swollen by new arrivals, friends of Paddy's, and had spread out, pressing into the next table.

'Oh, for fucksake,' said Liz, as Paddy grinned at her from what had been her seat. She stormed over, punched him on the arm, punched Kevin on the other arm, then made him move over so she could squeeze onto the seat beside him.

'It's his birthday,' said Kevin. 'He begged me.'

Orla pulled Sinéad back by the arm until they stood behind the jukebox again.

'What?' said Sinéad.

Orla pointed discreetly at the table and one of the boys, a clean-cut youth, out of place in a tweed jacket and a checked shirt. He had squeezed in beside Christy.

'It's him,' said Orla.

Sinéad looked blankly at her.

'For Godsake, Sinéad, it's Peter Harkin.'

Now Sinéad was interested and leaned forward carefully to see. 'So it is,' she said, smiling. 'What are you going to do?'

'I don't know. I can't stay here.'

'Brass it out – you didn't do anything. You went with him, you didn't see him again. That's it.'

Two months earlier, at a concert in Belfast, Orla had, to use the technical term, 'got off' with Peter Harkin on the back seat of the bus that brought the crowd back to Derry. It was an hour of fevered kissing that ended at the bus stop, but she was smitten. Oh, he was gorgeous, and Orla, for all her worldliness, was not one to go easily with anyone.

They met one more time, on an arranged date, and spent the evening walking the streets and eating chips, followed by more kissing until she had to go home. Since then, there had been radio silence as Sinéad called it.

'Mmm,' groaned Orla, chewing her nails.

'Jesus Christ, Orla! We can't stay here all night,' insisted Sinéad.

'But what's he doing here?'

'I don't know – he's talking to Christy. Come on.' Sinéad pushed her from the jukebox and back to the table, where their seats had also been taken by other drinkers.

'Budge over,' said Orla. Liz shifted her bum on the seat, enough for Orla to perch on the edge, avoiding eye contact with Peter.

'Talk to me, Liz, for Christsake,' she whispered.

'What's wrong?' said Liz.

'That's the boy I went with on the bus, talking to Christy.'

'Hey, he's Paddy's friend from school. He's a lovely fella.'

Peter must have heard. He looked at Liz, then got up and started to come over. Orla put her head down, trying not to look or smile, or do anything that would make it seem as though she remembered him.

'How's Liz?' said Peter. 'All right, Orla – long time, no see.'

'All right, Peter,' said Orla quietly.

He crouched down beside them. 'This is the first time I've been in here. Your Paddy's in some form.'

Paddy and Christy were arguing across the table a few feet away from them.

'Does your da still give people a hard time when they call for him?'

He touched Orla on the arm. She looked over at Sinéad – the move hadn't gone unnoticed.

'When we called for Paddy, their da would answer and he'd say, "There's no Paddy lives here." Does he still make everybody call him Elvis?'

'Sometimes, when he wants to wind him up,' said Liz.

'Watch this,' he said to Orla, and shouted, 'Hi, Elvis!' across the tables. Paddy didn't react.

'Elvis – do you want a pint?' he shouted again, louder.

Paddy looked over, registering who had called him. 'Fuck off, Harkin – aye, why not.'

'See,' said Peter, smiling at Orla. 'He's Elvis when there's a drink in it.' He went to the bar to get the promised beer.

'Aww, he's lovely,' said Liz. 'He fancies you, Orla.'

Sinéad was over immediately. Orla blushed with embarrassment and pleasure.

'What are you going to do?' said Sinéad.

'Shh, he's coming back.' Orla watched over Liz's shoulder as Peter wormed his way through the crowd. He passed the pint to Paddy, over the top of Christy's head, and came back to them, standing awkwardly beside her.

'I need another pee,' said Liz, looking at Sinéad. 'Are you coming?'

'We've just been,' said Sinéad.

Liz took her by the elbow and pulled her away.

'So, what's happening after this?' said Peter, squeezing onto the seat beside Orla.

'There's a party in a flat down the street. Do you know Noel?' she said hopefully.

'I do now,' said Peter with a grin. He sipped his drink.

Orla didn't know what to say to this and several uncomfortable seconds passed. She looked in desperation at her friends, lurking by the jukebox.

Peter nudged her with his shoulder. 'I never saw you again, not after the last night,' he said. 'I was kind of raging about that.' He ran a hand over his short, dirty-blonde hair, a sheepish look on his face.

'What – were your legs broke?' said Orla sharply. She had spent an agonising fortnight laid out on the sofa, wondering what she had done to put him off. 'What do you mean, you were raging? It was you that vanished off the face of the earth – not me.'

Peter was about to say something, but she raised her hand and silenced him before stating clearly, 'It wasn't up to me to go running after you.'

'OK,' said Peter. 'I should have made an effort.'

'An effort?' Orla's arms folded tight as she turned her back on him. 'You're some craic, hi.'

'Can I leave you home tonight?' said Peter, to the back of her head.

'No!'

The girls came back and Liz perched on Kevin's knee. Sinéad sat behind Orla and Peter. She nudged Orla in the back.

'Everything OK?' she said.

'No!' said Orla. Peter had his elbows on his knees as he looked the other way.

Sinéad turned back to Liz. 'Oh, dear,' she said.

'That girl's throwing daggers at you,' whispered Liz from her vantage point on Kevin's lap. 'I think she might be your man's girlfriend.'

Sinéad looked across to the place where she had left Dave the biker. Six or seven hairy men sat with their girlfriends, in a rough huddle. One of the women, red-haired, bursting out of an Iron Maiden T-shirt, was glaring at her. Sinéad realised that she still had the biker's colours on and Dave was nowhere to be seen.

'Shit, I forgot about him – is that her?'

'Do you know Dave the biker's girlfriend, Kevin?'

'No,' he said, turning to Sinéad. 'But you might want to get rid of the evidence – give the mouse-eater his vest back.'

'I don't know where he is,' said Sinéad. Very slowly, she shrugged it off her shoulders, letting it fall to the floor.

'Who calls him the mouse-eater?' said Liz, as Sinéad kicked at the waistcoat until it was under the table, out of sight.

'He's the man who found the mouse on the floor in here and ate it for a bet,' said Kevin.

'That's not true,' said Liz.

'I'm going to boke,' said Sinéad.

'It is,' insisted Kevin. 'The mouse was lying under that seat.' He pointed to the table around the corner.

'Somebody dared him, so he held it up by its tail and dropped it into his mouth. It was a Saturday afternoon. All you could hear were bones crunching.'

A shudder convulsed Liz and Sinéad.

'Was it alive?' asked Liz.

'No, it was dead.'

'And you had your tongue stuck in that same mouth, Sinéad,' said Liz.

'Lovely.'

Kevin and Liz left the party early and were standing in the derelict building that had become a kind of home to them, en route to Liz's house. It offered privacy and darkness, a place that belonged to no one else.

'I have to go,' said Liz. Kevin wasn't listening.

'Kevin,' she said, pushing him away. 'I have to go.'

Her bare stomach caught the chill of cold air as he reluctantly took his hand from beneath her jumper.

'What time is it?' said Kevin, before returning to the curve of her neck with a muffled, 'Do we have to?'

'Yes, we do. I said I wouldn't be late.'

Taking her hand, he helped her over the stony ground and they walked through the back streets, their steps guided by light from the windows of the surrounding houses that cast yellow squares on the ground.

'Do you want me to meet you tomorrow?' said Kevin.

Liz was eighteen and still finishing her A levels at the local tech. Kevin, seven years older, had left school when he was fifteen.

'I was thinking about going to the library,' said Liz.

They walked in silence, climbing the hill towards her home, past houses that had been built a century before.

'Do you know . . .?' said Kevin. She sighed inwardly and waited. He always started with this when he had a nugget of information to pass on, some revelation he had come across in the paper, or on the radio – Kevin loved the radio.

'Do you know, these houses were built for Scottish dockers, so they could bring their families over here when they worked on the docks?'

He waited for her prompt to go on. 'Really?' Liz obliged.

'That's why they all have Scottish names – Glasgow Terrace, Argyle Street, Argyle Avenue.'

Liz lived in the new houses beyond these, up behind the factory and beside the school.

'So where did all the Scottish people go?' she asked.

'They married us,' he said, with a smile.

At her front door, Kevin dipped his fingers between the waistband of her jeans and her soft skin.

'Your hands are freezing,' she said, with a thrill. 'Do you want to come in?'

The thought of making conversation with her mother was enough to put Kevin off.

'No, I'll go,' he said. 'See you tomorrow.'

'OK,' said Liz. She turned the key in the door. 'See you tomorrow.'

The promise of warm skin lingered in Kevin's thoughts. He had waited for this girl longer than any other, because she was young and lovely, and worth waiting for, he hoped; so unlike the girls his own age, the single ones and the ones who were not single but were up for it anyway.

He considered her his best chance in a world that had little to offer, the hope that persuaded him from his bed some mornings. He would wait and she could take as long as she needed. He wouldn't risk this for anything, certainly not for a cheap fuck.

'Stop there, mate. Where are you going?'

Lost in his thoughts, Kevin almost collided with the heavily padded torso of a British soldier. Suddenly, there was a rifle pushed against his chest.

The rest of the foot patrol spread out behind them, taking up defensive positions as the soldier questioned Kevin's presence on the street.

He took a step back.

'Home,' he said.

'Where's that then?' asked the soldier, his accent hard, foreign.

Keeping his hands firmly in his pockets, Kevin indicated with a nod the direction he was going.

'Down there.'

'Where are you coming from?' There was a definite Liverpool twang.

'Up there.'

He nodded again, in the general direction of behind.

The soldier produced a notebook. 'Right, smart-arse – name and address?'

'Kevin Thompson, two hundred and twenty-one Carnhill.'

His tone was dry enough to irritate but not enough to entice a dig in the ribs from the end of that gun.

'Arms out.'

Kevin knew the routine and stood rigid, arms wide, legs apart. As the Brit patted him down, he watched the rest of the patrol, shadowy figures crouched in doorways along the street, keeping point behind them and up ahead. The soldier's hands rubbed briskly along his arms, down and around his chest and waist, down each leg.

Hurry up, he thought, with a sigh. This one was younger than him, early twenties, maybe. When he straightened up and they stood face to face, he fell only slightly shorter than Kevin in height. Two grey eyes looked out from a face smeared with black camouflage.

As a final flourish to the search, the soldier stuck two fingers in the top left pocket of Kevin's jacket, pulling out a foil packet creased from age and lack of use. Looking at Kevin he smiled, then slid the condom away again.

'We'll let you keep that,' he laughed, patting the pocket and stepping back. Kevin was free to go.

He walked on a few steps, his head down, then turned to watch them.

'Liverpool' gave the signal. The squaddies on the other side of the street sprinted across and the patrol resumed.

The rearguard moved cautiously past him: the radio operator, burdened with a bulky backpack, a thin antenna protruding and swaying above his head; the final soldier, walking backwards, swinging his rifle from left to right as he scanned the street, bringing up the rear.

The retreating soldier raised his weapon to his shoulder and took aim, keeping Kevin in the rifle's sight until he turned the corner and Kevin turned for home.

★

Liz was immediately enfolded in the lights, the noise, the smells of the house. Her mother was still up, ironing a mountain of clothes in the kitchen and listening to a story on the radio. The air hung with the scent of the hot iron on cotton, the almost indistinct scent that was as much a sensation: hot metal, the slightly scorched cover of the ironing board, the lingering essence of washing powder enhanced by steam, dampening the fabric – an ironing air.

'Are you in?' her mother called. Mammy was settling herself for the night. Only Paddy was expected now.

'Where were you?' she asked as Liz came through the living room and into the kitchen.

'Just out,' said Liz.

'Did you see your brother?' She had five, but Liz knew which one her mother meant.

'Yes,' she said. As they left the party, Paddy was sitting on the floor, rolling a joint. But her mother didn't need to know that. 'I think he's staying in Noel's, so don't worry.'

She went into the living room and sat in the armchair opposite the television. Johnny was slumped in the other one, his leg hooked over the arm.

'Where were you?' he said. Four years older than her, he thought he had the right to know.

'Out,' said Liz, not in the mood for an interrogation.

'With your man, Thompson?'

'What's it to you?'

'He was three years ahead of me in school – I remember him,' said Johnny, not trying to disguise his disapproval. He made every effort to let her know, at every opportunity.

'And what?' said Liz. Johnny had never had a girlfriend, would never leave the comforts of the family home. He had no life.

'Where's me daddy?'

'Out,' he said.

It was after midnight. With a sigh, Liz got up again.

'I'm going to bed, Mammy,' she shouted, already halfway up the stairs. 'Night night.'

She lay under the covers and thought about school the next day, and Kevin. Something in the back of her mind niggled at her, making her feel sad; so what if he was older? It didn't matter to her. Although sometimes she wondered why was he with her, when older girls could offer more?

The sex stuff scared her and though she tried to ignore it, she knew that he wouldn't wait for ever. She wasn't consciously saving herself, the way the nuns in school suggested they all would, or should, for her husband – like they'd know anything.

She pulled the blankets up to her chin. She was eighteen. This was coming, and she would have to decide about it. But the idea, the physicality of it . . . she rolled onto her side and turned off the bedside light.

'I'll have to do it sometime,' she said, her voice muffled by the blanket. 'But not yet.'

Not yet.

The following morning, Christy woke up on the sofa in Noel's front room. He reached over the side, lifted a half-full can of Harp and took a drink to loosen his tongue from the roof of his mouth. He had pulled his leather jacket over his shoulders during the night, but there wasn't much warmth from it.

Lighting a cigarette, he tried to piece together the end of the evening, raising himself on one elbow to see the chaotic room. Paddy lay under the window, his arm wrapped around the waist of some girl, his head resting on a bundled-up coat. Empty beer cans littered the floor. An ashtray had fallen from the coffee table, spreading butts, ash and matches across the filthy carpet. The room glowed red, as early sunlight forced its way through the stained curtains.

He lay down again, trying to ignore the queasy hangover pangs in his stomach and the pains in his head, but it was no good. Finally, he went to the kitchen to put water in the kettle. Noel was nowhere to be seen, and the debris of the party continued into the kitchen where a bin had keeled over, spilling cans and empty cider bottles on the grubby floor. An empty whiskey bottle sat by the sink; Christy put it to his mouth, seeking the last drops, but it had been drained.

Dozens of people had crammed into the small flat and the joints had circulated through the crowd quicker than he could smoke them. The place thrummed to deep bass reggae and people sat or stood everywhere, talking, drinking. Couples, new and old, vanished into the bedroom, returning later crumpled and smeared.

As he stood watching the kettle fill, he could still see Orla, pressed against the sink, wrapped around that straight-looking friend of Paddy's. Great craic.

With three teas in hand, Christy went back into the living room and nudged Paddy with his foot.

'McLaughlin, wake up.'

Paddy muttered something and rolled against the girl, who turned out to be Sinéad. She raised her head, hitting it on the underside of the table.

'Ow, shit, what was that?' she said, rubbing the sore spot.

'Do you want tea, Sinéad?' said Christy, putting the mugs on the table.

As they struggled into a sitting position, Sinéad looked at Paddy. 'We were just talking, right?'

'I don't know,' said Paddy, getting to his feet and slumping quickly into the chair, still perfectly drunk. Sinéad stayed on the floor. 'What time is it?' she asked.

'After eight, I think,' said Christy. 'Here, have your tea.'

But Sinéad was on her feet, frantically searching for a missing shoe and repeating, 'I'm dead, I'm dead.' She found the shoe, put it on and was out of the flat before they could stop her.

'Did you get off with her last night?' said Christy.

'Not as far as I remember, but who knows? And what about you and our Liz? You were well into her.'

Christy remembered Liz laughing. He maybe even remembered trying to persuade her to go upstairs with him, when she passed him on her way to the toilet.

'I was stupid drunk.'

'Tell that to Kev, 'cause he was watching you. They didn't hang around, did they?'

'Throw us a fag, for fucksake, and shut up,' said Christy.

If Kevin and Christy's friendship was marred by anything, it was their continual, competitive sparring; their desire to outdo each other made for some entertaining nights, and some violent disagreements. Christy was in his final year at the local boys' grammar, but he still saw himself as Kevin's equal in every sense. This flirtation with Liz was his latest challenge.

Paddy gave him a cigarette.

'I wouldn't push that button, Christy – he looked seriously pissed off last night,' he said.

But Christy wasn't listening. He was on his knees, studying the books on Noel's shelf. He pulled one from the collection.

'*Sombrero Fallout*,' he read aloud, sitting back on his heels. With the cigarette between his lips, he sat down to read the blurb at the back of the slim novel. 'What is this?' he said, flicking through the pages.

'Let me see it,' said Paddy, trying to snatch it from him.

'Wait a minute,' said Christy, still reading. 'Look – there's only three words on this page.' He flashed the book at Paddy. 'I might take this,' he said.

21

'Noel won't like that,' said Paddy. 'He's my heart broke about his *Freak Brothers* comic – I keep forgetting to give it back to him.'

'You have it?' said Christy, looking up from the page. 'That's not just a comic, Paddy – it's really rare. And I've been waiting to read it for weeks.'

He got to his feet, pulled on his coat and shoved the book into his pocket.

'I'll leave him a note,' he said. 'Are you ready to go?'

They stuck two Rizla papers together and Christy scrawled a brief note, *'Took your book,'* then left the flat, stopping at the bakery on the corner to buy four sausage rolls. They ate them as they walked. Red sauce ran between their fingers and down the front of Paddy's coat.

At the end of William Street, they paused and reflected on the smouldering remains of a Transit van and someone's precious Cortina: two scorched carcasses, stretched across the road, slumped on the steel rims of their melted wheels with smoke and ash still rising around them.

2

Paddy lay on his back, looking at Ian Curtis's pale, sombre face.

The slats on the bed above him were permanently bowed by the weight of Gene's bulky body and curved down unevenly towards him like crooked floorboards. Lying under the blankets in the dim light, he was reluctant to move. Ian stared into the distance, mic grasped in one clenched fist, and, once again, Paddy tried to comprehend the singer's death at the age of twenty-three, hanged in his own kitchen when he had everything going for him – it was all to live for. Apparently not.

The photo was starting to yellow. He had cut it from the pages of the *New Musical Express*, and a rip had appeared along one corner, where the soft newspaper had begun to disintegrate. Reaching up, he moved the tack to pin it back in place, then ran his finger around the Anarchy sign, scored into the wood with a black biro, and picked at the grey lump of hardened chewing gum.

Five brothers had shared this bedroom, as boys and men, until Jerry, Carl and Gene married their girlfriends in quick succession, leaving Johnny and Paddy with the pick of three sets of free-standing double bunks.

It never occurred to his parents to dismantle the beds, just as it never occurred to them to take away the extra bunk; it was always there, never used but kept in readiness. Perhaps Bernie expected her boys to return some day; abandon wife and wains for the comfort of their mother? Perhaps she believed there was a remote chance of another one?

The beds gave the room the look of a prison cell, like *Cool Hand Luke* but without the good weather. The atmosphere was never light or airy, despite the two large windows that looked onto the street. The dark wooden bed frames, the brown-and-orange bedspreads, killed any light that filtered through to reach the blue linoleum floor. A lingering scent of farts and antiseptic, accumulated over the years, was woven into the fabric of the walls.

Paddy reached over to the windowsill where he had left his tobacco and papers. He rolled a cigarette, lit it and lay back on the pillow, flicking ash into an ashtray balanced on his chest. As he smoked, he thought about the night before.

Christy had stayed for dinner, lured to Paddy's home by the thought of Bernie's spuds. They were listening to records, passing a joint between them as they lay on parallel bunks. The smell of dinner, cooking below, drifted up the stairs; cabbage and sausages and rich gravy.

'I'm starving,' said Christy.

'You can stay if you like – she always makes too much,' said Paddy. He went to the landing and shouted.

'Mammy, is it OK if Christy gets his dinner here the night?'

'That's all right,' said Bernie, from the living room. 'It's ready now, so you'd better come down.'

'See, I told you it would be OK,' said Paddy.

'Thanks, Mrs McLaughlin,' said Christy as they walked through the living room to the kitchen where they found Johnny at the table, reading the paper, and Liz preparing the potatoes.

Bernie and Jim sat, side by side, on the sofa, watching the news.

'You're grand, Christy,' said Bernie, trying not to look too closely at the state of the boy. He was a looker, for sure, but thin. He needed a good dinner inside him.

No mother in the house, she thought, getting up to put the dinner out.

Christy watched Liz standing over a huge pot of buttery mash, to which she added splashes of milk and liberal sprinkles of salt.

'Look at you, all domesticated,' he said.

'I wouldn't go that far,' said Bernie, lifting a sausage from the pan with a fork and dropping it onto the nearest plate. 'You'll send her to town for a loaf of bread and she'll come back with a bunch of daffodils – she'd need to buck up her ideas.'

Christy snorted with laughter, then put his head down as Liz shot him a savage look.

The McLaughlins, Jim and Bernie – the Teddy Boy and the Good Girl.

After twenty-seven years together, each kept to their role: Bernie set the rules and Jim kept the faith, in the form of a Brylcreemed quiff and a record collection in the bottom of the hot press.

They met when he was the coolest guy in the dance hall; he worked at it, getting his hair just right, perfecting his hunched-over 'James Dean' stance.

His cousin Jim (their common grandfather was James, and so every branch of the family had at least one Jim), who had emigrated to America, sent him records that other people couldn't get, from Memphis mostly where he worked as a store man on a farm; rock and roll platters made of heavy vinyl with the Sun label's yellow cockerel in their centre. The songs made his stomach lurch and came accompanied by visions of long cars and dry, dusty streets.

He had stalked the shadowy edges of the dance floor and saw Bernie, small and neat, with her dark hair curled and clipped to one side and her skirts as voluminous as she could afford and her mother could make. He walked across the floor and asked her, 'Do you want to dance?'

After that it was every weekend, jiving on the dance floor, kissing in the dark, between stacks of crates behind the hall. He bought her a mineral to sip while the band took a break, and sat with her instead of the other men, smoking a cigarette, his arm draped around her shoulders.

After much searching, he found a job and proposed within a week. 'Yes,' said Bernie, without hesitation. When she told her mammy, they both cried.

The babies started coming within a year of the wedding and it was then that Bernie realised the extent of Jim's musical passions, because he had vowed that any child of his would have a great name, a name of significance, something to live up to and inspire.

Their firstborn, a boy, they named Jerry in tribute to Jim's hero, bad boy Jerry Lee Lewis. Bernie told her mother and the priest that it was short for Gerard. But at the christening, Jim made sure that the origin of the name was no secret when he announced, by the font, that his son was to be called Jerry Lee Lewis McLaughlin. The priest mentioned that it wasn't exactly a saint's name, but Jim got his way: the child was Jerry Lee Lewis McLaughlin or there would be no christening, that day or any other.

Jim had many heroes and the next child, also a son, was Carl (Perkins). Bernie didn't mind so much; it sounded like a Hollywood cowboy.

In the year that followed she gave birth to yet another boy, and now she was faced with a choice; she could accept little blue-eyed Gene Vincent or face another font-based debacle.

So she said nothing and longed for a girl.

It was not to be. Gene was followed by Johnny and then Elvis Patrick – the baby was born on St Patrick's Day.

When Liz arrived, to the relief of her mother, Jim was stumped until it occurred to him that Priscilla was a nice name. But enough was enough, and this time, Bernie stood her ground.

'That wain will be called Elizabeth, for my mother. That's her name, Jim, not Priscilla, not Betty Lou – aye, that's right – and I know the way you're thinking. There will be no second name.'

Recognising defeat when it stood in front of him, in the form of his wife's dead mother, Jim could only submit. Elizabeth it was.

'Here,' said Bernie, handing Liz a plate piled high with food. 'Take you that in to your father.'

Liz held the hot plate in a tea towel and carried it to Jim, who was still on the sofa, immersed in the latest hunger-strike news.

'I don't know where this is going to end,' he said quietly, taking the plate from her hand without looking at her.

Liz glanced at the screen and said nothing, before going back to the table to sit and eat with the boys.

Dinner was over, and Paddy and Christy went for a walk, talking and smoking, whiling away an otherwise dull Monday evening.

In the centre of town, a man stopped them in the street. They couldn't see his face, but he clearly wanted something.

'Give us a light, hi?' he asked.

It was risky, since 'Give us a light' meant one of two things: either a straightforward request to light a cigarette, or a threat, the precursor to a slap in the mouth.

Paddy weighed up the situation, before pulling a matchbox from his pocket and taking out a match. He struck it and held it out to light a cigarette. The flame lit up the stranger's face; he was eighteen, maybe nineteen, the same age as Paddy. There was no cigarette.

'I meant the box, if that's OK? We're trying to get something going,' he said.

Paddy thought he looked vaguely familiar: they might have been at the same school or passed in the street, too often to remember. Reluctantly, he handed the box over, the slap in the mouth seeming more likely if he was to stand and argue over a box of Swan Vestas.

Christy stood back and watched. Neither he nor Paddy were the fighting kind – more the give-them-what-they-want-and-run-away kind – and the two joints they had rolled and smoked left them softened like happy drunks, without the reflexes to put up any kind of defence if one was called for. And in this tense city, there was no need for another potential confrontation; the grumble of a riot echoed a street away from where they stood handing over their matches to a stranger.

The fella turned.

'Here, try these,' he shouted, throwing the matchbox at two figures squatting at the base of a doorway. Littlewoods, the store, full of clothes, food and birthday cards, was about to be burnt – again.

One of the hunkered men held a plastic bottle full of liquid. He was pouring it gently under the shutter, through a gap where the metal grille met the concrete pavement and where they had pushed a piece of rag.

The rich smell of petrol rose around them and the liquid ran down the shutter, along the ground and back in the direction of the arsonists' legs. It bubbled against the plastic soles of their shoes, splashing the hems of their jeans. As one tried to push the flooding liquid back under the door with his foot, the other frantically fumbled with a lighted match, flicking it at the puddle. It was promptly caught by a swift breeze and extinguished.

After watching this sad attempt at destruction repeated twice more, Christy and Paddy walked on.

'The only thing them boys will set alight is themselves,' said Paddy.

There were eight thousand men and women unemployed in the city, but that wasn't the reason for the riot that had kicked off around the corner. It wasn't why the three men in their anoraks were burning a business and no one was trying to stop them. It was more fundamental than that – more tribal. In a prison near Belfast, the Republican hunger strike was in its second month.

As they turned a corner, the lower part of the street ahead was dark and quiet, curving towards the violence along a pathway littered with debris and rubbish, and splashed with dried paint. 'Do you want to go back?' said Paddy. It sounded fairly fierce, up ahead.

'Wise up,' said Christy, walking on.

They reached the corner at the other end. Christy looked left, then right. 'It's not too bad,' he said.

To the right, two army vehicles sat side by side, their doors open wide. A grey police jeep was parked beside them. Together, the three Land Rovers closed the road to any traffic brave enough to try and enter the Bogside. The helmeted heads of the army and RUC could be seen moving behind them, happy to withstand the barrage of whatever the fifty or so combatants in the street had to throw at them.

Suddenly, Christy ran across the road and picked up a brick.

'Here,' he shouted, throwing it to Paddy, who caught it awkwardly in his arms. Then he picked up a second one and ran into the road, throwing the brick at the Land Rover barricade, before searching the ground for another.

Paddy ran across, swinging the stone with both hands. He hurled it as hard as he could, laughing when it hit the ground not five feet away. The crowd surged around them. Caught in the energy, he reached for a plank of wood and threw that, watching it sail through the air and land, nearer the mark, right in front of the shielded enemy.

Soon they were both sweating. Paddy paused, doubled over, his hands on his knees. They had come to the fight unprepared. His overcoat and jumper were heavy, and he had a stitch. He was also, crucially, aware that the rioters around them had their faces covered with scarves and masks, while he and Christy were easily recognisable without even a handkerchief to cover their identity.

'This is a mistake,' he said, looking for Christy to tell him so.

The energy of the fight had dissipated. The Guildhall chimed ten o'clock. There he was, talking to a couple of lads not far away, even easier to pick out in his leather biker jacket. A huddle of women walked, arm in arm, along the pavement on the other side of the street; it was the bingo crowd, heading for the bus home. Suddenly, there was a rattle of gunfire. The women grabbed each other and ran, grasping their handbags. A cheer went up from the boys in the road.

Paddy ran over to Christy. 'Hey, me and you are out of shape,' he said. 'This is hard work.'

'I'm going home,' Christy said. 'I've school in the morning.'

'All right, college boy,' laughed Paddy.

'Patrick, aren't you meant to sign?'

It was eleven o'clock. Jumping out of bed, he stood in his underpants and gave himself a long, satisfying stretch. Then he pulled on jeans, T-shirt and jumper and sat on the bed to put on his shoes and socks.

He reached under the bed, feeling for the tin caddy where he kept his savings, a few quid each fortnight that would, one day, get him across the water, and a round nugget of cannabis.

Leaving the money, he took the dope and pushed it firmly to the bottom of his jeans pocket, then ran downstairs, two steps at a time.

In the kitchen, Bernie gave him a piece of toast and a mug of tea. She looked up at her youngest son, licked her thumb and rubbed at a smudge of dirt on his round cheek. Then she tried to smooth the tuft of dark hair at the back of his head.

'You haven't even washed your face,' she said despairingly. 'What were you at last night?'

'I'm nineteen, Mammy – you do know that, don't you?'

'I'll keep asking until you start acting like it,' she said, gathering a load of clothes for the twin-tub. But Paddy, coat half on, mouth full of bread, had disappeared through the door. He slammed it behind him. His mother flinched as she felt the house vibrate.

3

The concert, in an art gallery, had attracted a lot of attention.

Anyone who could string two chords together on a guitar, had a friend with a drum kit, and the nerve to sing in front of people, gave themselves a name and called themselves a band. Half of them were friends, the other half were people they sort of knew. For some, tonight was the first time they would entertain a crowd.

'What does this look like?' said Sinéad, pulling on yet another top. This time she had changed her red stud earrings for large silver hoops she had bought in the market the Saturday before. The woollen sweater, with its broad grey and blue stripes, fitted neatly at the waist, and the sleeves just met the tops of her wrists: it was one size too small and it suited her.

Orla turned her head to see Sinéad's skinny bum, twisting in the reflection of the mirror.

'That looks great,' she said. Her interest had waned after the third change of clothes and now she lay across the bottom of Sinéad's bed, her feet on the covers and her arms behind her head, looking at a crack in the ceiling and thinking about Peter.

Last night had been their third date; proper dates, that didn't involve her hanging around the bar at the end of the night, waiting for him to notice her again and leave her home. They went to the pictures and he paid; they met up for a walk when the evening was warm, and the sky was light, after the clocks went forward. He held her hand.

And last night, Peter arranged to babysit for his sister. They curled up on the sofa, watched TV and kissed. As the night went on, she let him put his hand down inside her jeans and, although she felt kind of guilty, like it had gone too far, if she was honest it was strange and exciting. She had spent today in a haze of blissed-out imaginings. She really liked him.

This was her first proper boyfriend. The boys at the youth club, when she was thirteen, didn't count – just stupid wains. Half of them didn't know how to brush their teeth, never mind kiss a girl. Those small boys, with their wide parallel trousers, short enough to show their skinny ankles sticking out from broad, black brogues, their hands dug deep into their trouser pockets or their orange-lined parkas. They sucked on butts and tried to look hard, standing apart from the girls, huddled together. Until someone sent his friend over to say, 'My friend really likes your friend.'

There had been boys as she got older: those she liked for a while until they irritated her, and she dumped them after a day or two; those who finished with her in the same way, but were easily forgotten after an hour of mourning.

Then there was the one she went with one night but, in the cold light of day, thought, 'Good God, no . . .' That had been a fun fortnight, avoiding him until he got the message that it was not going to happen again.

'I'm changing these jeans.' Sinéad rummaged through the pile of clothes on the bottom of the bed, pulling out a pair that differed from those she was wearing only by the width of the legs; these were tighter, the kind that end up inside out when you take them off. She lay on the bed beside Orla, flattening her already flat stomach and pulling at the zip as she held her breath.

There was a light knock and Liz's head appeared around the door.

'Your mammy said to come up,' she said, out of breath from

the run upstairs. She threw herself on top of the clothes and surveyed the mess that was Sinéad's room. 'So, you still love Adam then, Sinéad?' she said.

One wall of the room was dedicated to the magnificent Adam Ant, from his *Kings of the Wild Frontier* phase to the current 'dandy highwayman' ensemble. The wall was a patchwork of photos torn from *Jackie* and taped to the wallpaper. Several, Liz noticed, were stained red with lipstick; there were little scarlet puckers on Adam's lips. Sinéad paused, mid-eyeliner, and looked at the wall.

'I'm besotted, but he doesn't know I exist – it's so sad, Liz. What am I going to do with him?' She returned to the precise task of getting a clean black line on the inside of her lower lid.

'So?' said Liz, nudging Orla. 'How was last night?'

'I think I'm besotted too,' said Orla.

'So it was good then?'

'His sister's house is lovely,' said Orla.

Her friends laughed. 'Right, that's what you did all night – admire the decor?' said Sinéad.

'No,' laughed Orla, embarrassed by their interest. 'It was great. He said he'd meet us up the town. What time is it starting at?'

'First band's on at eight,' said Liz. 'What are we waiting on?'

'Her,' said Orla, rolling her eyes in the direction of Sinéad, who was backcombing her hair into a rough beehive.

'I'll be five minutes,' said Sinéad, ignoring the bored tone. 'Let me brush my teeth.'

Liz made space on the bed by pushing more clothes onto the floor.

'Me mammy's still fighting with Paddy for throwing stones – it's nearly every night. She says she can smell the rioting off his clothes. He was shouting that he's leaving to go to England and she's all, "Over my dead body."'

34

It was true. In the intervening weeks since that first night, Paddy and Christy had caught the rioting bug and they weren't alone. The hunger strike continued and the young men of the city were gripped by an urgent need to get involved. They turned out in higher numbers and took greater risks as each day passed.

'What's that about?' said Orla, sitting up on the bed. 'I don't get it, Liz – they never cared before.'

Liz shrugged. 'I think he's bored. If I was a boy I'd probably do the same.' She stood to examine herself in the mirror. 'I'm thinking of getting a fringe,' she said. 'Look.'

She pulled a strand of hair forward from the back of her head, and spread the fine dark hair over her forehead, turning to Orla. 'What do you think?'

'It makes you look like your mother,' said Orla, lying down again. This boy thing, this need to fight, irritated her. 'It's all that "White Riot" crap,' she said, following the crack in the ceiling until it reached the wall. 'Anyway, I thought the whole point of us was, we didn't believe in the Provos?'

Liz let her hair fall and sat down on the bed again.

They listened to Sinéad in the bathroom, rinsing her mouth, spitting out, the water running into the sink. 'Hi, Liz,' she called. 'Do you remember Deirdre Doherty that sat behind you in school?'

'Aye,' said Liz, picking a shirt off the floor and folding it. Deirdre was a plump girl with thick red hair. Never had a pen with her and was always borrowing one from Liz. 'Why?'

'Pregnant . . . apparently.'

'Nooo . . . really? Who to?' said Liz, stopping mid-fold to listen.

'Don't know,' said Sinéad. 'I never heard that part.'

Orla and Liz looked at each other. Once, in the toilet in the Cave, Liz heard a girl, an older girl, a woman really, talking to one of her friends. She thought she might be pregnant. She said she would go to England, if she was. Liz thought that she meant to have the baby over there. But Orla told her it meant going over to get an abortion. Liz was uncomfortable just knowing someone who knew about this stuff – not Orla, but the girls in the toilet.

Of course, like all of Orla's acquired knowledge, she had 'read about it somewhere', probably a magazine her mother had. *You wouldn't read that in* Ireland's Own, *that was for sure,* thought Liz. *Ireland's Own* was the only magazine Bernie ever bought.

'Are you two ready?' said Sinéad, standing expectantly in the doorway. 'Come on!'

The gallery was full of sweaty men throwing each other around the floor. Onstage, the band thumped out a deep bass line and heavy drums, all a bit Siouxsie, a bit Gang of Four. It was ten o'clock and Kevin hadn't arrived; Liz was not a happy girl.

She was about to leave when she saw him coming down the steps at the gallery door. He didn't look drunk, but agitated. He stopped to talk to Noel, who pointed her out to him, and came straight over.

'Where were you?' she said, immediately angry.

'I got held up.' He tried putting his arms around her, but she shrugged him away and pushed past him. 'I'm going home.'

'Come on, Liz. I'm sorry. I'm here now.' He could feel the night slipping away, and he needed it to be a good one. He had to retrieve it, to tell himself that it was all here, all OK. 'You weren't on your own. Paddy's here, and Orla and Sinéad.'

She was starting to relent; it was stupid to be angry, childish that she felt like crying. He put his arms around her.

'What happened – where were you?' she said.

'In the house,' said Kevin. 'I fell asleep.'

*

36

He had been standing at the bus stop, with the warm sun on his face: blinding as it dipped towards the west. A man was walking along the street with a suggestion of a stoop to the shoulders; Kevin felt a shiver of familiarity as he came towards him.

It was Brendan, Ciaran's brother. They were very alike: the slight build, the same dishevelled brown hair, the same eyes. Brendan was fourteen when his brother was killed on active IRA service. Kevin hadn't seen him since, but he knew him immediately. He was expecting him to nod and walk past, but Brendan stopped at the bus stop and spoke to him.

'How's things, Kevin?'

'All right, Brendan. What about yourself?'

It's like looking at him.

'Not bad.'

There was silence until Brendan spoke again, friendly, wanting to chat.

'I think the last time I saw you properly was at our Ciaran's funeral – it's six years this summer, you know?'

'I remember,' replied Kevin, not knowing what to say next. He needn't have worried; it seemed Brendan had plenty to say.

'So you're into music big time, these days? I always remember you and our Ciaran, playing records in our house, in his room – I used to sit on the stairs, listening.'

Kevin smiled, remembering the tussle at the door as Ciaran stopped Brendan entering the bedroom they shared. Brendan would wait, at the halfway point on the stairs, until they left to go out on the prowl.

'You were involved then too, weren't you? You did everything together,' said Brendan. Kevin smiled and said nothing.

Where was this going? Even in known company, some things were not discussed. But the tone of the conversation had changed. With little tact Brendan began.

'Had you thought about signing up again, with the hunger strike and all?'

There was no stopping him.

'Seriously though, we need everybody we can get right now. Would you not think about rejoining?'

'What do you mean, "we"? Are you serious?' said Kevin.

'Totally serious. It's important, Kevin – we need to support the men inside. The hunger strike is just one strategy. They can't do it on their own. The Brits think they can ignore them, so it's important we keep the pressure going on the outside. This is going the whole way and we need as many boys as possible to keep it up. Think about it, Kevin.'

He listened in silence, watching Brendan's earnest face, remembering how the fourteen-year-old boy had cried at his brother's graveside, had clung to his father, devastated and confused. He sounded like a recruiting officer, so sincere, so sure that Kevin would understand and accept what he was saying. There was no fear, no nerves, no embarrassment at this intrusion into Kevin's life, and it was this certainty that made him suddenly so angry.

'Don't give me that crap, Brendan. I listened to all that shite years ago and I fell for it then. I'm not falling for it again and I'm fucking surprised at you, after what happened to Ciaran.'

If Brendan was shocked by this, he didn't show it. 'Ciaran would have been with us one hundred per cent, if he was alive,' he said. 'He's an Irish martyr – he gave his life for his country.'

'You're wrong, Brendan,' said Kevin. 'He didn't give his life for Ireland. Ciaran was a wain and so was I. He gave his life for fuck all.' He caught his breath. 'Your Ciaran – your brother – should be here now. Not dead – here! Do you think any one of them bastards that recruited us gave one flying fuck for him after he blew himself up – really? Get the fuck out of my way.'

Brendan backed off as Kevin pushed past him. He was shaking. By the time he stopped, he found himself by the river, shaken and upset.

The Foyle stretched out on his left. The broken sheds of the derelict docks were empty and silent. Sitting down on top of a stack of rusted steel girders, he thought about what had just happened. Tears rose, and he tried to shake them off, to button down this bloody trembling in his body. The lump in his chest threatened to suffocate him with anger and fear. Across the river, the green bank of trees caught the final rays of light as the sun finally dipped behind the hills. He heard their leaves rustle in the cool breeze, and he shivered.

Sound carries across water. His father had told him that.

For many years, he had refused to think about Ciaran Rafferty. Ciaran was the one with the looks, the one all the girls wanted. They were best friends. For two years they did everything together, even briefly joining the Fianna, the youth wing of the IRA, once they decided they had had enough of being harassed in the street. The official term was that he died 'on active service', a romantic facade that glossed over his death at seventeen, two weeks after he took the oath.

When Kevin lost his friend, he lost everything for a while. He was a shadow, a stammering wreck, dragged in for regular questioning by the army, helplessly abused, confronted with photos of Ciaran, his bloodied remains – the boy he thought of as his brother. And abandoned by the organisation he had signed up to, which saw him as damaged goods.

He created a new future for himself when he discovered punk; a future that came with carefully constructed defences. A future that relied on never looking too closely at the past.

'Are you OK there, son?'

A man stood above him, looking worried. His dog sniffed around the rusted steel and lifted its leg to pee against it. Kevin looked at him, but couldn't make out his face in the now dim light.

'Aye, I'm fine,' said Kevin. He didn't want a conversation.

'Don't you be thinking about jumping, now,' the man went on, pointing to the river with the stick he held in his hand. 'There was a boy went into there after Christmas, and sure they haven't found him yet. He'll be down there by Moville, by now,' he said, moving the stick along the length of the water, as if to trace the progress of the body, swept away by currents in the direction of the village that clung prettily to the mouth of the Foyle. Kevin's eyes followed it sadly.

'I'm not jumping,' he said, smiling at the man. He forced himself to stand, and realised that he towered over him.

The stranger tugged on the peak of his flat cap, nudged the dog with his stick, and walked away, whistling softly in the night air. The dog ran behind him obediently. Kevin remained by the river for a long while, looking down into its depths, wondering what it must be like to lower yourself into the cold water and then not struggle to live.

As one group ended and another prepared to perform, music was played to fill the gap until the next live act, and the crowd milled around waiting for them to start. Paddy stood by the stage with Peter and Orla, watching them set up. Suddenly, Orla turned on him, her arms folded.

'Why are you and Christy rioting? You never did that before, so why now?'

Orla's big eyes were edged with spiky eyelashes, dark like her black hair. She looked like a very angry doll, frowning up at him.

'Why are you shouting at me?' he asked.

'Because I want to know,' she said. 'Because I thought we were different.' She waved her arm at the surrounding crowd. 'I thought we didn't do that stuff?'

She was waiting for an answer, but Paddy didn't know why.

Peter answered her before he could. 'He's doing it for the boys inside, Orla.'

Now she turned to him. 'Really, is that it?' she said.

'It's for people like our Liam,' said Peter quietly.

'Well, if that's the case, Peter, why are you not out there?' she said.

Peter was silent.

'It's just a laugh,' said Paddy.

Kevin came over to them. 'What's wrong here?' he said.

'Nothing,' said Paddy. 'Do you want to go up the street for a pint?'

'I really do,' said Kevin.

Liz wasn't happy at all about that. 'You're really going to leave me here on my own again?'

'One pint, Liz – that's all. I'll be back.'

She watched them leave. 'Night Boat to Cairo' blasted out, and Christy dragged her out to a space on the floor. They danced around and the song ended in laughter and hugging. Liz felt Christy hang on, his arms embracing her for perhaps a second too long.

'You know he fancies you,' said Sinéad when she returned to where they had been standing.

'No, he doesn't,' said Liz. 'Christy's like that with everybody.'

She watched him move through the crowd, chatting to people. She liked how he looked, his broad shoulders. Kevin was taller but hadn't that athletic frame.

Sinéad was watching her. 'Aye, right,' she said.

As the next trio of young desperados lashed out with their guitars, Christy hung around, whispering smart remarks in her ear about the people in the audience, the boys on the stage.

When Kevin came back he stood at the top of the steps, getting his bearings. He saw them through the haze of sweat and smoke, saw Liz near the front of the stage, saw her laughing as Christy whispered, saw something in her attitude, in her eyes, and he knew – bastard.

He pushed his way through to them. 'All right, Christy?' he said, not smiling. He pulled Liz close. She felt the tension in him, the threat of violence – what was wrong with him tonight?

'You decided to come back then. Did you enjoy your drink? Was it really nice?' she said, pushing him away.

'You were having fun,' said Kevin, watching Christy.

'Oh, fuck off, Kevin,' she said. 'You left me and now you have the cheek to be jealous? I'm going home.'

'Go then!'

Liz stormed away. Christy stood with his hands up, as Kevin turned on him.

'I was just being nice, mate . . . there was nothing going on. I know the score between you two.'

Kevin went after Liz, looking up and down the length of the street, but she was gone. How could the night sour so quickly?

In the choice between going after her or going back to the bar, the bar won. He turned and walked up the hill to the Cave.

4

At the end of William Street, in the early-evening lull, a dusty dry air hung below the street lights. Christy had become embroiled in the violence of the day. *'Embroiled'*, he thought. *That's a good word – like being boiled, scalded by rage.*

Across the street from where he stood, the rough wooden shape of the H-Block sign loomed, counting the days of the strike. Christy passed it every day. It played on his mind.

He knew what hunger felt like. In the culture of the big Derry family, it was a fact of life that if you didn't eat when and where you were told, then you might not eat at all. The rules were drilled into small children sent out to play in the street; if you want food in the middle of the day then you need to be home at twelve o'clock. If you want your dinner, then you'd better be home by five.

The street was quiet – it was the teatime lull. A riot might rage through day and night, but even the worst disturbance would calm to the point where the streets almost emptied, tools were downed, or bricks, and people went home in the clear knowledge that if they didn't, the food wouldn't be kept for them. It would, without a doubt, be eaten by a sibling, or more likely by a hungry da.

This wasn't Christy's life. He wasn't like Paddy and Liz, with a warm home and Mammy and Daddy always there. He lived with his father and his older brother, Martin. He was eleven when his mother died from cancer. She was thirty-two.

His father failed to cope, not only with his wife's death, but also with the needs of the two boys left to his care. As the neighbours described it, he 'took to drink', in a big way.

The house, and the boys, fell into a rapid decline and while Martin took the brunt of his father's rages at the terrible betrayal done to him by God and the universe, Christy stayed quiet in the house, or ran the streets, hoping for a few minutes' shelter in the homes of other boys. Martin might have got the fist, but Christy was ignored. And, while his brother shielded him from the violence, the empty drain in his stomach ached from a lack of food, and the cold, dirty house where his mother once was, now only served to drive her memory from him. Despair filled the hollow space.

Granny Christine had intervened when Martin turned up at her door one day and asked if he could stay. They lived with her for six months, while their father tried to drink himself into the ground. It was only when he realised he was about to lose what was left of his family that he dragged himself to seek help.

The boys came home, but life was hand to mouth, the house little more than a roof over their heads. Christy's grandmother remained his source of love and money, who bought him books at Christmas, who made him stay at school, made him study.

Yes, Christy knew what it was like, how hunger and despair went hand in hand. *They go blind in the end, the body eats itself,* he thought, reading the painted numbers. *They want to wear their own clothes.* They were boys caught up in a war. It might have been him, had he been older. What was the point of exams, when injustice burnt in the streets around him?

Leaning against the fence, he sucked on a butt and looked from the sign to the surrounding street and the wreckage of a month of running battles; burnt-out cars, rusted from the rain, pavements mined and used as ammunition, their broken slabs misplaced, strewn around, to be lifted and thrown, again and again. And glass, shattered glass everywhere. He pulled on the roll-up again, but it was cold.

Fifty-two days, that's what the sign said. No one was backing down in this stand-off. They were entering Holy Week and the violence was as bad as anyone had seen.

Bobby Sands was an elected member of the Westminster Parliament and still the strike went on. Others joined the hunger strike in quick succession; there was a continuum of suffering. Caught in the maelstrom, Christy and Paddy had gone from occasional stone throwers to full-on rioters, battling in the streets.

Last night, and this afternoon, saw a fierce street war played out throughout the city.

In the centre of town, the smell of freshly ignited petrol hung in the air, soaked into the fabric of the street, into concrete, wood and metal, until it seemed the air itself would explode, with only a single spark.

Bottles and bricks had rained on the defensive positions of the army and police, five minutes from where he now stood, smoking. The night before, he had listened to the echoes from the surrounding buildings – dull thuds, as missiles slammed the trundling heavy armour of the Pigs, grinding across roads, over pavements and through stretches of wasteland. One swerved into the centre of the mob, scattering it down laneways and over walls.

Don't get caught – it means three months inside, if you do.

An impromptu Molotov cocktail bar was operating in an alleyway behind the shops. Glass bottles that once held lemonade were filled with petrol, syphoned from parked cars, and laced with sugar or washing powder to add a viscous quality. Ragged wicks were lit and then, with a hand on the base of the bottle and an arm held wide of the body, they were hurled into the air.

Flames trailed and dipped, then glass shattered, spilling fire across the ground. Plastic shields were torched, the bonnet of a jeep engulfed in a splatter of burning fuel.

The response from the military came in plastic: stubby, hard bullets that slammed their target, bruising, breaking bones, leaving a trademark red circle on skin; a tactical weapon for crowd control, a non-lethal response, but not to a human head at close range. Of course, eighteen-year-olds are both invisible and indestructible, and dodging bullets was part of the skill set of a practised rioter.

Getting the bullet that hit you, to keep as a trophy – that was another.

Paddy was the reckless one, the one at the front of the crowd, itching for the first reaction, throwing the first missile. He walked home elated, laughing.

'You're a madman, McLaughlin,' Christy had said. For the briefest of moments, he wondered, *What the fuck are we doing?*

It was getting dark now. The '*52 days*' was dimly lit. He was hungry and thought about calling on his granny – she always had something for him, a pound, a good plate of dinner. But if he went there, he'd never get out again.

He felt in his pocket for money, but found his remaining tobacco and matches. Rolling another slim fag, he sat on the kerb and waited for it to kick off again.

5

Kevin was careful about friends.

Those he had, like Paddy and Noel, he kept at a distance. It didn't pay to invest too much in anyone. He trusted Liz, yet even she didn't know everything about him. So, when Peter Harkin became a fixture in their small circle, he kept a civil distance.

On the morning when this changed, he walked through the rain to the record shop, under a sky thick with grey clouds that hung low enough to touch. His head ached from lack of sleep and the bad dreams that coloured his mood.

Behind the counter, Mike the hippy drank coffee from a chipped Led Zeppelin mug and watched the rain run down the window. It was Thursday; he had served no one so far and his morning had been disturbed only by the postman. The door dinged. He watched, over the rim of his mug, as Kevin came in and stood inside the door, shaking the rain from his hair.

The shop smelled of paper and plastic, the covers of a thousand albums, warmed in their wooden stands by a single gas heater – the best smell in the world. Water ran off him, forming in puddles around his feet. He pulled his tobacco pouch from his pocket, wiped the condensation from it. Some bleak folk/rock tune, almost painfully offensive, filled the air; 'whimsical', it would have been described as, back in the day of long hair and moustaches; 'Tolkienesque'.

'What's that shite you're playing, Mike?

'Jethro Tull . . . it's not shite,' drawled Mike. His thick,

47

southern-states-of-America accent stretched the vowel until the word lost its bite.

Kevin rolled his cigarette and stood for another minute, lighting up and giving the music a second listen. 'No, it's shite,' he said, this time to himself.

Mike retreated to the storeroom at the back of the shop and Kevin began to finger through the records, his fag held between his lips, flicking rapidly to the next one and the next, working methodically. There was the dross, the prog rock, the heavy metal, the already bought. He slipped into a rhythm, like a Catholic at prayer, absorbed in the Stations of the Cross.

Kevin's musical taste defined him. He could pinpoint the moment, the exact point in time when he was struck by his love for music.

He was fifteen. He had passed an open classroom door on the last day of term, and heard a radio playing. Inside, boys shuffled cards and smoked cigarettes. The opening chords of 'Get It On' brought him to a halt in the corridor outside. And he had waited, listening, until the song ended. Years later, he had a similar experience, a life-changing revelation. In his bed, alone at night, he listened to Peel play 'New Rose' for the first time; the guitar riff shot through him like a bullet. It changed everything.

As he got older, he moved through genres, pushed himself, delved into the weird, the extraordinary, even the necessarily tuneless. He discovered the Pop Group, a band designed to frighten the innocent, determined to shock. He loved the ability music had to challenge – threaten even. And although any band might have already broken up by the time he discovered them, it didn't matter; their value lay in the product and that could be kept, and enjoyed, for ever.

It was true that music was his emotional compass, the conduit through which he related to others. He truly hated that

Jethro Tull track, but appreciated Mike's quest for truth through music, his uncompromising search for authenticity. The Pop Group strived for the same truth, and it was at the outer reaches of that boundary that he found his connection.

The bell above the door dinged again and the blue flame on the Superser spluttered and hissed in the draught. Kevin didn't look up, not until he heard his name.

Peter Harkin stood at the counter, watching him. 'Is anybody working here?'

Orla had confided in Liz about the new boyfriend. She said he had a brother in prison, but didn't know why. Harkin was a common name, and Kevin suspected that he knew Peter's family. Or to be specific, he knew the brother, Liam.

Liam had run the same streets as Kevin, on the edge of their gang and on the edge of the paramilitaries. An irritation, he was always trying to insinuate himself into his and Ciaran's company. As they got older, Liam had graduated to a nasty barfly, semi-alcoholic, on the tap for drink and cigarettes. One night, after Kevin refused him, Liam sucker-punched him, landing a blow to the back of the head that knocked him off his seat. It was the finish of them.

And Peter was the wee brother – interesting. If it was the same family, Kevin also knew why Liam was inside; it wasn't for anything political. He had been robbing houses. From what Kevin heard, Liam was lucky the Provos hadn't got him first.

'Mike!' called Kevin. 'You're wanted.'

He would have preferred to return to his browsing, but Peter looked keen to talk, so he asked him, 'What are you looking for?' This would be good.

'Aww, I'm just looking for a copy of "Jealous Guy".'

It was tempting to slag him, but fuck it, it was a good song. Even so, Kevin couldn't resist a slight prod.

'So, you're into Roxy Music, then? What else do you have?'

'It's not for me – it's for Orla's birthday,' said Peter, slightly panicked.

'You don't like Roxy Music, then?' said Kevin.

Peter didn't know how to answer. He was saved by Mike's reappearance behind the counter, mug and fag in hand.

'This boy's looking for "Jealous Guy", Mike,' said Kevin helpfully.

'Good track,' Mike nodded. He put a copy in a paper bag and accepted Peter's money.

'So, you're a Lennon fan?' he asked. Peter looked blank, his hand held out for his change.

'I like the Beatles,' he said.

'The Beatles are crap,' said Kevin. 'There's plenty of better music from the sixties.'

'If it came out before '76, you think it's crap,' said Mike. He lounged back on his stool and pulled on his cigarette, exhaling a thick cloud of smoke.

Peter was out of his depth. He thought the best band to come out of the sixties were the Monkees, but wouldn't risk the ridicule that would surely bring. Still, he had enough nerve to put up an argument.

'So, you don't like the Beatles?' he said. 'And nobody else is supposed to?'

The challenge was cast. Kevin was quick to counter with a well-honed rant on the overplaying of 'Love Me Do', the sickening 'Hey Jude'.

'Lennon produced some good stuff with the Plastic Ono Band. I think McCartney held him back,' he said, starting another roll-up.

'What about Dexys? I've been listening to them,' offered Peter carefully.

Kevin lit up.

'Northern Soul, Geno Washington. You should be listening to the Bureau too – great brass section. Put on the single, Mike.'

Mike shrugged. He wasn't sure he liked being ordered around. He strolled slowly to the singles racks and returned with the 7-inch, then took off Jethro Tull and replaced it with a blast of horns that belted out from the speakers. Then he walked back to the storeroom – it wasn't his kind of thing.

'They split from Dexys last year,' said Kevin. 'Didn't like Rowland's control. I'll do you a tape, Pete. What else do you want on it?'

Peter was naturally chatty, but all his chat had failed on Kevin, who came across as uninterested, too cool for his own good. He liked this change.

'Ah, I don't know – what do you think?'

He'd called him Pete.

Kevin smiled at the question, and his guard slipped; the musical evangelist let loose. He mentally scoured his record collection, curating a beginner's guide to everything this boy needed to know about music.

'What are you doing now? Do you want to get something to eat? I was heading to Noel's after this, to tap some tea and toast, but I want to finish off here first.'

'What are you looking for?' said Peter.

'Whatever I haven't got, Pete,' he said. He returned to his search as Peter watched, then began his own, at the other end of the shop, listlessly flipping through the reggae section.

'Your brother's inside, is that right?' said Kevin after a few minutes.

'Aye, he's doing three years in Magilligan – membership.'

Is he fuck, thought Kevin.

Peter was still talking. 'I'm just glad the hunger strike is in the Kesh.'

It was respectable to be a political prisoner and not a common criminal. Either Mammy and Daddy had spun the rest of the family a story, or Peter himself was rewriting the facts.

'Have you been over to visit?' The prison wasn't that far away.

'No. Me ma and da take turns.'

Kevin looked quietly at Peter. He was round-faced and very young, his expression relaxed at that moment, far from the quick, cheeky front he normally put up.

He remembered the family as rough. Liam was the eldest and, like a lot of children back then, he was dragged up, reared in the street. But Peter seemed cared for. Maybe they had got the hang of it, his parents? More likely one of the sisters had stepped in. There were two girls, he remembered – not lookers but nice enough. It was better not to let on he knew them.

Mike was playing the Allman Brothers; it was his shop – he didn't have to pitch for sales. Kevin handed him an album to hold until the weekend, and he put it under the counter.

When they got to the flat, Noel opened the door, muttering, 'Don't let the heat out,' before he went inside again, leaving the door open for them. He was surprised to see Peter. 'Where were you two?' he asked.

'In Ken's Records,' said Kevin. 'Here, give us your single.' He took the bag from Peter's hand and put the record on, then sat back to listen to it.

Noel shouted, 'Who bought that crap?' from the kitchen.

Peter wanted to take it off again, but instead he sat on the vaguely damp sofa while Kevin examined the sleeve and listened to the soft melody.

'That's a great song,' he said, as it ended. Noel came in with tea. He sat the cups down and removed the record from his player, handing it back to Kevin as though it was contaminated.

Peter watched anxiously. It was a present; he didn't want the cover ripped or marked. He needn't have worried. Kevin gave the surface a wipe, replaced it in its sleeve and bag and handed it back to him.

'Skin up, Noel,' he said, before leaning over to lift a King Tubby album from the stack and put it on.

Kevin and Noel walked their new friend through town, to the place where Peter was to meet Orla. She watched them walk down the hill, towards her, twenty minutes late.

When they arrived at the bottom of the street, it was obvious that all three were wasted. Peter grinned, pasty white.

'He bought you a present,' said Kevin, pointing at Peter's hand. He and Noel laughed as Peter handed the bag to Orla.

'We're going up to McLaughlin's,' said Noel. 'Are you coming?' he asked. Peter looked at Orla's unsmiling face and said, 'No. We have stuff to do.'

'Okey-doke,' said Kevin. 'Come on, Noel.'

As they walked away, Orla turned to Peter. 'When did you become close?'

Just now, thought Peter, smiling at her.

6

Bernie was in overdrive. The house had to be cleaned: beds changed, floors polished, curtains taken down to be washed, dried, ironed and hung again, and all the woodwork washed down with soapy water. It was Easter.

Easter meant three things in Derry: the religious festival and, with it, Easter eggs and new clothes; then the Derry Feis, a festival of Irish culture held in the week following Easter Sunday. The schools of Irish dancing were in a frantic state of rehearsal for the highlight of their year. Finally, there was the commemoration of the 1916 Rising, marches to the cemetery and speeches over the graves of the Republican dead, lying beneath their tricolours.

But before all of this, the house had to be cleaned. The curtains and blinds were already down in the front room; it felt bigger, now that unobstructed daylight flooded in. Liz stood on a chair, washing the windows with vinegar and water. She polished them to a streakless shine with a piece of crumpled newspaper that left her hands black with ink. When she saw Christy turn the corner at the end of the street, she climbed off her chair and stood back, watching him walk towards the house.

He was in his school uniform: black trousers, blazer, white shirt and striped blue tie. He had his school bag slung over one shoulder and his hair was shaved above his ears, in a low-rise Mohican that he had seen modelled on Joe Strummer, on the cover of the *New Musical Express*. He thought it looked cool. She thought it looked stupid.

She had found herself thinking about him, ever since Sinéad said that he fancied her. Unbidden thoughts about his hair, the way he dressed, how they could talk about exams and books and he was interested in what she had to say. She was still with Kevin, though. The fight was short-lived; she was more hurt that he hadn't run after her than about his stupid jealousy, so she accepted his apologies. And perhaps he had reason to be jealous? Someone else – Christy – was interested in her.

Anyway, something was up with Kevin. But of course, something was wrong everywhere. Things had overheated.

There was the continuing battle of wills between Paddy and their mother. Liz thought it would be a passing thing, this interest in the war, but it wasn't. She avoided the war and its daily grind of suffering. The details were upsetting; she didn't want to know about the grief. The politics passed her by and, if she were really pushed to give an opinion, it would have been that she felt removed from it, even slightly above it.

And Kevin? He was withdrawn, tired. If she was removed from the trouble, he was completely absent – from it, from her. He wouldn't say what was wrong, but he was drinking, a lot. Last night, when they went for a walk, he pulled a can of beer out of his coat pocket and drank it in the street. She didn't like that – it seemed crude. She tried telling him about the latest slanging match between her mother and her brother.

'Fuck him,' he said. 'He doesn't know what he's doing.'

'Kevin,' she said. 'They're worried that something will happen. He might be a friend of yours, but he's my brother.' This wasn't the kind man she loved.

Sometimes, the years he had on her were a gulf she couldn't reach over. She didn't have the words to bring him around. She was too young.

'Are you thinking of finishing with me?' she asked him once, when he was buried in his own thoughts. 'Kevin?'

'No, not at all,' he said finally. 'I'm sorry. I'm just tired.'

That again, she thought.

He took her hand. 'Everything's OK.'

She was no fool; everything wasn't OK. She watched him, in those subdued moments, and saw him worried and preoccupied, sad.

Christy knocked at the door. Liz shouted upstairs before she opened it.

'Paddy, you're wanted!'

'How do you know it's not you I'm here for?' grinned Christy as she let him in.

Liz smirked. 'Nice haircut – do you want us to get the guy that did it to you?'

'You don't like it?'

She looked over the thick auburn hair, feeling an urge to touch it. The rich red was deeper in contrast with his pale skin and ran from his forehead to the nape of his neck in a wave.

'It looks better on Strummer. I'm surprised the school let you in, with your hair like that,' laughed Liz.

'There've been some comments,' he said, throwing his bag on the floor. 'Is he still in his pit?'

'I heard him moving around. Go up, if you like,' she said.

Christy pulled his bag up by the strap and stuck his hand inside. 'Here, look at this,' he said, pulling out a paperback and handing it to her.

'*Bury My Heart at Wounded Knee*,' she read. 'What's this?'

'American Indians,' he said. 'It sounds great. It's the real story of the Battle of Wounded Knee. You can read it and tell me what you think.'

'No Errol Flynn, then,' she said. She sat down on the bottom stairs and ran her thumb through the pages, stopping to look at the photographs.

There was still no sign of Paddy.

Christy sat beside her, watching her face. She opened the book and read down the page.

'It's meant to be a great read,' he said.

'Are you on your Easter holidays now?' she asked, still reading. 'You'll need the time for revision.'

'If I do the exams,' said Christy. 'I haven't done any work for them.'

'You can catch up,' said Liz.

He didn't reply.

'Christy? You're doing them, aren't you? What's the point of wasting two years?'

'Yeah, well, we'll see,' he said. 'I've a mountain of work to do.'

'You can study with me, if you like?' offered Liz. 'Moral support? Safety in numbers?'

He had his elbows on his knees, his chin resting on his hands, a smile on his face. 'Do you think that would be wise?' he said, looking sidelong at her with a wicked grin.

'Moral support, I said – nothin' else,' she smiled back. He held her gaze and, for a minute, there was a definite heat between them. Liz flushed. He was about to say something else when her father appeared behind them, at the top of the stairs.

'You may go up and waken him,' she said, getting up.

'All right, Mr McLaughlin?' said Christy, rising to let the father pass.

Jim looked with suspicion, first at him, then at his daughter.

'Just going up to see your Paddy.'

Her father followed Liz into the living room. She kept her face turned away from his gaze and started on the windows again.

'Are you all right?' he said.

'Aye, Daddy,' she said, then put down the polishing paper. 'Mammy, I'm going over to Sinéad's for a minute,' she shouted. Grabbing her coat off the banister, she left the house quickly, just as Bernie came out of the kitchen.

'Where is she away?' she asked Jim.

'Sinéad's. That Christy fella is upstairs – I don't like that boy,' he said.

'I told you,' said Sinéad.

'Oh, Sinéad, don't.' Liz sat on the bed and pulled her friend's pillow over her face. No, it was nothing. Nothing was ever going to happen.

'So, what are you going to do?' said Sinéad.

'What do you mean? Nothing, of course – nothing's going to come from it.'

Liz lay down on the bed and pulled the pillow over her face again, until lights began to flash behind her eyelids from lack of oxygen. She sat up quickly.

'I can't go back to the house yet. Not until I know he's gone. Come for a walk with me.'

'Let me get me coat and we'll go to the park,' said Sinéad.

They sat on a bench, the sun warm on their faces. The weather had taken a nice turn and a week's worth of rain had given way to warm spring weather. A late Easter was always good. The pond in the park was a ruin of broken glass, but the grass was cut and some of the beds had daffodils in bloom.

'You know I got an interview with the denim factory?' said Sinéad.

Liz opened her eyes and looked at her friend. 'You never said you applied.'

'Two weeks ago – I didn't want to jinx it. The interview's in two weeks' time.'

'I hope you get it, Sinéad. The money will be good.'

'And the cheap jeans.'

They were quiet again.

Liz stared at the clouds. 'I got an offer too,' she said.

'For a job?' Sinéad asked.

'For a place at a university,' she said, sitting forward on the seat. 'You can't tell anybody. I haven't said – not even to him, or Mammy and Daddy. I won't get in anyway.' She shrugged, feeling the grip on her stomach again, the one she felt every time she thought about it.

'Aye, you will – you're dead smart.'

'Even if I got good marks, I don't think I'd go.'

She already regretted telling her friend.

Sinéad closed her eyes again and crossed her legs. 'I'd take that stuff with Christy as a compliment,' she said with a sigh.

They sat in silence. The skyline of the park was dominated by the cathedral spire, an ornate, Gothic spike at eye level with them, and, facing it, the hollow shell of Gwyn's Institute; the old building once housed a quiet library and a musty museum, both destroyed in the flames of a fire years ago. It was fenced off from the public and guarded by a siege cannon that pointed towards the spire.

Liz could remember the children's library. The entrance was on the side of the building. She recalled the silence, the smell of books and the door that led to the main reading room, where the grown-ups sat among the wood-panelled walls; it was a door she longed to go through, but was afraid to, because someone had told her that children were not allowed. Once, she gathered her nerve and crossed the threshold, creeping into the room where a few men sat at tables, reading.

The books she saw there weren't picture books. Only their spines showed on the shelves, with dark colours and gold-imprinted letters. When she saw the librarian, towering over the high counter and looking down at her, she quickly made her way back to the children's books and the way out, pursued by guilt.

Thinking about it now, it wasn't just her age that was the

barrier to that room; it was the feeling that her sort didn't belong there, the people she came from. Maybe the people who had burnt the place to the ground felt the same; but that didn't make the burning right. Her teacher had been fierce in her anger about it, and sad, because so many books were lost.

'Is Kevin buying you an Easter egg?' said Sinéad.

Liz laughed. 'You know, I don't know? I haven't asked him for one, so probably not. I haven't even thought about buying one for him.'

'You can ask him now – there he is.' Sinéad pointed in the direction of the park gates and sure enough there was Kevin, walking up the hill.

'Oh, God,' said Liz. 'I can't see him now.'

'Yes, you can. Walk down the hill and surprise him. I'm away home,' said Sinéad.

Liz sat for a minute, watching as Kevin got closer. He was pulling on a cigarette and seemed absorbed, lost somewhere in his thoughts.

His slim face was thinner, paler than usual and stark against the crop of short dark hair. She saw the sadness in him, the dull expression that came into his eyes when he was alone and off guard.

As she stood and walked across the grass towards the path he was on, he saw her and smiled. She was glad that was still there, the wide smile that gave him a real boyish look. He wasn't that much older than her, not really. He didn't take his eyes off her.

'I was coming to see you,' he said. 'To give you this.'

From the inside pocket of his long raincoat he produced a chocolate egg, wrapped in gold foil and encircled in gingham ribbon. Liz was taken aback.

'It's lovely, Kevin. Thank you.'

'You're not allowed to eat it until Sunday,' he laughed, as she kissed him. 'I supposed that I should be the good boyfriend and get you one, so there you are. Where are you going?'

'Me and Sinéad were just sitting. She's gone home again.'

Kevin looked up the hill, but Sinéad was already out of sight. 'So,' he said. 'Do you want to go to your house? You can make me tea.'

She couldn't risk the chance that Christy might still be there.

'Me mammy's taking the house apart, cleaning. Let's sit here a while, in the sun.'

Kevin looked down at the egg in her hand. 'We would need to get that into the shade before it melts.'

'Or hatches,' said Liz, holding it up to look at it again.

She comforted him. Just being close helped. He couldn't explain the nightmares to her. It would only make him sound mad. In truth, he didn't want to talk about them; they scared him enough to make him avoid sleep.

For weeks he had sat up, reading and smoking until it was light. Only then would he let his eyes close. But it was taking its toll. That morning, his hand shook as he tried to shave; even now, there was a tremor. This had to stop – he had to get back some measure of control.

They lay on the patchy grass and Liz rested her head on his stomach. He watched the clouds pass overhead, then his eyes closed and sunlight glowed red through his eyelids. He felt the warmth of sleep blanket him.

'Kevin, wake up.' She was leaning over him and he stared through her, to the sky and the trees above their heads. It took a second to remember where they were. 'You were sleeping.'

'No, I wasn't,' he said.

'Yes, you were,' said Liz. 'Come on, let's go. I will make you that tea.' She held out her hand to help him to his feet and he got up with effort.

As they passed the ruined institute, Paddy and Christy came

through the park gate. There was no way to avoid them. Liz paused – only for a second, but it was enough for Kevin to notice the hesitation as they held hands.

'You two heading down town?' asked Kevin.

'Aye,' said Paddy. 'Are you going out tonight?'

Kevin looked at Liz, but she shook her head. 'I have revision to do,' she said, with a look at Christy.

'Aye, well, I'm not sure if we'll be there anyway. Tell me ma I'll not be home for dinner,' said Paddy, walking away.

'Bye, Kevin, bye, Liz,' said Christy, with a grin.

'What was that with you and Christy?' said Kevin, once they were out of earshot.

'Nothin',' said Liz.

That night, in the Cave, a gory horror film was reaching its blood-drenched climax. A dozen blue-lit faces gazed, enthralled, at the screen on the shelf, above the entrance to the bar.

The door swung open and Paddy and Christy ran in, coming to an abrupt halt as the faces turned from the television to them. A scream of terror drew the faces back to the video nasty, where the women in the woods had come to an untimely, but not unexpected, end. The boys put their heads down and walked through to the inner bar.

Paddy had a black scarf wrapped around his neck. He had fallen at some point; the knee was out of his jeans and there was blood. Christy came behind him and they sat down at the table, where Kevin, Noel, Orla and Peter were drinking.

'We were here all night, right?' said Paddy to Kevin. 'We just got chased up High Street.'

'By who?' said Peter, confused.

'What do you mean?' said Paddy, distracted by the surroundings.

'Who was chasing you, Paddy?' said Peter.

'The Brits – who do you think?'

Christy thought he should clarify. 'There was a charge. Everybody cleared. We ran up High Street and through the checkpoint and then in here.'

'Do you have any money?' said Paddy.

'I have enough for a drink,' Christy replied. He went to the bar.

'I don't know what you're doing, man,' said Noel. 'Why are you into all this shite?'

'It's just a laugh, Noel,' said Paddy, rubbing the blood off his knee with a wet finger.

'But it's all bullshit, all the crap you said you didn't believe in.'

Not this again. Paddy stopped cleaning the wound to look up.

'They're using you, man,' said Noel. 'You're cannon fodder.'

Paddy looked around at the rest of them.

Orla shrugged. 'You know what I think?' she said. 'He's right.'

Christy came back with two pints of lager and looked around at the tense faces.

'What? What's up?' he asked, still holding the pints.

'Nothing,' said Paddy, taking his drink out of Christy's hand. 'Noel is just letting us know that he doesn't approve, that's all.'

'Fucksake, Noel,' said Christy, taking his seat. 'Lighten up.'

Noel pushed his chair away from the table and walked to the bar, obviously annoyed. Kevin watched him and said nothing.

'Fuckin' hippy,' muttered Paddy, also watching Noel as he stood with his back to them at the bar. 'Fuckin' middle-class hippy. He's a Prod – what the fuck does he know?'

'Leave it, Paddy,' said Christy. He could feel Paddy tensing for a fight.

'That's not fuckin' on, McLaughlin,' said Kevin angrily. 'I've no time for this. They're right and you're wrong, OK? This is what happens when you let that crap into your life, all that fucking "Wrap the Green Flag Round Me" bollocks.'

Across the table, Paddy fumed. Kevin leaned over to look him in the eye. Tapping the table, he said, '"Guerrilla war struggle is a new entertainment", Paddy – don't you know that? Here.'

He pushed Noel's gear towards him. 'You don't mind smoking his dope, do you? Calm down and skin up.'

'All I'm saying is, you can't pretend that stuff isn't going on,' said Paddy, tearing three Rizlas from their pack.

'I can,' said Kevin. 'There's more important stuff in life.'

Orla went home. With no Liz and no Sinéad, the evening had worn thin on her. Kevin had a word with Noel and persuaded him to let the subject drop.

The bar closed. Back at the flat, Noel produced a bottle of rum, stolen from his father on his last visit home. It was dark and rough, too strong for them. They took turns, swigging from the neck of the bottle, as it was passed around the room.

Kevin had put the Gang of Four on the turntable. He was telling Paddy about the band.

'What is it?' said Peter, lifting the album cover to read it. 'Entertainment!'

'I'll let you borrow my copy,' said Kevin. He had given Peter a few of his records to listen to, over the few weeks since that morning in the record shop.

Paddy looked quickly from Peter to Kevin.

'You never lend me any of your records,' he said. He knew Kevin's enviable collection and had asked, more than once, to take one home.

'You don't give stuff back,' said Kevin.

'I do!' said Paddy, offended.

'Freak Brothers,' said Noel from his chair, where they had assumed he was sleeping.

'Oh, for fucksake,' said Paddy. 'You'll get it back – OK?'

'Heard it before,' said Noel, closing his eyes again.

'See?' said Kevin. 'Pete returns things.'

Christy had been quiet, smoking and watching Kevin and Paddy talk. 'Did Liz like the book I lent her?' he said suddenly.

'What book?' said Kevin.

'I gave her a book today – did she not say?' Christy took the rum as it was passed to him and put it to his lips, watching Kevin's reaction, the doubt developing behind his eyes.

Kevin didn't answer and changed the subject, but his silence said everything Christy needed to know. The Gang of Four played on in the background.

'I want to see them playing live,' said Kevin, taking the cover out of Peter's hands. 'No other band sounds like them. Or writes like them – it's all about capitalism, exploitation, even about over here. They call themselves anarcho-syndicalists. They think wages should be abolished, work is slavery – this is revolutionary stuff. Listen – it's hard, real, industrial.'

'Where'd you read that – the *NME*?' said Christy drily.

'Same place that you get all your nuggets of genius from,' said Kevin.

'Art-school boys, playing at being revolutionaries,' Christy said to Peter, handing him the bottle. 'There's a revolution going on here – but he's not interested in that.'

'Don't start that crap,' said Noel, his eyes opening suddenly. 'Not in my flat.'

'Why not? You can't ignore it,' insisted Christy.

'If you take enough drugs you can,' said Paddy.

'So, is that what you need – more dope?' said Peter, with a laugh.

'There's nothing funny about men starving themselves because they want to be treated as political prisoners,' said Christy. 'I don't think it's OK, allowing them to die.'

'Do you know something? I'm sick of this crap,' said Kevin, getting up and going into the kitchen. His head ached. Peter followed him.

'Are you all right?' he asked. Kevin had his head in both hands.

'I've drunk too much. I don't need to listen to his shit tonight,' he said. He reached for a cup to get a drink of water. The pain in his head was crushing.

'I don't think it's OK, you know – the hunger strike?' he said. Peter was leaning against the fridge, watching him with folded arms. For some reason, Kevin felt the need to explain. 'The whole thing's a disaster – a fuck-up.'

In the other room, Paddy and Christy had decided to leave. The depleted bottle of rum lay on the floor. Peter and Kevin said goodnight to Noel and followed them out the door and down the empty street. Kevin concentrated on walking straight. Up ahead, Paddy was laughing at something Christy had said.

'Meehan thinks he's fucking great. Fuckin' books . . .' muttered Kevin.

'Leave it,' said Peter. 'Let's just get home.'

It was three a.m., and the Bogside was silent. Paddy had found a sheet of corrugated iron leaning against a wall by the road. He and Christy began throwing rocks at it, watching them bounce off the metal, with a clang that echoed off the surrounding houses.

When Kevin and Peter caught up with them, Peter joined in. Kevin watched them through a rum-induced haze, the ground undulating before him. Christy had his back to him, shouting, laughing.

'Meehan,' he said, but Christy didn't answer.

'Meehan!' This time Christy turned in his direction. Kevin staggered forward. 'What's going on with you and Liz?' he said.

'Nothin',' said Christy, turning away.

66

'There is,' said Kevin, grabbing his arm. Christy pushed his hand down, releasing the grip on his sleeve.

'Be straight with me,' said Kevin. He could hear the words slurring from his mouth. 'Tell me the truth.'

'There's nothin' goin' on!' shouted Christy. 'Go home, Kevin.' But Kevin couldn't let it go.

'You think you're so fuckin' smart,' he said, but Christy had already walked away. He bent unsteadily, grabbed a piece of stone paving from the ground and threw it. He was too drunk to do harm, but the rock hit Christy, hard, on the shoulder blade, and he yelped in pain. As he swung around, Kevin glared at him, his hands at his sides, the word already formed in his mouth. 'Cunt.'

'What's going on?' shouted Paddy. Peter ran between them, forcing Kevin back.

'Cunt, yourself. The bastard hit me,' said Christy, rubbing his shoulder.

Kevin pushed Peter away and staggered up the hill.

7

The long vowels, rich, Jamaican, mingled with a serious dub beat.

Madness . . . madness . . . waar.

He heard it in his head first, then he was awake, and for a moment he didn't know where he was, so he lay listening to the music, eyes shut. When he finally opened them, Paddy was on the bed opposite, smoking a fag and looking at him.

'Wakey, wakey,' he said, amused. Kevin looked around the room.

He was on a bottom bunk, in the boys' room of the McLaughlin house. Vague memories of the previous night came back to him: struggling up the hill with Paddy, Mrs McLaughlin in her dressing gown, the cool cotton pillow as he collapsed into the bed. He was relieved to discover that he was fully clothed, apart from his shoes and coat. 'What time is it?' he asked.

'After ten,' came the reply.

His mouth was thick and dry. 'Give us a fag,' he said. Paddy passed him his pouch.

'We got in about four – Meehan's ragin' with you.'

Paddy lay back on the bedcovers, his hands behind his head. Kevin rolled his cigarette and lit it.

'It was a good night, apart from the fight. I still think Noel was out of order though,' said Paddy.

'Noel's right,' said Kevin. 'The Provies are wankers.' He stubbed his smoke out in the ashtray on the windowsill. 'Did you say Christy's ragin' with me? Why?'

'You don't remember firing a stone at him in William Street? What was that about?'

He had a flash of memory, of Christy's face close to his. 'What did he say?' he asked.

'He said you accused him of trying it on with Liz,' said Paddy.

'He's always sniffing around – I lost the rattle.'

'Anyway,' said Paddy. 'He's not happy.'

Kevin lay down and rolled over to face the wall. The ill-advised tobacco had made his head and stomach worse. He needed less stimulation. Paddy was still musing on the night's events.

'Orla's annoyed with me, too. I think that's why she went home. Her and Harkin are full on, aren't they? Always thought Orla was so quiet – who knew?'

'He got further with her than you ever did,' said Kevin. Paddy recalled the very brief encounter with Orla, on the living-room sofa downstairs, only a year before. Despite his best efforts, she was not for letting him do anything.

'Don't say to Liz about Christy, Paddy,' said Kevin, rolling over again.

Paddy looked at the bleary face, the flattened hair. 'You look like death warmed up,' he said.

The pulsing music shook the speakers. 'Do you hear that vibration?'

Paddy held his hand over the front of the speaker. 'I'd love to hear a big sound system,' he said. 'Like you read about.'

'You'd have to go to London,' said Kevin.

Funny, Paddy had forgotten about his plans, about the money in the tin under the bed; his precious savings, his escape plan.

'I used to think about it all the time,' he said. 'But you need someone to go with, don't you?'

'And you need a place to live I've thought about it plenty,' said Kevin.

Raising himself up on one elbow, Paddy looked over at him.

'What?' said Kevin. Paddy had a look on his face, an idea brewing. 'What?' he said again, laughing this time.

'Why don't we go?' said Paddy. 'I've got money saved, you know? About fifty quid. That's enough to get over there and then all we need to do is sign on, until we get work. What about our Elizabeth? Do you think she'd come too? She could go to university.'

Having someone to go with – that had always been the missing piece in his plans. And Kevin was a good guy, no fool. They could do it, just book their place on the ferry and go.

'Who do you know over there?'

His round face beamed with hope. Kevin was thoughtful, witnessing his excitement. He had a cousin in Kilburn who might put them up, for a while anyway. Could he suddenly decide to leave, up sticks and go like that? And what about Liz? Would she be prepared to take the risk and go with him?

'I know some people,' he said finally. 'But let's think about this, Paddy. It needs planning.'

'So, you would go?'

'I would, if it was organised right – aye, I would,' said Kevin.

It was after three o'clock when Bernie heard them come in, Kevin falling down drunk and Paddy not far behind him. But it was Liz who called her, Liz who asked if he could sleep on the sofa. He had crashed there already.

Thinking he would be better off in one of the boys' beds, she gave him a good shake and ordered him up the stairs. He clambered to his feet and climbed the stairs, like a lamb.

She kept Liz in the living room for a decent interval, then told her to get herself back to bed. Liz knew her mother would spend the rest of the night half-listening for movement between the rooms.

And now she was still in bed, listening to the music and the voices through the wall. He was laughing.

When she was dressed, she crossed the landing and opened the door, feeling ridiculously shy.

'Did you sleep?' she said.

'Aye. Is your ma angry?'

She sat on the bed by his feet, and he pulled her down to lie beside him. He reeked of stale spirits and tobacco.

'I haven't been downstairs. She'll be all right. It was her idea for you to stay.'

'We're going to London,' said Paddy.

Kevin laughed uncomfortably. 'Jesus, we were only talking about it,' he said.

Liz sat up again, her eyes darting between them. 'What do you mean?'

'We're leaving and going to London.' Paddy was running with this as a fact.

'Are you serious?' said Liz, turning to Kevin.

'We were only talking about it,' he said. 'Paddy, you can't just get up and go – you have to plan it. You might have money saved, but I don't – you're talking September, October, at the earliest.'

Paddy was not to be put off by minor practicalities and was charging on with it.

'Then we'll get organised – it's going to happen,' he said.

'Can I come too?' said Liz. If Kevin was going, and the offer for university fell through, she was damned if she'd be left behind.

'Under no circumstances!'

Paddy entered the front room and announced their plans to

their mother, without thinking what kind of a reaction they would provoke in her.

'Neither of you are leaving this house, to run off to some foreign country on your own! Are you off your heads?'

Kevin sat on the sofa, deeply uncomfortable, deeply hung-over, and tried to eat a piece of toast as fast as possible. He gulped scalding tea. He was sure Bernie had glanced briefly in his direction when Paddy told her the three of them were, for definite, moving to England.

He was more than a little afraid of Liz's mother; she would blame him for putting the idea in Paddy's head. He was unwashed and sick and all he wanted to do was leave. He turned to Liz and whispered, 'I'm going.'

She walked him to the door. 'Will I meet you later?' she asked, after a brief kiss.

In reply, her mother shouted from the fireside, 'There's a service in the cathedral at three o'clock, Elizabeth. Make sure you're there.' Liz translated this as, *Make you no plans – I'll tell you what you'll be doing today.*

'See you later,' said Kevin, backing away from the front door.

8

Bobby Sands MP lay in the hospital wing of his prison.

He had received the Last Rites on 17 April, Good Friday. This information filtered through the streets and the violence flared ever stronger, coinciding with the solemn ceremonials of the Easter vigil and the resurrection of Christ. It was the end of Lent.

Liz, Orla and Sinéad wandered into town that Saturday, to witness the disorder for themselves. It was late, somewhere between ten o'clock and eleven.

As they approached the edge of town, they passed boys standing in doorways and on street corners, in small, tense groups. The deep, tiled entrance to the council swimming pool sheltered a dark huddle of youths with scarves covering their faces. But the shadows couldn't disguise them, and Sinéad recognised one as a friend. They solemnly acknowledged each other.

'All right, John?'

'All right, Sinéad.'

At the edge of the rioting, the girls hung back, far enough to be identified as mere spectators. They were not the only ones. Older couples and other girls observed from the footpaths. They stood with folded arms, chatting and pointing; close enough to feel the warmth from the burning bus that lay across the road by the high-rise flats, but out of the line of fire for any incoming missiles.

The three friends sat on a wall at the bottom of the street, swinging their feet; nervous, but intrigued all the same.

In the middle, Sinéad threw her arms wide, welcoming the chaos. 'How can you think of leaving all this, Liz?' she declared.

'She's not going anywhere – are you, Liz?' said Orla, watching her closely.

Liz was sure she was going, sure she was not going, depending on the company she was in.

Her mother was devastated by the thought and would hear nothing of it. Her denial of it as a ridiculous idea was enough for Liz to rule it out too – it was stupid and impossible. But when Paddy talked about it as real and imminent, she was on the boat already, with him at her side and excitement surging through her.

Living with Kevin? An entirely different set of pictures swam through her head. Suddenly sex was at the top of her list of worries.

There was a general cheer as two men walked confidently to the front of the army cordon, petrol bombs aflame in their hands. They threw them over the roofs of the Land Rovers and onto the soldiers behind. The girls laughed at their brazen, cocksure attitude.

They stopped laughing when, a minute later, the Land Rovers split apart and two armoured cars tore from the void. With a terrifying roar, they hurtled down the road towards the mob.

'Oh, fuck!' squealed Orla. Everyone, spectators as well as rioters, ran. The army vehicles careered into the crowd. When the girls stopped running, they were at the top of the street again, on a traffic island in the middle of the road. They looked back; from below came the dull sound of gunfire – plastic rounds.

'I'm going home,' said Orla, gasping for breath as she held her sides. 'This is too dangerous.'

Men carried crates full of bottles into the town as they climbed. One pushed a wheelbarrow filled with rubble. A priest stood at the cathedral gates, nervously watching the road and the developing night of trouble.

'Get yourselves home, girls,' he said as they passed.

'OK, Father,' they answered.

At the top of the hill they turned and looked back. It was quiet where they stood.

'No Peter tonight, Orla?' said Liz. It was rare to see her without him.

'He said he'd call, but he didn't. He could be in the middle of all that, for all I know. Where's Kevin?'

'Me mammy didn't want me to go out; she's annoyed enough as it is, so I said I'd stay in and help with the dinner for tomorrow. He's probably in the pub. But the bars close early tonight, don't they – or is that just Good Friday?'

The bars closed at their usual time of 11.30 p.m. and numerous men with a charge of drink in them came onto the street, swelling the crowds already involved in the conflict. Kevin rolled out of the Cave, where the evening had been quiet. He walked down the hill with Noel and through the town; they passed a joint between them. They, too, were drawn to the spectacle on the streets below.

'They're not going to back down, Kevin. Cold fucking bastards,' said Noel, sticking Rizlas together. Kevin gave him a wry smile; here they stood, the two of them, withdrawn from the traditions that spawned them – and increasingly isolated in this bedlam of a country.

The smell of smoke hung in the air as they got near the distinctive clamour of a riot: shouts, engines, thuds, the sudden retort of plastic bullets – bang, bang, bang.

Turning the corner, the scene opened out before them, illuminated by the glow of burning vehicles and reflected in the windows of the flats and maisonettes on either side of the road. Fire shimmered off shattered glass, a thousand flecks of brimstone falling from the sky. The air was heavy with ignited petrol and the rage of hundreds of men moving, bending, reaching, running, all with a single purpose, joyous in their collective.

Fire engulfed the petrol tank of one burning car and it exploded suddenly, sending a shockwave that knocked one unlucky rioter onto his back and caused the rest to flinch, then turn towards the noise and cheer.

Observed through a haze of cannabis and alcohol, there was a surreal quality to the scene, heightened and yet dulled as if viewed through the lens of a camera.

It was a new experience for Noel to be up close like this. Kevin watched his excitement, feeling the urge in him to have a go, to experience the anarchy of lifting a stone and throwing it at authority.

'It's like being in a film,' said Noel. 'All it wants is a really good soundtrack.'

Kevin needed to get away. He was nauseous and dizzy; his head spun from the noise and the smell of smoke and burning oil. The sides of his mouth filled with saliva and he knew he would be sick.

'Come on,' he said. 'Let's go.'

They moved into the road, hurrying past the exploded car, stumbling over bricks and craters of torn-up tarmac. Halfway across, there was a surge of roaring engines. Turning, they stopped, transfixed by the three huge army vehicles that were speeding towards them from the left.

The crowd surged as one and ran. From the right, soldiers charged on foot, shields and batons raised. Shots rang out; everyone ducked and crouched down as they ran, tilting forward, half falling, scattering into side streets and down alleyways. There were shouts behind, an angry, distant roar, and Kevin knew someone was hit, perhaps more than one, as a barrage of live rounds and plastic bullets were discharged recklessly, over and over.

'Come on!'

Noel was shouting at him and he realised that he had stopped running.

'Kevin!'

Noel grabbed his arm and dragged him out of the way, as a Pig swung dangerously close to him in the middle of the road.

'OK,' said Kevin, shaking him off and running again, through the garden of a house and down a dark lane, into a car park at the rear of a block of flats. They stopped between a brick wall and several parked cars.

'I thought we were dead,' said Noel. 'You froze there, man. Are you all right?'

Kevin couldn't answer. He leaned forward, hands splayed on the roof of the car in front of him. His head was down between his shoulders, then his stomach heaved and he vomited.

Out on the road the army had succeeded, at least temporarily, in 'stabilising the situation'. The area was clear; only the fires remained, dropping lower as the bodies of vehicles were consumed.

On the corner, at the junction of the road, someone lay facing the clear night. The stars were set in the dark sky, hazy through brown, smoky drifts. With eyes open and unseeing he lay, his head bloodied, smashed on one side, his pale face unmarked.

As the soldiers approached to look and to take charge, his friends crouched down, sheltering him. One stood up to face them, arms by his side, his fists clenched in shock and anger.

'Look what you've done, you bastards!' he was shouting, but the soldiers walked past, unheeding. One of them spoke into a radio, reporting back on events. An elderly man, dressed in a shirt and tie, ran across the road and the Brits instinctively lifted their rifles to their shoulders, taking aim. The man stopped and raised his arms, holding up the towel he was carrying as a white flag.

'I live across the way there and I know a bit of first aid. Let me have a look at the wee lad,' he pleaded.

The boy who'd stood up heard this and shouted to him, past the soldiers, 'I think he's dead.'

'Let me look, please. He's only a wain, for Christsake.'

The soldiers stepped aside, and the man knelt quickly by the injured boy. He looked closely at his face and held the towel to the side of his head. Blood seeped through the cloth. He felt for a pulse but shook his head.

'What's your name?' he asked the friend, who now knelt with him. The others stood by, watching silently, with arms folded.

'Paddy,' he said.

'Give me your coat, Paddy.'

He took off his jacket and handed it to the man, who covered the boy's face with it. Paddy began to cry.

The man looked up at the soldiers standing above them.

'Call an ambulance, will you?' he said. 'He can't lie here.'

9

'Will you just do it and get it over with?' said Christy.

It was five o'clock the next morning. He and Paddy were standing outside Orla's house, debating whether they should knock or not.

Paddy had been fine up to the point where they had turned the corner onto Orla's street. Then, the impact of what they were about to do hit him. He didn't want to be the one to break the news. He didn't want to deal with a crying girl. He didn't even know what to say.

They had spent the night at the hospital, long hours sitting in the waiting room, expecting Peter's parents to arrive. Neither wanted to leave him on his own. Peter's family didn't have a phone and so the hospital had the priest call to the house with the news that their son was dead. It took hours to organise.

'I'm not doing it – not on my own,' said Paddy.

'You aren't on your own,' Christy pointed out.

'Let's go to our house first and get our Liz. It'll be better if she's with us. She'll know what to do.'

'All right then,' said Christy, relieved that they had a plan, one that included reinforcements.

The McLaughlins lived two streets away. Paddy used his key to open the door quietly, and Christy stood at the bottom of the stairs while he went up to Liz's bedroom.

'What?' said Liz, when he called her softly. He was standing by the door, his hand still on the handle. The room was beginning to lighten, and she knew, when she looked at his face, that something was very wrong. For a moment, she thought it was her mother or father. 'What is it?' she said.

Paddy's voice trembled as he spoke. 'I need you to come to Orla's house with me, 'cause Peter Harkin's dead, and I have to tell her.' He was crying again.

Liz got out of bed and immediately went to her parents' room. Her father was already sitting on the edge of the bed.

'Daddy, our Paddy's crying and there's blood on his shirt. You'd better come.'

'Is he hurt? What's happened?'

'He says that a fella we know is dead,' she whispered.

Now Bernie was out of bed. She pushed past them to find Paddy still standing in the other room, and put her arms around him.

'Come downstairs,' she said. 'We'll get you a cup of tea and something to eat.'

They found Christy sitting on the bottom step, in the dark. As Bernie and Liz took Paddy into the front room, Jim stopped by Christy.

'What happened, son?' he asked.

'A friend of ours was hit with a plastic bullet.' He raised his hand to his temple and pulled an imaginary trigger. 'He's dead. He's going with Orla, so we were on our way to tell her – but Paddy wanted to get Liz, to help.'

Jim felt him tremble.

'Come in here,' he said, guiding Christy by the arm into the room. He lit a fire from the warm ashes in the grate and Bernie made tea and toast for all of them. They sat for a minute, no one eating or drinking, trying to take in what had happened.

'So, you two were at the hospital?' said Jim.

'Aye, all night,' said Paddy.

Christy nodded.

'You were lucky you weren't lifted out of the place.'

'There were police there, but nobody took any notice of us,' said Christy.

Bernie looked from him to her son, both washed out and exhausted.

'Will the wee boy's family not get in touch with Orla, Elizabeth?'

Liz shook her head. 'I don't think they know about her – she's never been to the house and she definitely hasn't told her mammy and daddy about Peter.' She stopped and stared into the cold cup in her hand. Orla and Peter; the names ran together, like one. Poor Orla.

'I don't want her to find out on the radio, Mammy.'

'Jim, these two can't do this. Look at them – they're too young, and they're in no fit state.' She got to her feet and looked through the blinds at the early morning. People would be starting their day soon.

'Right,' she said, decision made. 'Where does she live, Elizabeth? We'll go, you and me. It would be a sin for the wee girl to find out on the news, and us know already.'

'It's going on for six o'clock, Bernie. Give it another hour,' said Jim.

'It's Easter Sunday, Jim,' she replied. 'Somebody will be up for Mass.' Turning to Christy, she asked, 'Does your house have a phone?'

'No,' said Christy, suddenly overcome with a desire to lie down.

'Well, you're not going home yet. Bed, both of you,' said Bernie. 'We'll take care of this.'

A shaken Liz vanished upstairs, to cry and then get dressed. Paddy and Christy climbed into the bunks and quickly fell asleep, grateful to have the burden removed by the grown-ups downstairs. In the front room, Jim and Bernie sat side by side, listening to the clock tick loudly on the fireboard and the coal fire hiss and spark. The coal was damp.

'Some Easter this is going to be,' said Jim, after a few minutes. 'How did we get landed with this?'

'I'm just glad it's not the other way around,' said his wife.

Jim watched her as she rose stiffly from the seat to go and dress herself. Bernie was good with bad news; she would know what to say to the mother, how to put it across.

But he knew from her face that a bit of her was defeated by this task, maybe a piece of her that was still a girl, mad about a boy; how do you break that heart in someone else's child, and not die a bit yourself?

Like the boys upstairs, he too was glad it didn't fall to him.

Orla's mother heard the quiet tap on the front door and nudged her husband.

'Did you hear that, Malachy? There's somebody at the door.'

Malachy lay still, beneath the covers.

'Malachy,' she said again, pushing him with both hands so that his body rocked from side to side. 'Wake. Up.'

'Is everybody in?' mumbled Malachy, wanting to be sure before committing himself to rise from a warm bed.

'Aye, they are. Go down and see what's wrong. Maybe it's the police.'

'You would know if it was the police, Peggy. They'd bang the house down,' he said, pulling the bedcovers back and reaching for his trousers at the foot of the divan.

He looked through the crack in the curtains; the path below was empty and for a second he considered getting back into bed. Then the soft tap came again.

Outside, Bernie and Liz shivered. The sun had risen but there was no heat in it this close to dawn, and the anticipation of passing on bad news made them shake with adrenaline.

'Knock harder, Mammy,' whispered Liz. 'They won't hear you.'

'Aye, they will,' said Bernie, pulling her coat around her.

At last, they heard movement and a figure appeared in the hall behind the glass. The door opened an inch or two. It was Orla's father, his face creased and stubbled. He looked from one to the other and then recognised Liz.

'Hello,' he said, puzzled. Then he turned to Bernie. There was a passing familiarity between them, from the street. 'How are you doing, missus? Is there something wrong?'

'Is your wife there – can I speak to her?' said Bernie.

He looked at them, then turned and went to get Peggy. She was already on the landing, leaning over the banister to listen to the conversation.

'It's that wee girl our Orla goes around with, and her mother's with her – the mother wants to talk to you.'

'Stay you there,' said Peggy. She went back to the bedroom, took her best dressing gown from the back of the door, and put it on. Then she fixed her hair in the mirror, before returning to where Malachy waited, now at the top of the stairs. A cold draught crept up from the open door. With a worried glance, she passed him and went downstairs.

Before Peggy could speak, Bernie said to her, 'We've had some bad news.'

Peggy paused, then moved aside. 'Come in,' she said.

She ushered them into the living room and sat stiffly on the edge of a seat, facing them.

'Are you all right, Liz? What's up?'

But it was Bernie who replied; this was a conversation for two mothers.

'Has your Orla ever mentioned a wee boy that she's seeing?'

Oh, God. Peggy shook her head. 'No, she hasn't – what is it?'

'Right . . . your Orla is going out with a wee boy who is a friend of my Patrick, and last night he was hit by a plastic bullet and he's died. Elizabeth didn't want Orla to hear about it on the news, so we thought it would be best to let you know, as soon as possible – so you can break the news to her.'

Peggy was silent. She looked at Malachy who had stayed behind her and was sitting on a hard chair, just inside the door. He listened quietly, his head down, his big hands resting on his knees.

'Did you know about a boy?' she asked. He shook his head.

'How long was she going with him?' she asked Liz.

'Two months – almost,' said Liz. She couldn't help but feel this wasn't her secret to tell. And although it had to come out now, it seemed underhand, behind Orla's back. When would they go and get her, so she knew she was there?

'Does she really like him?' Peggy was asking her, in a voice beginning to break with emotion.

'Aye, she really does – she's wile about him.'

Peggy ran her hands over her face, pushing her hair back off her forehead.

'I don't know what to do – what do I do?' she said to Bernie.

'Do you want to go and wake her now, and tell her when Elizabeth is here? Or do you want us to go first?' said Bernie.

Finally Malachy spoke, from his chair by the door.

'Is he definitely dead?'

'Our Patrick was at the hospital all night – he is definitely dead,' said Bernie. 'I'm so sorry to bring this to your door. You don't know the boy, but if it was me, I would have wanted to be told straight away.'

'What do you think, Malachy – should we wake her now? It's never going to be easy, whatever time she finds out.'

Malachy stood, making it clear that the conversation was over.

'Thank you for coming over to let us know, missus. We'll tell her ourselves, when she wakens on her own. You've enough to be getting on with,' he said, looking at Liz.

'We'll leave you to it then,' said Bernie, rising to leave. 'Come on, Elizabeth.'

Liz looked at her mother – was that it? She wanted to see Orla, to make sure she was all right. 'Will you tell her that I was here and that I'll call over later?' she said to Peggy.

'Don't worry, sweetheart. I will. Thank you for letting us know,' said Peggy, reaching out to touch Liz's arm. 'Go home with your mammy and then go to Mass for that wee boy and his poor family. That's all any of us can do now.'

IO

Kevin arrived home at three o'clock, after a walk from Noel's flat. There were no buses.

'Did you get to Mass?' his mother asked. Not, 'Where were you?' Just Mass.

'Aye, Ma. I went last night.' He hadn't, but she was fine with the lie.

Over dinner his father asked, 'Did you hear who it was that died last night?'

'No,' he replied. 'What happened?'

'Wee fella hit with a plastic bullet,' said his father, a forked carrot held poised in his hand. 'Eighteen years old – Mickey Mullan was saying this morning, outside the chapel. No name given out yet – they'll wait till all the family knows.' He ate the carrot and started on his ham.

Kevin recalled the previous night, when the crowd surged and he heard the shift in tone – that roar, a groan of common distress. Was it this that he had heard?

After dinner, he slept on the couch until his mother shook him awake. Then he changed to meet Liz, not at her house but at the junction of Northland Road and Duncreggan. He stood for a long time before he realised that she wasn't coming.

At her house, he knocked but there was no answer and then he was worried. An eighteen-year-old killed – he thought of Paddy. But surely, if that were the case, he'd be standing out-side a wake house now, not an empty one. And Paddy was nineteen.

When he finally made it as far as the Cave, sweating and

thirsty from the walk, he found his friends sitting inside and laughed with relief.

'You're here,' he said to Liz. 'I've been halfway round the town, looking for you. What happened? In fact, hold that thought till I get a drink.' He went to the bar, ordered a pint and turned to find Liz behind him.

'You don't know, do you?' she said.

'Know what?' He paid the barman and took a sip from the glass. 'Why didn't you meet me – what don't I know?'

'Peter Harkin's dead.'

He put the glass down carefully, and looked at her. She had that washed-out, no-make-up look of someone who had been crying sore all day.

'I went to your house and there was nobody there. I thought maybe it was Paddy,' he said vaguely.

'Mammy and Daddy are at Jerry's tonight – Kevin, where are you going?'

He couldn't look at her. The dark, smelly bar closed in on him. Paddy, Christy and Sinéad watched him walk past them and out of the bar again.

'What's wrong with him?' said Paddy, as Liz watched him leave.

'I don't know – I think it's shock. You were right, he didn't know,' she said.

She followed him out and looked up and down the street, ran through the arched gate in the Walls. If he had gone to Noel's she would see him on the way, but there was no sign. She ran across the road and down the narrow curve of Bridge Street, and there he was, sitting on the doorstep of an empty house.

'Christ, you can shift when you want to,' she said, sitting down beside him. 'Are you OK?'

'How the fuck do you think I am?' he said, looking straight ahead.

'Come back to the bar.' She tried to take his hand in hers but he pulled it away.

'Go back yourself,' he said. 'Leave me alone.'

'Why are you having a go at me, Kevin? I haven't done anything.'

He didn't answer her, but leaned his head against the door behind, staring into space. Annoyed, Liz got up and left him, but when she was outside the bar, she stopped and walked back to him. He was sitting in the same place, in the same position. She sat on the step again. This time she said nothing and they stayed like that for a long while.

Eventually, Kevin spoke.

'Was he the one from last night?'

She nodded. 'Yeah. Christy and Paddy were with him.'

'Jesus,' he said. He put his head down to his knees. He couldn't breathe. Tears fell and cooled on the backs of his hands; he watched them drop, then run off, followed by more.

He was destroyed. How could he explain it to her, when he could hardly grasp it himself?

He saw himself in the street, in the shadow of the building with the Easter sun fading. He knew that this was an extreme reaction and he chided himself, told himself how overly dramatic he was being. He couldn't control it, this reaction – this anger with himself, with his friend.

Stupid, fucking stupid.

Then somewhere deep, beneath the rage and the grief, a thought grew like a cold point of light.

They die – the ones you love die – and there's nothing you can do about it.

Liz's hand was on his back; he felt it, warm through his clothes.

'Ah, Kevin, it's OK,' she was saying. She didn't know what to do; he could feel that she was at a loss. She had expected him to be strong, to put his arm around her and tell her that it would be all right, he would look after her. Right now, he wasn't certain he could even stand up. He really wished she would go away again.

That decision he had taken, somewhere, at some undefined time, to guard against this very thing – it hadn't necessarily been a conscious one. He had cut his hair, changed his clothes, built a new relationship with the world. In that way, he had put aside the past, somewhere final, somewhere it was not to be disturbed or opened or looked for too closely.

He never spoke of it to his friends. It was why he liked them. More than that, it was why he had chosen them. His friends were part of his protection. No one was to die; life was not serious; sex was for fun; music was the most important thing in the world.

Fuck – he'd loaned him those records – how was he supposed to get them back now?

Peter Harkin – he had sneaked in.

That wet morning in the record shop. Was it because Peter's brother, bastard that he was, was inside? Or did he see himself in this boy, this teenager with a life before him – funny, happy? Whatever it was, Peter had crept in under the carefully placed defences and now he was dead.

Kevin, who had tried so hard to shield himself, was engulfed by the truth that it had all been in vain. He had no power to stop the bad stuff. Anger and grief ran through him, cold, like water in his veins.

She hadn't ever expected Kevin to cry. Not that she thought of herself as a child, but the possibility that she would have to look after him, to console him, had never entered her head.

He sat like a young boy on the step, withdrawn.

She wanted to leave him there, but she didn't. Instead, she said, 'Let's go for a walk.'

Taking his damp hand, she urged him to his feet. 'Come on, Kevin.'

He stayed silent and she was relieved. She suspected that Kevin would run again if she tried to talk about it. He was calm and absorbed in his own thoughts as they passed through the city.

'Where do you want to go?' she said. After an hour of silent wandering, they were on the outskirts and it was getting chilly and dark.

'I want to go home,' said Kevin.

Not sure if she was invited or not, she continued to walk with him, to the family home she had never seen. His firm grip on her hand was enough recognition of her right to be there as she was likely to get.

There was a light on in the front room as they walked down the path. His parents were at home and she was suddenly nervous, but Kevin opened the door and walked in front of her, into the brightness inside. Liz followed shyly and waited to be acknowledged.

'Mammy, this is Elizabeth,' he said to the small, solid-looking woman sitting in a chair by the fire.

His mother turned to see her and smiled. 'Come on in, love, till we get a look at you.'

He had called her Elizabeth.

She moved to the centre of the room, hoping he would make some excuse and they could go to the kitchen or some-where, but he sat on the sofa so she sat beside him, on the edge of the cushion, facing his mother.

He was there, in her face; her eyes an older version of his.

'Where's me da?' he asked.

'He's gone up already,' said his mother. She looked Liz over. 'Take off your coat, Elizabeth. Are you not going to get the wee girl a cup of tea, Kevin?'

'Aye, in a minute. That wee fella from last night, the boy that died. He was going with Liz's friend.'

'Ah, dear, that's so sad,' she said, with warmth in her expression. 'Is she OK, your friend?'

'She's not great,' said Liz.

'And how long was she going out with him?'

'Only a couple of months,' said Kevin.

'A couple of months is a lifetime when you're young,' said his mother. 'And was he your friend too?' she asked Liz.

'Aye, he was.' His mother was being kind; Liz didn't want to cry but could feel it coming. She looked to Kevin for rescue.

'Tea?' he said at last, and she nodded gratefully. 'We're going to sit in the kitchen, Ma – do you want a cup of tea?'

'No, thanks, too late for me,' said his mother, smiling at Liz.

In the cool kitchen they ate leftover chicken sandwiches and drank tea.

Kevin was different in his own house. She had never seen him do anything domestic before, unless you counted rinsing out a mug in Noel's kitchen. She watched him buttering bread and slicing meat.

He was pleased she was there and keen to make her welcome. His kitchen, much like her own, was small and slightly grubby, with tea towels and cups about the place. The smell of the day's dinner lingered, mixed with detergent and something metallic and damp from the place under the sink. This was his home. When he was hurt, this was where he wanted to be. Seeing him here, watching him move around the kitchen, she felt that something had shifted between them – a barrier had fallen away.

There were no alleyways here, or pubs. She was inside his life and she observed him, seeing him for the first time – smaller, kinder, more real. She watched him make the food and pour the tea and she didn't want to be anywhere else than here, with him, right now. She thought later that perhaps this explained what happened, after his mother called to them that she was going to bed. With the room free, they moved to the warmth of the embered fire.

'Are you all right, Kevin?' said Liz. They were lying on the sofa. He hadn't said anything about Peter since he'd told his mother and then he had carefully distanced himself from the story.

Now, in the quiet, she knew it was in both their heads and she had to say something.

'Not really,' said Kevin softly.

She turned her body until she was looking in his eyes, stretched out against him on the sofa, and kissed him. It didn't matter now, she wanted to make him feel better; she knew that this could change, could, in fact, be lost in an instant and regretted for ever.

Something fundamental altered in her; everything was wide open and at the same time, very simple and real. Kevin felt it in her and responded, and then the sex was just happening, there on Mrs Thompson's good sofa, with no one trying to stop it.

II

Bobby Sands died on 5 May; it takes a long time to die of hunger.

Liz had been woken from her sleep by banging bin lids and harsh whistles. The helicopter droned in the sky, sometimes faint, sometimes loud, threatening to land on the roof of the house. There were noises, shouts in the street, as people emerged from their homes. She didn't get up – she knew what it meant.

Instead, she lay in the dark listening to the growing noise and rattle, and thought of Kevin. He would be home already and she longed for his presence. Hours before, they had lain on crumpled, unwashed sheets in Noel's spare room, curled into each other. His breath was warm, his body curved around her as he slept.

That was last night, but she could still feel the weight of him.

She made herself look at the notes again. *Bloody Emma Woodhouse, and bloody Jane Austen.* Having struggled to finish the book in time for the exam, she had resorted to reading *Cliff's Notes*.

'*Emma experiences several major revelations in the novel that fundamentally change her understanding of herself and those around her. Which revelation do you think is the most important to Emma's development, and why?*'

She read the practice question, then lifted the novel again, hoping to find some relevant passage she could copy from. But it was hopeless. Placing the book back on the table, she rested her cheek on it, letting her eyes close; the pages smelled like oatmeal. She breathed deeply and allowed *Cliff* to take the weight of her tired head.

That morning she had found Johnny downstairs on the sofa, reading the paper.

'Why aren't you at work?' she asked.

'No one is working today,' he said, without looking up from his reading.

She didn't think this concerned her, and so she went to her class in the tech as normal. She sat alone in the classroom for forty minutes, until the lecturer finally arrived.

'Oh,' he said, pausing in the doorway. 'I wasn't expecting anyone to come in today.' Now that a student had shown up, he was obliged to stay.

They sat in silence, on the pretext that someone else would arrive and the lesson would begin. He didn't want to be there and she knew it, but she remained stubborn; she wasn't leaving. After all, this had nothing to do with her.

Eventually, feeling that it was his job to say something significant about the events of the day, the lecturer leaned forward, elbows on his desk, fingers interlaced.

'It's the ultimate sacrifice though, isn't it – to give your life like that?'

Liz looked at him in his creased tweed jacket, his 'country gent' elbow patches, the greasy locks of curling hair, and thought, *That's sentimental crap.*

It was an effort to have an independent political thought, one that didn't match the rules of the world she had grown up in. But Liz realised how angry, how thran, she felt; she refused to go along with this general mood. The truth was that she did not want to be associated with this struggle. It repelled her.

'I think it's stupid,' she said. 'What's the point of killing

94

yourself like that? What's the point of dying for a piece of land?'

The lecturer looked at her and said nothing. He checked his watch – the assigned hour for the class had come to an end.

'I'll see you next week,' he said, and he got up and left the room.

As she walked out of the building, Liz was glad in a grim kind of way. She had made her point. She had made him sit. And she didn't care about exams now, or university. She would leave this town anyway, with or without a university place.

So now she was lying with her head on a book that smelled of oatmeal, and she wondered why it had not occurred to her to stay away from college, like all the other students. Was she so far removed from the politics that she didn't know what everyone else obviously did?

The helicopter cut through the sky above her; it was a constant presence, a whining, distant rumble that made her shiver. It had been there all her life, marking out the days: tense and ordinary days, sunny Sundays and tiresome school mornings.

Today she had taken a position, exercised a clear thought about the political situation; it was for the first time, and it was against, not for. Seventeen days had passed since Peter's death. In the week immediately after, they had attended the wake and the funeral, not because they wanted to, but because they had to. White-faced, Orla had stood by the grave, not part of the family but not like the rest of them; she was stuck in the limbo of the new girlfriend. The wake had been the worst.

Because she had never met Peter's parents, she didn't want to go, but her own parents persuaded her on the second night; it would be the right thing to do. They would go with her, as would Sinéad and Liz, for moral support. They were right, of course; she couldn't pretend it wasn't happening.

When they were introduced, Peter's mother stared at her through drugged, dead eyes. His father was polite, shaking her hand in the way people do at wakes – firmly, without eye contact. Liz and Sinéad held a hand each, as Orla approached the coffin.

Candles sucked the air from the warm, packed room. There he lay, on white satin, a Rosary twisted through his thin fingers. His face was unmarked, young, with an unreal, waxen quality. They heard her whisper, 'It's not him.' Then her knees buckled and arms surrounded her and withdrew her from the room and the house.

In the days that followed, her friends didn't know what to do with her. It was a task beyond their experience.

'All you have to do is be a friend,' Bernie told Liz. 'Sit with her and talk to her.'

But Orla didn't want to talk. She was moody and sullen. So they did what teenagers do, and got her drunk. Then she cried and threw up, and they had to take her back to Liz's house to sleep it off. Since that night she had refused all invitations to socialise with them again.

But the strange part was how everyone else had got on with things. One of them had died, but it hadn't changed anything, at least not that she could see. It was as if this episode had slipped through their lives; they had looked at it, seen it and gone on. There wasn't another option: an option B to fall apart; an option C, stop there and do nothing, ever again; an option Z – whatever that would be?

The only thing they had was A, it seemed – to go on; not true for Orla, of course and, now that she thought about it, not true for her either.

Perhaps the effect was more a ripple than a tidal wave. She had made a stand, and she wondered if it had been inevitable all along; would she have arrived at that point anyway, even if Peter hadn't died in the horrible way he had?

Her eyes closed. The oatmeal scent soothed her as her cheek warmed the page.

Kevin also heard the bin lids rattle the night.

He was at his door when the whistles blew, hard and shrill, in the distance. Close by, on the corner of the street, a man shouted, 'Bobby Sands is dead!' It was a call to arms.

He pulled his door key from the lock and turned towards the street again, in search of a confrontation on which to cool his rage.

12

Noel had been in his granny's bathroom cabinet, coming home with a selection of blood-pressure tablets and Valium pills of varying strengths. He carried a sample of each in a small tin box that he had also removed. The same box lay, depleted of much of its stock, on the table in his flat.

An afternoon that had started out with a few cans of beer quickly became a chemistry lesson; an ideal chance to try some of Granny Baxter's nerve tablets, perhaps one of the lower-strength tranquillisers. With one Roche in him, after half an hour Paddy was complaining.

'What is it these are supposed to do? I don't feel anything.'

'They're supposed to make you feel calm – do you not feel calmer?' said Christy.

'No, I don't. Here, give us one of them stronger ones, Noel.'

Noel threw a pill across the room. It landed with a bounce. Paddy retrieved it from under the sofa, picked the fluff off it and swallowed it down with a gulp of lager. He sat back and waited to feel the effects. To keep up with him, Christy and Noel also helped themselves to the contents of the little box.

The dead were coming in a rush. Not even a month since Peter had gone and three more hunger strikers were out of the picture. Others were dead, too, in town and outside of it. What else was there to do but get off your head?

In the prison, they were waiting for another one to go soon. They had planned the strike well, to space the deaths two weeks apart. If it wasn't settled soon, it was in danger of becoming routine.

Everyone knew how a hunger striker progressed, from life to ultimate death; the move to the hospital wing, the lapse into coma, then the few uncertain hours when it was still possible for someone to intervene, or stand aside. Everyone knew how long it would take for death to come. As the days started to number into the sixties for each of them, people began to tell each other, 'It won't be long now.'

It was grim.

Christy and Paddy had seen enough of death. They had been scared off. Of course, neither said this, but then they hadn't said much at all; not about what had happened, not about how they felt. Drink and drugs, the two great killers of pain, were the way to go.

Noel had been experimenting for years. Christy might have talked about Vietnam vets and their drug-taking prowess but hadn't strayed beyond cannabis and mushrooms – maybe a bit of acid once. Paddy was the same.

This was new. Noel watched them slump under the effects, slumping himself, glad of the company. The narcotics were strong, untested for tolerance. Neither cared that they were going somewhere new. Surely that was the point?

Paddy sprawled across the sofa, staring at a beer stain soaked into the once crisp, freshly pinned Bob Marley poster. Christy rested his head on a cushion and stretched across the floor. The hair on the sides of his head was growing back rapidly, but the stubble itched. He scratched at it as he lay there.

Noel had his armchair, surrounded by crushed beer cans and cups growing mould on cold tea. He rolled a joint on the arm of the chair; tobacco spilled over the side, missing the cigarette papers. The record that had been playing in the corner ended, and the needle began to skip over in the final groove.

. . . *t-tic t-tic t-tic.*

'Somebody change the record,' slurred Christy. 'Put on

something good.' Everything had slowed. Speaking the words was an effort.

Paddy groaned, his arm a dead weight as he stretched it in the direction of the sound, then dropped it to his side.

'I can't move,' he said, and laughed at some private joke, sniggering quietly to himself before his head fell back and his eyes closed.

'I'll do it,' said Noel, through the papers he was licking.

. . . *t-tic t-tic t-tic.*

He put a light to the joint and inhaled. His head rolled forward on his chest and stayed there. The joint burnt along its length, ignored.

. . . *t-tic t-tic t-tic.*

As the drugs took full effect, no one moved.

. . . *t-tic t-tic t-tic.*

Christy came round, shivering in a draught that blew in under the door. The record was still skipping over on the turntable and the room was darker; the sun had moved from the window. How long had he lain there? He lifted his arm, heavy and numb from the crush of his full weight, and hit Noel on the shin with it.

'Hi, pass it on, will ye?'

There was no response. He reached up, took the cold joint from Noel's hand. 'You let it go out, Noel,' he said, looking at the stub between his fingers. 'Give us a light?'

Noel didn't move. Christy laughed until it occurred to him that he couldn't see him breathing and then he was scared. Climbing to his knees, he shook Noel to see if he was still alive. Noel snorted softly as he breathed in and muttered something that sounded like swearing.

'Give it over here,' said Paddy from the sofa.

'It's dead,' said Christy.

Paddy sat up, rubbing his eyes like a child. 'Jesus, that was strong,' he said. 'Skin up.'

Christy threw the lit joint and it hit Paddy on the forehead, burnt end first.

'Fuck off, Christy,' he shouted, holding his head. 'Where did it go – do you see it?' He found it in the crease of the cushions. 'That wasn't funny,' he said, lying down again. 'And take that record off to fuck.'

As Christy crawled across the floor, there was a sharp bang on the front door.

'I'm not moving,' said Paddy. There was another bang. With an effort, he clambered off the sofa and out into the hall where he pulled the door open. Christy recognised Kevin's voice. He hadn't seen him for weeks, not even in the pub. He had taken Peter's death bad.

Not bad enough to stop him riding Paddy's wee sister, thought Christy.

Noel had divulged that they had visited the flat several times, making use of the room upstairs. Noel didn't care – people had to have somewhere to go – but Christy was pissed off.

'What do you want them to do?' Noel had said. 'Use some back alley?'

He listened to Christy spout his outrage. They were taking advantage of Noel's good nature.

'Jealousy is a terrible thing,' he said in reply, with a mocking shake of his head. 'And there's no need to tell Paddy, right?'

Paddy was quite relaxed about it when Christy told him, at the first opportunity he had. 'I assumed they were doing it anyway,' he said, with a shrug. 'For a start, he's twenty-five. And it's up to her what she does.'

The sudden smell met Kevin when he entered; it was a stench beyond the rancid damp that seeped from the walls.

This was squalor, dirt. Noel had let his housekeeping go. Paddy returned to the sofa, relit the joint from the ashtray and handed it to him.

Taking a pull, Kevin looked at Noel.

'Is he alive?'

'Aye. We held a mirror under his nose – he's breathing,' said Paddy.

Christy was still on his knees by the turntable, trying to put the needle on the edge of a record. He swayed and lost his balance, lurching forward. The needle screeched through the album, scoring it as it rotated.

'Fucksake, Meehan,' said Kevin. He practically lifted Christy away before he could do any more damage. There was a three-inch gouge in the vinyl. All right, it was one of Noel's sad hippy LPs, but even Yes deserved better than this.

'What are you on? You're like three junkies,' he said, looking up from the damage.

'Noel's granny's nerve tablets,' said Paddy. 'Do you want one?'

'No, thanks,' said Kevin, sitting back up on the sofa.

Kevin knew Noel's tastes. He'd kept him company once or twice.

'What the fuck are you two at?' he said.

Paddy and Christy had crashed again, one on the sofa and one on the floor. Kevin leaned over Noel.

'Noel – are you OK?' To his relief, Noel twisted in the chair.

Kevin lifted the cannabis and tobacco, saying to himself, 'Might as well, as I'm here.'

He selected *Boy* from the pile of albums on the floor. The child's soft eyes gazed at him from the cover as he removed the disc and put it on the turntable. It was the final day of Liz's exams. The thought of a summer with her was very welcome. There was a tenderness to their relationship now, and a loving feel to the time they spent together, in bed and out of it.

He was very happy. This terrible thing had happened, and it had been bad there, for a while. He was sad when he thought of Peter; of course, that pain was real. But in recent weeks, sleep came easier; he had this very clear feeling that time had passed or, rather, that change had happened, as if he had travelled instantaneously forward in time. He could observe what was happening around him and see it for what it was – right now – instead of through the prism of the past. That thing he had feared most, the fear of pain, a fear that loss and terror could catch up with him and destroy him again, it hadn't happened. He had survived.

He grieved for his friend, but the grief didn't annihilate him. He wasn't the boy who had been terrorised and beaten – no one was coming after him, no soldiers, no police. He had carried the fear with him. He might have denied it, swatted it away, but it had never left. It erupted like a sickness, bringing confusion, leaving him unsettled and exhausted.

And now it was gone; its absence felt like coming up for air. He looked at his friends, trying to kill the pain with whatever drugs they could find, thinking they were winning by allowing themselves not to feel. For the first time, he knew he was wiser than them, felt the benefit of experience, good and bad.

The cannabis hit rose up through him and spread, tingling, through his limbs. Ignoring the smell of the room, he moved Paddy's feet out of the way, closed his eyes and, with his head resting on the back of the sofa, let the music take over.

13

Jim wasn't sure if it was his bladder that woke him. He turned over and looked at the clock on the bedside cabinet. Its hands glowed green in the dark – two o'clock.

The June sun had concentrated all its strength on the walls and windows of their bedroom during the second part of the day, and even now, the heat in the room stifled him. He looked across to the windows. They had left the curtains open and both windows wide, but it was just as hot, and not a breath of air circulated to cool him. The curtains hung, undisturbed.

Maybe he should take off his underwear and lie naked, the way the young ones did? His supposedly lightweight vest clung to his back and chest; he couldn't breathe.

Bernie would be scandalised if she woke up to a naked man in her bed. When was the last time he had been intentionally naked in this room – other than for dressing? With a house full of children who could walk in unannounced, even that didn't happen often. It had been years, many years, since he and his wife had lain naked together in bed.

The thought of her reaction made him smile; it would nearly be worth it, to see that. She snored softly beside him. He turned to see her dark head, her outline, curled under covers that were pulled up to her chin. The heat didn't bother her.

Like the brick in the walls, she seemed to absorb it throughout the day and radiate it during the night – he couldn't move far enough away from her in bed. Maybe if he left his drawers on, for decency's sake? They felt long and heavy, twisted around his groin. He really needed to pee.

There was an open window in the bathroom. Still no breeze, but the night air carried echoes from the street, shouts from far away, a passing car, and voices, a conversation that sounded close enough to be at their front door.

It was Patrick's voice, and another that he knew but couldn't place. Something, the tone perhaps, told him they were not talking about football. He waited, listening. The other voice, the one that wasn't Paddy's, started again.

'He was your friend.'

'I'm supposed to be going away.'

'Somebody told me who to talk to, the person you have to ask . . . They shot him dead in the street, Paddy. You can't let on you have nothing to do with it.'

'I know what happened. I was there too, remember?'

There was a long pause. Jim put the toilet seat down and sat on it, waiting to hear more.

Christy spoke again. 'I don't think it's OK to do nothing, not any more.'

'Why? What difference would it make?'

A pause again, then Christy's voice. 'I don't know . . . because of Harkin? Because to be honest, I agree with the hunger strike – they're not just criminals, are they? I've thought about it a lot. If more people get involved, maybe it'll be over sooner? Maybe me and you should do our bit? Do you really want to end up just being a druggy, in a squat in London?'

'Who said anything about being a druggy? I don't want that – I'm going there to get a job, which is more than I'll ever get in this shithole.'

Jim was relieved to hear his son get angry.

'All I'm saying is this,' said Christy. 'Peter Harkin was one of us and that could have been you, or me, lying dead. What's more important, Paddy? How long do we let them get away with it?'

Paddy said nothing for a long time, and Jim waited to hear his answer. Finally he spoke.

'I don't know. Maybe I'll think about it. You're not the only one who's angry, you know? I keep seeing his face, from that night – with his eyes open. Scares the shit out of me.'

Jim got up from his seat and left the bathroom. He had to be calm and he had to be quiet, and right now it was an effort because he felt like being neither. But Bernie couldn't know what he had just heard. He closed the bedroom door and turned on the landing light.

The bathroom was immediately above the front door and they would see the light through the glass panel. He wanted them to know that he was up. He walked downstairs and opened the front door. They were leaning against the wall outside, smoking.

Both boys jumped at the sight of him, standing there in his yellowing, saggy underwear.

'I think it's time you were away home, Christy,' said Jim.

The boys exchanged a glance. Had he heard? It was hard to tell – they couldn't see his face in the dark.

'He's going now, Da,' said Paddy. 'See you tomorrow, Christy.'

Jim didn't move from the door.

'All right, Da. I'll be in in a minute – you don't have to wait on me,' said Paddy, irritated. Jim turned and went into the hall. Christy started up the path, then turned to Paddy.

'Meet me in the town. I'm serious about this, but I can't make you do it. You have to make up your own mind.'

Paddy watched Christy disappear down the street. Before entering the house he listened to hear if his father had gone back to bed, but Jim was waiting at the top of the stairs and he caught him by the arm as Paddy tried to squeeze past him.

'What was all that about?' he said.

'All what?' said Paddy.

'I didn't like what I heard of that wee discussion, the one you and your man were having there.'

Jim held his gaze. His sullen, angry son tried to pull his arm away, but Jim couldn't let this go.

'That's not what I want for you, son – don't do it.'

'Do what, Da? What are we doing?' He was full of sarcasm. Jim spoke softly but with urgency.

'I know your friend died. And I know you two are angry about that. But joining up with the boys isn't going to bring him back. Me and your ma, Paddy, we've tried to keep you – all of you – away from all that bother. We want more for you.'

There was no escape.

Where's the privacy in this fucking house? he thought. How could they still be spied on at two o'clock in the bloody morning?

His back was to the wall, trapped by his father. He knew he would have to stand and take the lecture. But he refused to look at him.

Instead he watched the ceiling light where the moths had gathered. He watched their manic flutter, how they flung their fat bodies into the glass, slamming heedlessly and bouncing off. He watched as one went too close, hit the hot bulb with a hiss and a soft slap and fell, dead, on the carpet.

His da was never going to let this go. Why couldn't he just shut up and let him go to bed? But Jim had plenty still to say.

'Even calling you – and I know you've hated it, and people think it was just a laugh – but even calling you Elvis. I wanted . . . I want you to do more in your life, son. I want you to play music, travel, see the world . . . do something with the life we gave you.' He paused, glancing towards the door of his bedroom where Bernie still slept, he hoped. Then, more quietly, he pleaded.

'Please, son. I wanted my boys to go somewhere, do something more than I ever got the chance to. Don't go down that road.'

Paddy took his eyes away from the moths and looked at his father, standing there in his ridiculous underwear. He didn't know how to answer this stuff.

That stupid name. What was he supposed to be – a Boy Named Sue? Some kind of experiment?

He wasn't like his father – he would never be like him. What did his father know about anything, except to do what he was told by his wife, and go to Mass, and have too many wains?

Jim held him fixed to the wall, his arm in a firm grip. He looked down at the worn hand, thickened by rough work, the stain of tobacco that smudged the inside of the forefinger and its hard nail. How many fags did it take, how many a day, smoked over how many years, to generate a stain like that? Dirty, orange-brown, creased into the skin, the mark of an old man.

Suddenly he shrugged the hand off his arm.

'Leave me alone, Da,' he said and walked into his room, where the snoring Johnny turned over in his sleep.

Early the next morning Paddy lay in bed, staring in melancholy form at Ian Curtis, still there. He was avoiding his father and intended to stay in bed until he knew he had gone to work.

In the quiet, his thoughts returned to Peter; images of that night, the hospital, Peter's mother, her face as she arrived in the hospital casualty unit – the fear.

They had stayed because they couldn't leave their friend with strangers, but they had watched from a distance as the mother and father talked to the nurse, then entered the room where Peter's body lay on a trolley, waiting for them. Paddy dreaded, and expected, screams, wailing. He was afraid to hear their distress and at the same time he craved it. But as the door closed there was only silence.

They waited, watching. When no one came out, and there was no sound, Paddy remembered thinking, *He must be alive.* But of course he wasn't.

Christy said, 'Let's go,' and so they left the hospital.

On the walk home, they were tired and quiet, most of the time. And afraid. Afraid of running into the police and getting picked up.

When they arrived at the bridge it was clear of police and soldiers, and they crossed the river. As daylight returned it began to feel unreal, as if a long time had passed – years in fact. Just then, if he had wanted to, he could have believed that it was a dream and let himself go calm as they walked.

Did he feel calm now, really? All the drugs in the world, all the tranquillisers, couldn't disperse the thoughts that muddled his head, or the fear and anger that he was unable to explain to himself, or speak about to anyone, because he could never tie them down, mark them for what they were. He wouldn't allow himself to look in the direction from which they came, because with the anger came pain, and he could face neither.

The drugs didn't work. Paddy wanted to feel strong again; he wanted to be decisive, to take control. There was nothing fun in what he needed to do – it was no longer a game.

He met Christy in town. 'OK,' he said, before he could talk himself out of it. 'Fuck it – I'll do it.'

14

Lifting his head from his work, Jim looked down the street. That fella of Elizabeth's was bound to show up at some point, and when he did, Jim wanted to catch him on his own for a quiet word.

He was digging a bed in the front garden, a semicircle of dark, heavy clay underneath the living-room window. Bernie wanted flowers. The front of the house needed brightening and this was the solution; a display of orange marigolds and purple and white lobelias. It was back-breaking work, and hot with the summer sun shining down relentlessly. He could already feel the back of his neck was burnt; it stung when his collar rubbed against it. With an effort he straightened and once again was shocked at how stiff he was.

Too old for this carry-on.

Paddy was avoiding him. He had tried to get him on his own since that conversation on the landing. But it was hard when he was obviously determined never to be in the same room as his father, and spent most days out of the house.

Jim didn't know how this worked. How did you join an illegal organisation and what did it involve? Secret meetings, no doubt, but where? In a house, a field somewhere up the country, the back room of a bar? Would they take anyone, or did you have to apply, like for a job?

He was fairly certain that any fool could sign up. They weren't that flush with volunteers, not even now when the place was lit up with anger. But how could he know for sure?

This Kevin – the boyfriend – looked like his best hope of

breaking Paddy down, or at least finding out what was going on. He was older, and he was the one who came up with the London scheme, for them all to go across the water. At least, he was the one getting the blame from Bernie.

Maybe he could persuade him to start pushing the England idea again? Anyway, that was the plan, as far as it went. The fella was a regular visitor, now that Elizabeth had finished her studies. So Jim was waiting for him.

Of course, he hadn't appeared in three days.

Once more, Jim pressed with his foot on the top of his spade, edging around the crescent of soil, bending occasionally to pick out a rock or a weed, then straightening to throw it on the growing pile beside the doorstep. He had uncovered a large stone and was digging around it – a piece of cement block, left over from the time the house was built. There was a noise behind him, the rusted hinge scraping against itself. It was Kevin, holding the gate open and looking guardedly at him.

'All right, Mr McLaughlin?' he said as he walked towards the front door.

'Hold on a minute, Kevin. I want a word with you.'

It was the first time that Jim had spoken directly to him, or used his first name for that matter. Except when he answered the door to them, giving them a hard time, Jim didn't feel the need to involve himself with the comings and goings of his children's friends, romantic or otherwise.

Oh, God, here we go, was Kevin's immediate thought. *What does he know?*

'You lookin' for our Elizabeth?' said Jim, although it was obvious. He needed some way to open the conversation.

'Aye,' replied a puzzled Kevin.

'Aye, well, she's out in the back garden, sunning herself,' continued Jim, leaning on the handle of his upright spade.

'Is she?' said Kevin, before reaching to knock on the door.

'So –' Jim's voice sounded loud in his own ears. 'What are you doing with yourself these days, Kevin?' The boy couldn't get away from him quick enough, but was forced to turn again, to answer him.

'Nothing much,' he said.

'No work about?' said Jim, determined to keep him there.

'Nothing doing. I keep applying when I see anything, but sure, half the time they don't even write back to you.'

Was Liz's father about to ask him what his intentions were towards his daughter, or what?

'Aye,' nodded Jim. 'It was always the same in this town.'

He paused for a moment, and then spoke in a softer tone. 'Kevin, I'm looking to have a quiet word with you, and it's to go no further. Is that OK?'

He beckoned for Kevin to climb over the hedge, and come into the garden towards him.

'Here, take this,' he said, handing him a garden fork. 'If anyone looks out, you can tell them you're helping me with this stone.' Kevin took hold of the fork.

'What can I do for you, Mr McLaughlin?'

'I'm not sure you can do anything yet, son, but I'll ask you anyway. Are you still thinking about going over to England?'

'If I can get the money together, I am. Why?'

'Make sure our Patrick goes with you, right?'

Kevin vividly recalled the embarrassing living-room scene. 'I thought you and Mrs McLaughlin were dead against it?'

Jim looked at Kevin for a second, weighing him up. Could he say the unsayable to him? Right now, it didn't feel as though there was a choice.

'You're to say nothing to Elizabeth about this.' There was a hint of a threat as he paused, making sure that Kevin recognised the seriousness of what he was about to say next.

'I overheard Patrick talking to that friend of his, that Christy boy, about joining the Provos, the other night. Now –' he spoke in an even softer voice and looked quickly at the window – 'I've tried to talk to him about it, but sure, he's never going to listen to me, and now I can't even get him to stay in the same room as me, for fear that I'll have a go at him about it again. You don't strike me as stupid, Kevin, and you're close enough to him – to both of them, maybe – that you might have heard something of what they're up to.'

Kevin looked at Jim's worried face. He didn't know what shocked him more: what he had just been told, or that Jim was confiding with him in this conspiratorial manner. He looked at the living-room window. Liz's mother was standing there, watching them.

'Is it this stone you want shifting?' Kevin asked suddenly.

Jim stared at him until Kevin nodded, almost imperceptibly, in the direction of the window where his wife continued to stand, watching them.

'Aye, son. You try and lift it up and I'll get the spade underneath,' he answered, convincingly. The two of them made a show of working on the stone. Kevin pushed the prongs of the fork in and under, using his heavy boot to press down for leverage, and Jim worked around the edge, loosening the clay. It was buried deeper than it looked, with only the top third showing. By the time Bernie had moved away from the glass, they had succeeded in hoisting the stone out of its bed of soil. Kevin lifted it with his hands and carried it to the doorstep. He rubbed his hands together, shaking off the clay.

'I haven't seen Paddy for ages,' he said. 'Nothing was said to me about anything like this. I would have told him to catch himself on, if he had said anything. Are you sure about this? Because the last time I was with him and Christy, the two of them were off their faces on . . .' He stopped. Jim didn't need to know about the tranquillisers.

'On what – were they drunk?'

'Aye, drinking whiskey – but they were just normal, other than that.'

'Couple of eejits, the two of them, throwing stones at the soldiers and then that friend of theirs gets himself killed – a friend of yours too.' He stopped to look for a reaction from Kevin.

'Drunk?' he went on. 'Aye, and the rest, no doubt. You think I don't know what else they're up to? Maybe the boys wouldn't have them anyway, if they think they're a couple of junkies?'

'I wouldn't count on that,' said Kevin, surprised at the father's candour. He remembered Ciaran's brother, his brazen attempt to recruit him and the evangelical language he used, that evening in April. They'd have them all right.

'Talk to him, Kevin. You're old enough to know where this is going to lead – maybe he'll listen to you.'

'I can't promise anything, Mr McLaughlin, but I'll have a word with him and see what he says. It might just be big talk.'

'You and him are very chatty with each other all of a sudden,' said Bernie as Jim stood by the kitchen sink, scrubbing soil from beneath his fingernails. 'What was all that about?'

'I was just getting him to lend me a hand with a big block of cement in the new bed out there. Couldn't get it out myself. Fair play to him, he got stuck in and lifted it out for me. He's not a bad fella, that one,' he said. He watched Kevin and Liz in the garden, sprawled out on a blanket under the washing line.

Bernie came over to stand beside her husband: Kevin was lying on his back, hands behind his head. Liz was beside him, on her front, reading a magazine. They looked very comfortable in each other's company.

'You'll not be saying that if he gets that wee girl pregnant, Jim McLaughlin, or drags her off to England, to live in sin with him in some grubby bedsit. And let me tell you, he'll have me to worry about if harm comes to her, whether he has your good opinion or not.'

15

Five days later, Kevin squeezed through the turnstile at the dole office and there was Paddy, being searched by the security man at the gate. Kevin stopped to speak to him.

'I'm late,' said Paddy, rushing past.

'I'll wait for you outside,' shouted Kevin, not sure if he had been heard.

He kicked at the weeds that sprouted along the pavement, weeds old enough to have flowered. How to bring this up, that was the problem – Paddy would deny everything. And maybe his father had heard wrong; there was nothing to know. People talk shite sometimes – what they would do if they got a chance. He'd done it himself. But this was all about Peter; he knew they had been witness to some bad things. He knew how those images could linger.

Paddy finally came through the gate. They walked down the hill together.

'No craic then?' said Kevin, breaking the silence. He glanced at his friend, half hoping to see an outward change in him, some visible clue to a decision, longer hair or ordinary sensible shoes, something that would reveal an internal shift in his priorities. But he looked the same as he always did: puffy-eyed, thrown together, dragged from bed.

'I haven't been out,' said Paddy, without returning the look.

'Haven't seen you around the house, either,' said Kevin.

'No – I know.' Silence, again. *Just ask him*, thought Kevin. *Keep it light.*

'So, your da started talking to me, all of a sudden,' he began, thinking he could turn this into some sort of funny anecdote. He went six steps further, before realising that Paddy had stopped dead, and was no longer beside him. When he turned to look for him, Paddy started walking again.

'What was that?' said Kevin.

'Nothing. I just thought I saw somebody, that's all.'

'Are you all right?'

Paddy faced him full on. 'What do you mean, me da's started talking to you? Does he not always talk to you?'

'You know he doesn't,' Kevin replied. 'It's always your ma – your da sits in the chair reading the paper when I'm there.'

They were walking again. Paddy tried a laugh but could barely conceal his agitation. 'So why has he started, "all of a sudden"?' he said.

'He cornered me in the garden the other day. Had me digging out stones for him, for Christsake – and he was asking about you and Christy and some shite about you two volunteering for the 'RA. What the fuck, Paddy?'

This time Kevin stopped. A dumpy woman, carrying two bags of shopping, nearly ran into the back of him. She threw him a look and a rebuke as she manoeuvred around them.

Paddy sighed, 'For Christsake, Da.'

'I told him it was probably nothin',' said Kevin. 'But I'm looking at you now, Paddy, and it doesn't look like nothin' any more.'

Paddy didn't answer. He stood with his head down for an uncomfortably long time as Kevin watched him, and the tension built between them. This was not going to be good.

Finally, slowly, Paddy spoke in a low voice.

'You know, this is none of your business. It's up to me what I do, Kevin, not you. If I feel the need to take a stand on all of this, all these people dying on the street – in front of my own eyes – then I'm not going to wait around for your permission, or me daddy's, before I do.' His voice shook.

'That's fair enough,' said Kevin, just as softly. 'But it's not you. Aye, Harkin died. But you were rioting for a laugh, Paddy. Not a movement.'

'Well, it's different now.'

'What have you done? Have you spoken to someone yet? Have you actually joined up?'

Instead of an answer, Paddy started walking again.

'What about us going to London – what happened to those plans?' said Kevin, moving quickly to keep up. To his surprise, Paddy laughed.

'Do you think I could go and live among them murdering bastards? Is that really what you think, that I should just put it all to one side and forget?'

'There's nothing you can do that will bring him back. It'll ruin your life. At least England gives you a chance of more,' said Kevin.

Paddy exploded in fury. 'What do you know? When have you ever committed yourself to anything? Ever?' he sneered. 'The age of you – no job, no wife, no wains. Hanging around with us, like you're the same age as us – riding my wee sister. Don't be offering me advice about something you know nothin' about.'

Kevin stepped back, stunned at this unwarranted attack, the bitterness of it. Paddy's face was inches from his own; he felt the warmth from his breath, inhaled it. Then with both hands he pushed Paddy away, slamming him in the chest.

Paddy crashed against the plate-glass window of a café. The pane shuddered. Inside, a man got to his feet, banging the glass with his fist, mouthing some obscenity at Kevin who was now holding Paddy by the neck of his shirt, pressing him against the window.

'You're a nasty wee shite when you want to be, aren't you, McLaughlin?' he said. 'You don't know anything about me.'

He let his hand drop, stepped back from an alarmed Paddy, and walked away through the small group of bystanders which had formed around them.

When he called to the house two days later, Jim caught him again, this time in the front hall as he waited for Liz to ready herself to go out.

'Did you talk to him? What did he say?' he asked.

'I saw him, aye,' said Kevin.

'Keep your voice down,' said Jim, looking over his shoulder at the closed living-room door. They could hear the television. 'She thinks I'm only going out to buy fags.'

He opened the front door and pushed Kevin outside.

'So? What did he say?'

Kevin's inclination to get involved in this whole thing had waned considerably in the intervening days. Paddy's words hurt; was he some sad git with nowhere else to go? He had gone from *Fuck him* to *Maybe I should help?* and back again to *Fuck him*, since they'd spoken.

'He said it was none of my business.'

'You didn't say I told you?' said Jim.

'What else was I supposed to say?' said Kevin, his voice rising.

Jim pushed him further away from the door. 'For Godsake, did you have to mention me? Could you not just have wheedled it out of him?'

'Wheedled it out?' Kevin's exasperation was starting to show. 'It's not the kind of subject that you can just bring up out of the blue, Mr McLaughlin! What was I supposed to say? "Do you fancy a pint, and, by the way, did you ever think about joining the 'RA?"'

Jim sat down on the neighbours' wall with a sigh, looking up at Kevin.

'So, tell me what he said.'

'Well, he didn't deny it, and he gave me some very clear reasons why he felt it was the right thing to do. But he wasn't clear about what they had done so far – if they'd spoken to anyone or anything like that.'

Kevin reached into his pocket for tobacco and started a roll-up.

'And what about moving away – did you ask him about that?'

Kevin remembered the laugh that notion got. 'No chance of that happening,' he said. 'He called it "living in the middle of them murdering bastards" – sorry, his language, not mine.'

Jim put his head in his hands, distraught. His Brylcreemed quiff fell forward and Kevin suddenly felt sorry for the man.

'Is there not somebody that we can talk to – somebody in charge?' said Jim, his voice muffled behind his hands. 'If we talked to them and explained that they're just a couple of eejits, wains, maybe they'd tell them to go home.'

'I don't think that's the way they look at it.' Kevin was watching the front door. What the hell was keeping Liz? 'They need numbers to keep the pressure on. They didn't expect that the hunger strike would go on as long as this and people are getting lifted all the time.'

Jim took his head out of his hands and looked at Kevin with renewed interest.

'You seem very clued up about all this. Do you know any-one we could ask? Somebody that could even point us in the right direction?'

Oh, no – I'm not going down that road, thought Kevin.

Jim had the look of a hopeful man again.

'Look, I've done what I can, and that's it,' he said.

'Kevin, you have to help me. What's Elizabeth going to think, if something happens to Patrick and you could have stopped it? I know nobody – I wouldn't know where to start.'

Jesus Christ, was he blackmailing him, or what?

'Why do you think I know any more than you?' he asked.

'You sound like you do, for a start. You've talked to somebody – how else would you know they're feeling the pressure?'

Every impulse told him to say no. The thought of approaching the 'RA for a favour repelled him. He had no desire to revisit the past. But if something happened to her brother, what would Liz think?

It was with deep reluctance that he said, 'I might know somebody – but I'm going to have to think about this, and I'm not making any promises.'

'That's all I can ask of you, son. Just do your best.' Jim got to his feet. 'Right, I suppose I'd better buy some fags, or she'll be thinking I've a woman on the go.' He began to walk down the path.

'Ah – you have to let me back inside,' said Kevin.

'Oh, aye!' Jim laughed, as he got his key out of his trouser pocket and quietly opened the door to the house. 'This conspiracy lark's tricky,' he whispered, cocking an eyebrow. 'Keeps yeh on your toes, eh?'

'Did somebody come in?' said Liz. He was sitting on the bottom stair. 'I thought I heard the door.'

'It was your da, going out.'

'Right? Still not talking to you, then?' she laughed.

If only, thought Kevin.

16

It was difficult to decide where to put themselves. Christy and Paddy stood awkwardly in the middle of the small bedroom. The bed was already taken by two men, one of them about eighteen, the other in his mid-thirties. Feeling exposed, they squeezed themselves into the gap between the cot and the window, and tried hard not to look in their direction.

Paddy stared at the picture on the opposite wall, above the bed – a teddy bear's picnic, in faded pastels. When he thought about joining up, this was not the scenario he had visualised. In his head, he had seen wood panelling and maybe a tricolour on the wall, not Holly Hobbie bed sheets and baby clothes.

After a week of waiting, they received the word to report to this address, at six o'clock on this day. When they arrived, they were hurriedly shown into the bedroom by a small, prematurely bald man who told them to wait there. The worried faces of the other recruits turned to them as they entered, then dropped again when it was clear that they were not of importance. That was ten minutes ago.

Paddy turned his head closer to Christy. 'Maybe we should just leave,' he said, under his breath.

'It'll be all right,' said Christy. 'We're here now.'

There was another knock on the door downstairs and they all froze, listening. There were voices at the bottom of the stairs – male voices – and then heavy steps climbing the stairs. The bedroom door opened, and two men came in, both middle-aged and tired-looking. One stood by the door while the other tried to impose himself on the scene by standing in as central a place as possible in the tiny room.

'OK,' he said, after a pause. 'Let me begin by saying, if you are here for a bit of craic, if you're here because you want to be a hero, if you are here for any other reason than a strong belief in the right to conduct a war against the British forces of occupation, and unless you are prepared to risk imprisonment and possible death to achieve an Irish Socialist Republic, then you need to consider, very carefully, what you are about to do. Because this is not a game you are entering into. It could, and probably will, cost you everything.'

It was a very impressive speech. Paddy felt the hairs rise on his arms as the man spoke. He went on.

'It will not be fun. It will be lonely, scary and dangerous.' He looked at each one of them, individually, for the briefest of seconds. The man by the door, as broad as the door itself, shifted from foot to foot.

'There is no shame in deciding that this is not for you. Right – now we are going to leave the room for a few minutes. If you want to, you can go now, and there will be no comeback about it.' He turned and nodded to his companion to open the door. They both exited the room.

Paddy looked at the two on the bed. The young one sat with his head bowed, but the older man scanned the room with a panicked eye, then stared straight at Paddy. All the while, his hand searched inside his jacket pocket for something he couldn't find. Suddenly, he got to his feet and without saying a word left the room. They could hear him on the stairs, taking them two at a time in his rush to get away. Paddy and Christy looked at each other, but neither moved.

The door opened again and the big man came back in. He looked at the empty place on the bed.

'Right,' he said. 'Who's first?' No one spoke.

'You,' he said to the boy on the bed. The boy pushed himself off the covers and left the room with him.

Paddy turned to Christy. 'Are you sure about this?' he said.

'Christsake, Paddy, it's all we've talked about for weeks, and you were all gung-ho about it. I'm staying. It's up to you – you heard the man.'

'I know,' said Paddy. 'I know you're right.'

They sat on the vacant bed in silence. There was a carefully placed row of toys lined along the wall behind them. Paddy lifted one of the dolls. He turned it over and it drawled, 'Maaaa,' in a slow, dull voice, as though its batteries were running out. The cotton print smock it wore fell up and over its curly head. There were no knickers on its hard, plastic bottom. He was about to make a joke about it, but then thought better of it and resisted the urge. Where were the kids? Maybe the ma had taken them away for a wee holiday, he thought. The house was very quiet. He turned the doll over again.

'Maaaa.'

'Put the doll down, Paddy,' said Christy. He looked at the closed door. 'What do you think they're doing out there?'

'Having a talk with him – maybe getting him to take the oath. They didn't look like they wanted to hang around, did they?'

There was movement on the landing and stairs, and then the front door closed with a bang. 'Go you first, Paddy – you're going to bottle it, sitting here on your own,' Christy said. The door opened again.

'Who's next?' said the man. Paddy got to his feet.

'I'll wait for you outside,' he said to Christy.

On the landing, the man opened the door immediately opposite – the master bedroom. Inside, the man in charge was waiting. He stood in the middle of the room again and spoke to Paddy.

'You have made your decision and now we will administer the Oath of Allegiance to you. This is your final opportunity to leave, if you have doubts,' he said, his voice stiff and overly formal.

'Go ahead,' said Paddy. 'I'm ready.' The silent man handed him a worn and creased piece of card that looked as though it had passed through many hands; Paddy's shook as he held it, and he realised his mouth was dry.

'Read out the words on the card,' prompted the man, and he began, his voice shaking to match his hands.

'"I do solemnly promise to uphold and have belief in the objectives of the Irish Republican Army, and obey all orders issued to me by the Army Council, and all my superior officers."'

That was all. The man took the card from him again.

'You are now a member of the Irish Republican Army,' he said. He was given an address and a day to go there, at which time he would be assigned to a brigade in town. Then he was free to leave.

From across the street, he watched the window of the room he had just left. He had joined the IRA and he wasn't even sure what it meant. He couldn't fire a gun – would they train him? Would there be a boot camp? Obstacle courses?

Christy crossed the road to join him, and Paddy saw he was wearing an Echo & the Bunnymen T-shirt. His biker jacket still had *The Clash* painted across the shoulders. Was this consistent with the dress code of a Republican paramilitary, he wondered? A soldier of Ireland?

'Pint?' said Christy, when he arrived beside him.

'Pint,' said Paddy.

17

Such a strange summer. June was gone, and July was slipping towards August.

It was that lazy sprawl of time when exams are over, and there are weeks left before plans have to be made for the future. Warm days – sometimes sunny, often overcast – were spent in the park or on long ambling walks with friends. They lounged on bedroom floors, with the record players spinning. Evenings were cool and wet, the soft rain lifting the scent of grass, dripping from full, overhanging branches and hedges.

The rage of the rioters seemed to have calmed with time; the reality was that the methods of war had shifted away from the streets to a deadlier, more organised approach. But the bin lids still rattled, of course, for the passing of another person dying for Ireland.

Liz was moving, stretching. She could feel it in herself, the tension and the excitement in her stomach, spreading through her limbs as she lay on the sofa. She closed her eyes and listened to the judder of the twin-tub in the kitchen. She felt the cool air of the room, shady despite the sunny day outside. Kicking the cushion that covered her bare feet, she swung her legs off the sofa and spread her arms wide. Then she stuck both feet into her slippers.

In the kitchen, her mother was surrounded by washing: whites, coloureds and darks, waiting for the machine to stop spinning its last load.

'I'm going over to Orla's for a while, Mammy. We said we'd watch the wedding together,' she called.

'Don't know what you'd want to be watching that nonsense for,' said Bernie. 'Don't be late for your dinner.' She resumed her wait, resting her hands on the lid of the spinner as it thumped to a halt.

Orla was still in her pyjamas when Liz arrived. 'Has it started yet?' she said, sitting beside her in front of the television.

'Aye, it's on now,' Orla said, moving over to make room for her. The streets of London were filled with flag-waving hoards, embellished soldiers and carriages.

'Did you see her yet?' Liz studied the scene. 'What about the dress?'

'You can see just a wee bit of it through the windows. The wee bridesmaids are lovely, though. It showed you them arriving at the chapel.'

'Cathedral, Orla,' said Liz. She sat down and took her shoes off. 'Where is everybody?' she said, looking around at the empty house.

'Me ma's down the town and me daddy's away out somewhere. He says there's better things to be doing than falling for this old shite – says it's the government, dangling shiny things in front of us like wains in a pram,' said Orla, her eyes following the gold carriage as it went along the Mall. 'I just want to see what she looks like in her frock. Do you want tea?'

'Aye, go on,' Liz said.

It was nice seeing Orla more like herself. The last few months had been hard on her and she still never mentioned Peter when they were together. Sometimes it was a relief; Liz had no answers for her. She had taken her mother's advice and tried to be a friend as much as she could. They sat with mugs of tea, watching the parade that was bringing Diana to her wedding.

Out of nowhere, Orla asked, 'Do you think she's still a virgin?'

Diana was just visible through the glass on the carriage

door, a vision seated in the billowy centre of her dress and veil, leaning forward for a better view of the crowds lining the avenues of leafy London, waving and smiling at her as she passed.

'I bet she is,' said Liz, with confidence. 'They'd have made sure of it. They've probably made her take a test or something, before they allowed him to propose – in case she was already pregnant.'

'Really?' Orla looked at her in horror, imagining what a test like that would involve. 'That seems a bit much.' *Poor Diana.*

The carriage pulled up to the cathedral steps. As the door opened, yards of crushed ivory silk swelled through. 'Aww look, it's all wrinkled,' said Liz.

'Maybe it's meant to look like that,' said Orla.

'I don't think so – it's wile-lookin'.'

'No, it's not, it's lovely,' said Orla, feeling unexpectedly defensive of Diana and her dress, and her virgin-testing ordeals. 'There, she's smoothed it all out now. Ooh, look at her train. I'd love to have a train like that when I get married.' She stopped talking. Liz watched her sad face.

'Look at the oul' da,' Liz said, keeping the commentary going until the moment passed. 'Look at him – he can hardly get himself up them steps. She is beautiful, isn't she?' Liz rested her chin on her cupped hands. 'I sort of feel sorry for her. Look at the one she's marrying – he's hardly a looker.'

'That's why they're bringing her into the family – good genes. They don't want the wains ending up with Charlie's ears,' laughed Orla.

'Or his nose,' said Liz.

'Or that hair, with the side parting!'

When they had stopped laughing at the thought of ugly royal babies, they slumped into the cushions to watch the wedding service. The music swelled in the cathedral as the bride began her walk down the long aisle.

'Orla?' said Liz.

'What?'

'Are you OK?'

There was silence. Liz was afraid to look at her. When she did, she saw Orla lost in her thoughts, her head down. After an agonising few seconds, during which Liz cursed herself for asking, Orla spoke.

'I don't know what I am, Liz. I really don't.'

There wasn't much point in stopping now.

'Do you think about him much?' said Liz.

Orla looked so sad. She was her friend; it seemed cruel not to ask.

'Aye.'

Here were the tears, rolling down her red face, her pursed lips trying to contain choking sobs. Liz shuffled across the sofa and put her arm around her shoulders. Their heads touched, and neither spoke as Orla cried. On the screen, Diana stood clouded in layers of veil, pale as a ghost as she quietly took her wedding vows. The sobs subsided and the tears dried.

The sun had moved and now shone through the window, reflecting on the screen. It made it difficult to see what was happening. Endless hymns droned on, none of them familiar, and pompous sermons in clipped English.

'Why don't we go to the shop and buy an ice pop?' said Liz. 'Go and wash your face.'

Orla would rather have crawled into bed, but she submitted to Liz's suggestion and when she reappeared in a T-shirt and cut-off jeans, she seemed brighter. They walked into the sunny day, relishing the heat.

In the corner shop, which was dark and cool and smelled of dusty potatoes, children swarmed around the sweets, choosing from the cartons on display.

'Can I have . . . two Black Jacks? Naw . . . can I have . . . a

Blackjack and a . . . Refresher, and . . . can I have a Bubbly as well?' mused a small girl, putting her coppers on the counter in front of the bored assistant. Liz leaned over the heads of two dirty boys who were poking around deep inside the freezer. She lifted out two Giant Bars and paid at the counter. They walked back to the house, peeling the blue and silver foil from the ice cream. Orla stripped hers off and rolled it tight into a ball, which she flicked away.

'You know, Liz,' she said. 'That morning, when you and your mother came to our house.' She licked the end of the ice cream. 'I heard you, you know? The knock on the door woke me up. I heard your mammy's voice and I knew something really terrible had happened. Why else would she be there? And I didn't want to come down the stairs because I didn't want to know what it was.'

After months of silence, the big cry had released something. She couldn't stop it all coming out.

'Your mammy said Peter was dead, but then you both left, and they didn't come near me. They just sat downstairs drinking tea, and I didn't know what to do. I went back to bed.' She watched Liz for a reaction.

'I lay there for ages until I had to get up, and only then did she tell me. I let on I was hearing it for the first time . . . and I felt like a real faker, crying like I was putting it on for them.' Her voice was very low, as if she was confessing.

'They told us they wanted you to sleep, that you would know soon enough. They wanted to give you a few more hours of peace,' said Liz. 'I don't think they meant any harm, Orla.'

'I know that,' said Orla. 'But I lay in my bed all that time, thinking I wasn't important to them. That it didn't matter to them that I was his girlfriend.'

She was crying again. Liz pulled her onto a step and held her hand as she continued.

'Then it just felt like that was true, Liz. So I couldn't talk about it, not to you or Sinéad even. I had no right to be properly sad, like his family would be.'

Liz turned to her. 'We probably should have asked you, Orla, but we didn't. Because we thought it would be too sore on you. And we were useless and didn't know what to say. But you have every right to be sad – you should be sad. There'd be something wrong with you if you weren't, right?'

Orla nodded.

'And you can tell me anything. You can talk about anything you want, and I promise that I'll listen, even if you're driving me up the walls with your moaning and crying – OK?'

Laughing, Orla wiped the tears off her cheeks.

By the time they got back to the house, Charles and Diana were halfway down the Mall, waving and smiling from another carriage. The spectacle had lost its charm now that they had seen the dress. The rest was just horses and the Queen in a hat.

'It looks really hot in London,' said Liz. The fountain in front of the Palace was filled with paddlers. She would be living there soon, if all went to plan.

'It's hot here,' said Orla. There wasn't a breeze in the living room. 'Let's go to Sinéad's and get her out of bed.'

The front door to the house was wide open when they got there, so they went in without knocking and found Sinéad spread out along the length of the couch, eating a crisp sandwich. On the screen, Diana was looking pleased with herself, on the balcony of Buckingham Palace.

'Don't the English make you sick?' she said, sitting up to make room. 'Anyway, it's a day off work. Where were you two?'

'In Orla's, watching this,' said Liz.

'What do you think – nice dress, shame about the groom?'

She stretched and yawned. 'I'm so bored. What about tonight – are we out or what?'

Liz picked a magazine off the floor. 'Me and Kevin are out anyway,' she said, flicking through it.

'Do you never want to go out on your own any more?' said Sinéad. This 'couple' thing was getting on her nerves. 'I want to go out with us, for a change.'

'There's no need to whine, Sinéad. I'm meeting him there – the three of us can meet up earlier.' She needed to fill Sinéad in on the morning's developments. 'What do you think, Orla? It's just the Cave, and us.'

Orla smiled.

Sinéad was on her feet. 'Yes! I need to find something to wear.'

They had shared a litre of cider and were in high spirits when they arrived in the bar. It was dark and warm inside, and they found Paddy and Christy sitting at a table beside the jukebox, deep in conversation.

'I thought you didn't drink in here any more?' Liz said to her brother.

'Who told you that?' said Paddy.

'Nobody. You're so thick these days.'

Sinéad and Orla came up behind her, carrying glasses and more cider.

'How's Orla?' said Christy with a smile. 'It's nice to see you out.'

Orla smiled back. 'Thanks.'

'So, are you here for the night?' said Liz.

'For a while,' said Paddy. 'Where are you sitting?'

'Not with you, anyway,' said Liz, taking the hint and leaving them, to sit at a table close to the bar.

'Have you two fallen out?' Sinéad asked.

Liz looked over her shoulder at Paddy. 'I don't know what's wrong with him – the only person he's talking to in the house is Mammy.'

Orla stood up suddenly. 'I'm going to the toilet,' she announced.

'Fair enough,' said Sinéad, and she and Liz watched as Orla staggered slightly, making her way between the tables. She put her hand to the jukebox, steadying herself as she passed.

'She's drunk,' Sinéad observed.

'She was crying this morning, and talking about Peter,' said Liz.

'Really – what did she say?'

Liz filled her in on the story.

'Jesus,' said Sinéad. 'We got that wrong, didn't we?'

'How were we to know?' said Liz. 'She's coming back – don't say anything.'

'Aye, 'cause that's worked so far,' said Sinéad. Orla sat down again. 'Are you all right, Orla? I heard the craic about this morning.'

Orla looked at Liz, who took a drink from her glass and said nothing. 'Aye, I'm all right – I'm just embarrassed, that's all.'

'For what?' said Sinéad, in too loud a voice. 'Fucksake, Orla, you're only human. We were worried about you, but you know us – useless with the big stuff. As me Mammy says, it's better out than in.'

'Can we stop talking about it now?' said Orla, exasperated. 'Oh, Jesus, look at this!'

A cheer erupted from the drinkers by the front door as Bobby Curran made a staggering entrance, held up on either side by two hookers.

Bobby wasn't a transvestite, but he was gloriously gay. Tonight he had outdone himself. Dressed in a baby-doll nightie with matching knickers, both in the brightest pink Bri-nylon imaginable, he stood inside the door, his hands on his hips, and announced to the bar, 'Buy me a drink, boys. I'm celebrating!'

He was a man in his fifties, who no longer cared what people thought about him, his appearance or his sexuality. He drank with the prostitute, the punk and the rocker, ne'er-do-wells all, in the seedy bars of the area.

But the drink had a powerful hold on him and was taking a toll; beneath the pink nightie his belly rose, swollen like a pregnancy. He strutted into the bar on skinny legs, shuffling in matching fur-trimmed mules, and ordered a drink.

'Hello, girls,' he called to Liz, Sinéad and Orla, tottering over to sit with them. 'Here, shove over,' he said.

'I love the outfit, Bobby,' said Sinéad.

'Do you?' Bobby was genuinely pleased. 'I'm celebrating the Royal Wedding. Did you see? Wasn't she lovely? Getting sold into marriage like that, the poor girl.'

He reached over and covered Orla's hand with his.

'And how are you, wee Orla? Ach, your wee boy died, isn't that right?' He tapped her hand, slurring, 'Sure, you'll be grand.'

The barman called him to collect his drink and he was up again, swaying across the floor.

'There you go, Orla – if Bobby says you're grand, you're grand,' said Sinéad, watching him take his pint over to another table, where his companions sat with a group of bikers.

It was after nine when Kevin arrived. Before he sat down, he walked over to Paddy and Christy.

'How's things?' he said, leaning his hands on the back of Christy's seat. Paddy looked up at him but didn't answer. It was Christy who spoke.

'OK,' he said. 'Liz is over there.'

'I know. Why aren't you?'

'We're OK here,' said Paddy drily. Christy watched the exchange. 'Maybe later on.'

'What was that about?' Christy asked once Kevin had gone.

'He knows,' said Paddy.

'Knows what – about the . . .? How the fuck does he know?'

'He started me about it,' said Paddy. 'A couple of weeks ago.'

'Jesus Christ, Paddy. Remember what they said – say nothing to nobody.' He watched Kevin at the bar, talking to Bobby. 'What do you mean, he started you?'

'He had a go at me, in the street the week before last. He actually reached for me.'

'Really?' said Christy. 'Fucksake – I thought he'd be fair enough about it, too. He was as much a friend of Harkin's as we were. Probably more, in fact.'

'You know what he's like – "It's all bollocks" and all that crap.'

'I don't get how he knows, though. Did you tell him?'

'It wasn't me,' said Paddy. He wasn't taking the blame for this. 'Me da heard us talking, me and you. He said to Kevin and then Kevin started me in the street about it. That's all.'

Christy sat for a minute, watching him with suspicion.

'I swear to God, Christy. I said nothing,' said Paddy.

'But you didn't deny it.'

'What was I supposed to say? He really pissed me off.'

Christy seemed to accept this. 'What did your da say?'

'Nothing much.'

Someone put money in the jukebox, and the opening bars of 'Leader of the Pack' cut through the noise of the drinkers. Over Christy's shoulder, Paddy watched Bobby Curran dance in the middle of the floor.

'Look at this,' he said, nodding to Christy.

Bobby swayed through the crowd, then climbed onto a chair, mouthing the lyrics, acting out the words and lifting his nightie provocatively to reveal, to anyone at eye level, the hairy, swollen belly and those obscene little knickers, straining to contain their contents. Christy stood up to watch.

'He rid me round the Derry Waaalls!' howled Bobby, his arms thrown wide in an invitation to the room. He put his hand on top of Dave the biker's head and clambered onto the table. Everyone laughed, cheering him on, making *vroom-vroom* noises, but above them all was Bobby's deep thirty-a-day growl.

'I aaasked him for a faaag, but then he—'

He stopped mid-line.

Christy sat down suddenly.

A British soldier was standing at the front of the bar, his rifle against his chest. He stared open-mouthed at Bobby. High on the table, in his frills and heels, Bobby stared back.

Suddenly, there were six more big men in camouflage, blocking the light. Whether they had heard the cheering, or had come in for a routine scout, by their expressions they had not expected this.

The Shangri-Las faded and the bar became tense and silent, as everyone waited to see what the soldiers would do. Within the confines of the bar they looked ridiculously exaggerated, with their weapons and heavy uniform, their faces smeared with black paint. Bobby looked down at them. Undaunted by the interruption he thrust his belly at the soldiers, his hands on his hips.

'Come over here with your big guns, boys,' he called, with a curl of his finger. 'I'm Barbara and I'm going to show you a good time.' He swayed on the tabletop and rubbed his hands over his groin and belly.

They stood, transfixed. One or two started to laugh. The crowd remained quiet, watching. In the back, Christy and Paddy put their heads down.

Then a soldier pushed through from the entrance and spoke quietly to the officer in charge. With a quick hand gesture the order was given, and the troupe began to back out of the bar, accompanied by roars of laughter and abuse. Bobby kept up a stream of vulgar, loud propositions as they retreated.

'Show us your big cock,' he shouted at the last, terrified boy, as he vanished through the archway and out into the street.

Laughing, Kevin looked around the room and saw Christy pull his coat from the back of the chair as he and Paddy began to weave their way towards the door. They blanked him as they passed.

Outside, they ran into Noel.

'All right?' they said, without stopping. Noel watched them hurry down the hill. He pulled a joint from his breast pocket and lit it, sheltering the match in his hands. After a deep draw he pushed the door open, just as Bobby and the women were leaving.

'How's Mr Curran?' said Noel.

Bobby's foot slipped from its mule and he tumbled dangerously to one side. Noel caught him by his arm and righted him.

'Thanks, darling,' said Bobby, peering at him with yellowing, dimmed eyes. He steadied himself, grasped the arm of the nearest girl, and they click-clacked away, arm in arm, across the road.

18

'I didn't know you could drive.'

Kevin was sitting in the passenger seat of an old Escort. Jim sat in the driver's seat. They were parked in a housing-estate car park, waiting for Brendan Rafferty to make an appearance.

'Why would you?' said Jim. He adjusted the car seat to give himself more legroom.

'Liz – Elizabeth – she never mentioned it, that's all.'

They had arrived under a bright sky to a street full of kids kicking a football around the square. Now it was getting dark. The street lights had started to come on. Kevin watched them through a gap in the houses; orange lights stuttered to life, creeping towards them. When the smaller boys and girls had been called in to bed, the older ones remained, hanging around a garage door opposite, smoking cigarettes and watching the car.

It was Jim who had suggested talking to Brendan, after Kevin hinted that he might know someone. He had exhausted all other options. Of the limited number of people he remembered, or who remembered him, some were still inside; the rest were not involved and knew as much, or as little, as he did himself. And he had to keep it low-key. Asking too many questions was risky.

'Someone's going to look at us sitting here and think we're Special Branch,' said Jim.

'Or gay,' said Kevin, regretting it immediately when Jim turned to look at him.

'Don't say that,' he said.

'Well, it's hardly worse than them thinking we're cops, is

it?' said Kevin. They lapsed into silence again, each staring out of their own window.

'Where does Mrs McLaughlin think you are?' Kevin said eventually. He had the impression that Liz's mother kept her husband on a tight leash.

'At a wake up the country – with the brother,' said Jim.

This wasn't a total lie. At that moment, in a farmhouse some-where outside Raphoe, their father's cousin was laid out. He had died, in his eighties, the previous day. Under normal circum-stances, Jim would have been driving up there to represent their end of the family. As it was, he would still have to go the following night. But it was the perfect cover, since Bernie hadn't known the man and was more than happy that she wasn't expected to attend.

The last light faded, and Kevin considered calling it a night. He wasn't even sure that Brendan Rafferty lived on this street.

'So how do you know this boy?' Jim asked.

'I was a friend of his brother's years ago,' replied Kevin.

'Really – why could you not ask him, then?'

Kevin was silent for a minute before replying. 'He's not involved in anything like this any more.'

'He was the one with the good sense, then – getting away from it, I mean. Is he still in Derry?'

'No, he's not,' said Kevin.

Jim sighed, and Kevin knew he wanted to talk about it.

'So did he go to England? You should have had the sense he had and gone with him.'

'I don't know about sense, seeing as he's dead.'

Jim turned around in the seat to face him. 'Is that right?' he said, full of interest. 'What happened?'

'It was years ago – a bomb. We were only wains.'

'Was he caught up in it? Killed in the blast or something? Rafferty – I don't remember the name now,' said Jim, trying to recall a tragedy that would fit the bill.

'Yes,' said Kevin, trying hard not to raise his voice. 'In a manner of speaking, seeing as he was planting the bloody thing when it went off.' The atmosphere in the car was too tense for him – he wanted to get out and walk.

Jim was quiet again for a while, but he couldn't let it go. This wasn't the kind of thing that came up in normal conversation, but then, what was normal about any of this? And Kevin seemed upset. He had to ask.

'Is that when you got involved?'

Fucking Paddy, and fucking Christy too, for that matter.

'No, Jim. That's when I got out.'

Lights flashed in the rear-view mirror as a car passed them and pulled up further along the street. When the passenger door opened, the interior of the car lit up, illuminating two talking figures. One of them climbed from the car and rested his arm on the roof, leaning in to continue the conversation. Kevin rolled his window down. He could hear them – they were arranging to meet the next day. The man closed the door and stood back to let the car drive off.

'That's him,' said Kevin. 'Stay in the car, I'll go and talk to him.'

He got out quickly and called the man by name. Brendan turned around, as if he was about to run.

'It's Kevin Thompson.'

Brendan watched the figure silhouetted against the street light.

'What do you want?'

'I'm just looking to talk to you – to ask you something. Is there somewhere we can go, to talk?'

'Here'll do fine,' said Brendan, moving closer.

Kevin realised he didn't know what to say. 'I'm looking for some advice,' he started. 'About who to talk to – about joining up. Who's in charge of recruitment these days?'

'You've changed your tune since the last time I saw you.'

'It's not me that's looking to volunteer – it's two friends of mine.' Kevin walked closer to avoid being overheard. 'They're two eejits, too fond of the gear. And one of them's the girlfriend's brother. The da's going off his head about it.'

'Let me stop you there.' Brendan raised his hand to silence him. 'I'm not in the business of talking people out of stuff. If these two boys feel they have something to contribute, then they can. Sands said everyone has a part to play and he was right.' He turned to open the gate behind him.

'You don't want these two, Brendan. They're a couple of stupid young fellas. They're not political – their friend died, and they're angry.'

Brendan stopped. 'Who was the friend?'

'The wee boy who was hit with the plastic bullet before Easter. Harkin, his name was. Before that, it was all drugs and music with these two.' Kevin saw a change in Brendan, a softening in his stance.

'I remember that,' he said. 'Easter Saturday, wasn't it? I know the family.'

'So do I.'

Brendan paused, thinking. 'We all have friends that died, Kevin. Is that not the best reason to get involved?' He looked behind Kevin, to the car. 'Who's that?' he said.

'It's one of their fathers – he's worried. That's why I'm here, for him.' He moved closer again, trying to press his point. 'Look, Brendan, I know the score. But if anything, these two would be a security risk.'

Brendan was still watching the car. 'It might be the making of them,' he said thoughtfully.

'I'm not asking you to do anything here,' said Kevin. 'Just give me a name, point me in the right direction.'

Brendan looked straight at him again. 'I can't do that and – let's face it – I don't know who you're working for, either of you.'

'You know me, Brendan. You know my family – I'm no tout. Look, forget about it.' He turned to go back to the car.

'What's their names?' Brendan asked.

'Paddy McLaughlin and Christy Meehan. Thanks, Brendan.'

'I'm not promising anything, but I can ask about. Do they live around here?'

'Rosemount,' said Kevin.

Brendan paused again, looking at Kevin with interest. 'I have to get in here,' he said, indicating the house.

'How will we get in touch again?' called Kevin.

'You won't – I'll find you. Like you said, I know your family.'

'Well?' said Jim, when Kevin was back in the car.

'He said he'd ask about. He took their names,' said Kevin, relieved it was over.

'Good,' said Jim, smiling.

'If they've already signed up, there's nothing to be done, Mr McLaughlin. You know that, don't you?'

'We'll face that one when we know for sure,' said Jim, starting the engine. 'I'll leave you home.'

19

It was cold in the shade behind the factory, and Paddy shivered.

The helicopter was a distant buzz, hovering over some other area, but he wasn't taking a chance. He stayed in the shadows, out of sight.

His orders were to be here for nine o'clock, when he would be met by someone. That was the arrangement. Only then would he know what the job was.

But it was after nine, now, and no one had shown up. He moved to the edge of the wall and looked out across the green to the row of shops. Most of them had their metal shutters pulled down and locked. Only the newsagent was open; a crowd of teenagers loitered around the entrance. Paddy watched them for a few minutes, pushing each other, smoking, shouting crude remarks at girls as they passed.

There was his mother, walking quickly towards them. She held her cardigan closed, with one arm across her breast. Her purse and cigarettes were in the other hand. In a chill of panic, he wondered if she was looking for him.

No, she was only going to the shop. He watched until she came out again, this time carrying a carton of milk and a loaf as well as her purse. He was sure she paused, for the briefest of seconds, and looked across to where he was. Quickly he pulled his head back, behind the safety of the wall.

It was Sunday. Two nights before, they had been in another bedroom for a lecture on secrecy, what to do if they were arrested, and the basics of using a gun. Before this, the only gun Paddy had held was the plastic revolver from Santa, on

Christmas morning. He was seven. It had come with a cow-boy hat and a silver sheriff's badge.

The real thing was cold and heavy. They said it was a small handgun, a 'short', but it felt huge in Paddy's hand – much bigger than on television and heavier than he'd expected. It was covered in a sheen of fine oil and it smelled metallic. Hours later, when he sniffed his hand, he could still get the smell of iron.

There were three people in the room: himself, Christy and another man, Lexie, who was giving the lesson. They were shown in turn how to hold the gun, how to load and unload it, how to take aim and fire – without bullets, obviously. That would come later.

And now he was here, following his first order, and it looked more and more as though he was on his own. They hadn't told him what to do if the other guy was a no-show. Should he go home again or find someone to tell? Might they think it was his fault, if he didn't report the absence or if the action failed?

As he was thinking this, a man appeared around the corner and crossed the lane, head down. He came straight up to Paddy.

'All right?' he sniffed, shifting from foot to foot.

'I thought I was stood up,' said Paddy, and the man laughed.

'It's not a date we're on. Right, listen – there's stuff to be moved tonight and we need a car, so that's what we're doing. Is this your first job?'

Paddy nodded.

'You'll be grand,' said the man. 'Just do what I tell you to do and you'll be back in the house by eleven.'

Paul – that was his name – kept up a constant stream of talk as they walked.

'There's two ways of doing this, right? Either we go to a house where we know there's a car and we tell them we're tak-ing it for a job, or we wait in the street for someone getting in or out of a car and we walk up to them and take it. This one isn't for burning, so we need to be sure that it's not going to run out of petrol. It has to be reliable.'

'What if they don't want to give us it?' said Paddy.

'They'll give us the car,' said Paul. 'We're going to a garage – get one after they've filled her up. You'll go over before they get back in. You say, "IRA. Hand over the keys." Don't get into a discussion, right? And don't ask – tell. If you're nervous, don't show it.'

'I can't drive, you know – what do I do with the keys?'

Paul rolled his eyes. 'You give them to me and I drive,' he said.

'And where will you be while I'm doing all this?' said Paddy. A lot was falling on his shoulders.

'I'll be behind you, looking out for bother. Do you have something to cover your face?'

It hadn't even occurred to Paddy, obvious though it seemed. 'No,' he admitted.

Paul said something under his breath, something that sounded like, 'Amateurs.'

'Here,' he said. 'Stick this in your pocket and wrap it round you when we get there.' He handed him a woolly mass that unfurled into a Celtic scarf.

When they got to the garage, the forecourt was empty. They had arrived just as the sun dipped below the horizon. The petrol pumps were lit by the last two unbroken lamps that hung from the canopy. The rest was in near-darkness.

'Wrap that scarf around your face,' said Paul. They were standing between the garage and a wire fence, out of sight of the road. Paddy quickly obeyed, pulling the Celtic scarf from inside his coat and wrapping it over his mouth and nose. He tied it at the back of his head in a thick knot. It was suffocating.

Paul pulled out a black woollen hat and stuck it on top of his head. Then he rolled it down over his face, revealing cut-out holes for his eyes and mouth.

The pump attendant, a teenage boy, was responsible for serving the final customers of the evening and locking up the pumps for the night. Paddy could see him reading a newspaper in his hut.

'What about him?' he said.

'I'll look after him,' said Paul.

They waited. It was a busy road, with cars passing every few seconds, even the occasional van. The longer they waited, the more tense they became.

'When's the car needed for?' said Paddy, wondering what would happen should the garage close and they missed their chance.

Before Paul could answer, a car slowed down on the road and swung into the forecourt. It pulled up beside one of the pumps and a middle-aged man got out. He waved to the teenage attendant. Then he went to the rear of the car, removed the petrol cap and inserted the pump nozzle.

'Let him get the cap back on, then walk straight over and get the keys off him,' whispered Paul. 'No messing – you're the fucking IRA, right? Remember that.'

Paul moved swiftly towards the attendant's hut. At the pump, the man was watching the gauge and didn't notice him. He stopped beside the sliding window hatch. The attendant had returned to his reading.

Paddy watched this, then realised that his target had placed the pump handle back in its stand, and his key in the petrol cap again.

He walked out of the shadows and across the tarmac.

Give me the keys, give me the keys . . . he said, practising. And then he was beside the man, too close.

The man turned; he smelled of spirits and had that well-groomed appearance that came with money. A round belly rose beneath his expensive V-neck sweater. He opened his mouth to say something, but Paddy got there first.

'IRA – give me the keys!'

He had to shout to be heard through the scarf, and his voice echoed off the canopy above their heads. The man stared at him first, then he glanced around him.

'Get away to fuck,' he said, and started to open the car door, the keys in his hand. Paddy jumped in front of him.

'IRA – give me the fucking keys!' he shouted again.

But the man had the door open. Paddy didn't know what to do. Someone was coming up behind him. Suddenly, Paul pushed against the man, with a gun held at waist height. He made sure it was seen.

'Give him the keys,' he said quietly. 'We're taking the car.'

The hand trembled as Paddy took them off him.

'You'll get it back, don't worry,' said Paul, as the man continued to stare at the gun that was aimed at his ribs. 'The car will be behind the shops in Creggan, with the keys inside. Come for it after one o'clock – it'll be waiting for you. Here, give me them.'

Realising that the last order was for him, Paddy handed the keys over. He heard the noise of traffic on the road beside them.

'Get in, for Christsake,' said Paul, and he ran to the passenger side and climbed into the car. Paul had the key in the ignition. He revved the engine and they drove off. Looking through the rear window, Paddy saw the man standing in the middle of the forecourt, watching them drive away in his car. There was no sign of the attendant.

'What did you do with the young fella?' he asked Paul.

'Nothing – he's lying on the floor inside the hut, counting to a hundred. He'll not say anything.'

'I thought I fucked it up,' said Paddy. 'When he wouldn't hand over the keys, I didn't know what to do.'

Paul was silent.

'What happens now?' Paddy asked.

'You? You go home – you did all right. Go straight to your house and stay there.' He stopped and Paddy got out.

The car drove uphill, into the middle of the big estate, then it turned a corner and vanished. The helicopter droned, high in the sky. He put his head down and walked as fast as he could towards home.

In another part of the city, Kevin was walking home. He turned into his street and saw the car outside his house. Before he reached it, he knew that it was Brendan. The car window rolled down as he stopped beside it.

'All right, Brendan? You waitin' for me?' he said.

'I think you know that already, don't you? Your two friends – I asked about them. It's a done deal, both of them.'

'OK,' said Kevin, with a sigh.

'They're doing what they feel they have to, Kevin. The boys inside are dying.'

'I know. Look, thanks – you didn't need to do this, and I appreciate it.'

Brendan turned the key in the ignition and drove off.

He wasn't surprised how it had turned out; they had plunged right in. How quickly things could change. Nothing would be the same.

His thoughts went to Jim, and Liz; this would hurt her – the bang on the door in the middle of the night. The fear. They used to say, years before, that a volunteer had six months on average before he was either inside or dead. How much shorter were the odds now?

20

They did whatever was asked of them. Within two weeks, Paddy and Christy had carried out a brace of hijackings each.

Christy had been part of a gang who robbed a bookie's. He waited in the doorway, watching, while two others held up the girl behind the counter; it wasn't what he'd expected to find himself doing. But the organisation needed money, and this was, therefore, a legitimate action. He felt sorry for the girl, but it was a war and she would be OK.

After his first hijack, Paddy was considered reliable and was sent out, two nights later, on another one. This time they were looking for a van.

They stopped one in the middle of the road. Paddy pointed the gun at the driver, through his window. He didn't own the van, a works vehicle, and handed over the keys without argument.

'Here, you can have it – it's no skin off my nose,' he had said, walking away without a backwards glance. The van was used to transport some men on a job and ended up burnt out on a country road.

'Surprisingly easy,' mused Paddy.

And now they were to be trained in gun use, which meant crossing the border into the Republic, a border that was guarded by permanent army checkpoints.

'Get yourself to Buncrana next Monday, and you'll be picked up at the bus station,' they were told.

Christy and Paddy found themselves sitting side by side on

the back seat of a Lough Swilly bus, bumping along the road to the seaside town.

'Who's collecting us?' asked Paddy.

'Haven't a clue – they'll find us,' said Christy, looking out of the window at the sheep in the fields. The other passenger on the bus, an elderly woman in a plastic rain hat, sat with two heavy bags of clothes on the seat beside her. Paddy watched her head nodding as she dozed.

They were near the border and the bus slowed in anticipation. Concrete sangars loomed in front of them. The driver expected to be pulled in and checked over, but the soldier waved them through. He stood by the side of the road, his face upturned, watching the passengers behind the glass as they passed. Before they were out of the checkpoint, his attention was already on the car behind.

Buncrana, a sleepy seaside village full of slot machines and gift shops selling postcards, candyfloss and bright pink Buncrana rock, was an attraction for day trippers from Derry.

They came in busloads on Saturdays and Sundays; in family groups and teenage gangs they roamed the streets leading to and from the shore, strolled along the main street with an ice cream in hand, and returned home as the sun went down, with sticky, sandy kids falling asleep across their parents' knees. During the week, the streets and the beaches were quiet.

The bus drove into town past the shore front, and pulled up across the road from the station. The boys waited while the driver roused the old woman, who had slept for the duration of the journey – he walked along the aisle towards her.

'Come on, Sally – you're home,' he said.

She raised her face to him with a confused look, then gathered her bags with difficulty and struggled along the aisle to the exit, stopping every few seconds to put them down and lift them again.

'Do you need a wee hand?' said Paddy, more out of impatience than generosity.

'Aye, son,' she said. Paddy reached over her head – she couldn't have been more than four feet in height – and took the bags. He handed one to Christy and they shuffled behind her as she slowly walked to the front of the bus, climbing down only after a brief chat with the driver.

'Bye, Sally,' he said as she finally dismounted.

Down on the pavement, she gave them a toothless smile. 'Ye's are good fellas,' she said, taking her bags again. 'Are ye's going for a wee paddle?'

'Aye,' said Paddy kindly.

'But where's your towel?' she said.

'Ah, you know us Derry men – too hard for towels,' laughed Christy.

'Well, good luck to ye's,' she laughed, walking away with a wave of her hand.

There was no one at the station – a flat-roofed 1930s building – but the café beside it was open, from which came a pungent, vinegary aroma that set the saliva running.

'Smell the chips,' said Christy. 'Do you think we have time to buy a bag? Fuck it, we're gonna be here for hours, and I'd no breakfast.' He held his hand out to Paddy. 'Give us some money and we can split a bag.'

Between them, they pooled the seventy pence needed for a chip and a can of Coke. Christy ran inside and came out, minutes later, carrying a bundle of paper that held the greasy food. The two of them dived in, gulping the hot chips down as fast as the scalding fat would let them. They washed them down with the Coca-Cola.

Christy gave a loud burp. 'That's better,' he said.

A car pulled up; its blue paintwork was splattered with mud and eaten away at the edges by rust. Two men sat in the front. The driver rolled the window down to call them over.

'Meehan and McLaughlin?' he asked.

'Aye,' said Paddy.

'Get in.'

They jumped into the back seat. Paddy glanced at the passenger, a man in his late twenties with curly ginger hair and a ginger moustache. He looked familiar.

'Where are we going?' Paddy asked as they drove off.

'You'll know when you get there,' came the reply.

Green hills rolled by on either side of the road. Sheep and cows grazed. For a long time, no one spoke. It was an uncomfortable silence. Then the man in the passenger seat farted. As the stench filled the car, the driver put his hand over his face. 'Jesus, Mick, what in Christ's name were you eating?' he said.

'Open the window, for fucksake,' shouted Paddy.

'Open it yourself,' said the driver.

'I can't,' said Paddy, trying frantically to force the handle down. 'They're stuck.' Christy finally forced the window on his side open a couple of inches and the driver rolled his down. Air flowed through the car.

'It was all that Guinness last night,' confessed Mick. 'My guts are wrecked.'

Banter flew back and forth between them now. The boys were questioned about activities in Derry and how the fight was going.

'Are you two on the run?' asked Paddy. Red-haired Mick looked over his shoulder and laughed but didn't answer.

Paddy and Christy answered every question as best they could, revelling in the attention of the more experienced men who talked about strategy and what the leadership should be doing. Christy looked over at Paddy, grinning back at him.

This was great; the past was irrelevant, the Cave assigned to history, childish nonsense, from a time when they were stupid, directionless boys.

It seemed they had been driving a long time, and travelled miles, before the car turned up a narrow road, shielded on both sides by high hedges and overhung by trees.

The further they went along this road, the narrower it became, until a line of grass ran down its centre as tarmac was replaced by hard clay and rough stone. Finally they turned into a small yard, with several decrepit outbuildings at one end and a single-storey farmhouse at the other. Fragments of curtain hung at the windows, their tail ends clinging to the broken glass. The place looked for all the world as though it had been abandoned for many years.

Mick jumped out of the car and knocked on the door. It opened slowly, and an elderly man in a flat cap looked up at him. They spoke a few words, then the man stepped aside and let him in.

When Mick came out again, he was carrying a coal sack wrapped around a long, heavy object. Christy and Paddy swivelled to watch through the back window as he opened the boot of the car and put the sack in, slamming it closed. Once more in his seat, they reversed and drove out of the yard, back the way they'd come. The old man stood by his door, watching them leave.

The car climbed steadily up winding roads and into the hills. When they came to the top of a steep incline, it stopped, and they got out and walked across rocky ground until the four of them stood looking down on a curved expanse, a bowl carved into the rock of the Donegal hills. It fell away in a sweep below their feet. They began to climb down.

Halfway into this hollow the men stopped. Mick had carried the bag, and a piece of cardboard, from the car. About fifty yards ahead, there was an out-thrust of rock, a natural ledge with a flat surface. He strode across to it and propped the card against the rock, then drew a crude circle on it in white chalk. Once he was happy with his work, he strode back across the grass, grinning.

'That's what you're aiming at,' he said, pointing at the target.

Robbie, their driver, unrolled the bag and took out a rifle. Its long wooden handle was nicked and scored with rough use.

'This is an M1 carbine – American. Do you two know anything about guns?' he asked.

'Only what we've been taught so far,' said Paddy. 'So not a lot. But I've seen ones like that in war films.'

'Aye, you would have,' nodded Robbie. 'Who wants to go first?'

Paddy had his hand in the air immediately and almost jumped on the gun when Mick told him to come forward.

'Right,' he said. 'You're going to shoot from a kneeling position, so get down on one knee – hold the gun like this.' He dropped onto one knee, demonstrating.

'Put it tight against your shoulder and support it like this.' He aimed at the target, looking along the length of the barrel. Paddy tried to memorise each detail – how to turn his body, where to place his hands – left underneath, right gripping the wood, finger on the trigger.

'You try,' said Robbie, handing him the rifle.

Paddy felt the trigger against his finger and looked through the sights to the target in the distance. 'Is it loaded?' he asked, feeling the urge to pull.

'Not yet,' said Robbie. 'Give it here.'

The bullets gleamed in their cardboard box, their nibs blunt and shiny, reflecting the sun. It seemed strange that the gun had appeared from a crumpled bag, but the bullets were pristine. Robbie removed the magazine and they stood close, watching him load it: five brassy rounds clipped into place, one at a time.

'Always check the barrel of the gun – make sure there isn't a round left in there from the last time it was used.'

'Why?' Christy asked.

'Because,' said Mick, 'if you don't, and it goes off, you're going to kill someone – maybe your mate there.'

He nodded at Paddy. 'Or yourself. Always, *always*, check.'

He clipped the magazine in place. Robbie raised the gun to his shoulder again and fired. The retort echoed off rock and stone. Without thinking, Paddy and Christy put their hands over their ears.

'Get used to that sound, boys. This is a shooting war,' said Mick.

'Here, give us a go,' said Paddy, reaching out for the rifle.

'There's four shots left in it,' Robbie said, handing him the weapon. 'Take your time, take a breath and squeeze the trigger – don't pull it.'

'It's like *The Magnificent Seven*, when they're teaching the Mexicans to shoot,' said Paddy, holding the gun to his cheek. He took a breath and held it behind tight lips, saw the board caught in the sights, then squeezed. He had braced for a strong recoil, but the gun was light. As he lowered it he squinted, trying to see his handiwork. 'Did I hit it?'

'Just about,' said Mick.

A delighted Paddy swung around to face them with a grin and the rifle held loosely in his hands. The two men and Christy backed away quickly.

'Whoa! Don't point that at us, you mad bastard – point it up or down!' shouted Robbie.

'All right, Steve McQueen, take your other shots,' said Mick, hungover and in no mood for stupid kids.

This time, Paddy focused. He held his breath and let himself relax before firing, again and again and again.

'That's better,' said Robbie. 'Look.'

It wasn't exactly a bull's eye, but Paddy could see where the bullets had hit; there were dark, ragged holes in the distant cardboard. Two bullets made it within the circle and the other two had at least hit the board. The sound left a terrific ringing in his ears.

'Make sure you put the safety on,' warned Mick.

It was Christy's turn. Mick handed him the gun.

'Let me see you load it,' he said. Christy knelt on the ground and laid the rifle across his knees.

'Take out the magazine, like this,' said Mick, showing him how to release the clip. 'Now, what's the first thing you do?'

Christy looked blankly at him, then remembered. 'Check there isn't a bullet in the chamber.' He looked inside – there wasn't.

'Good. Now load the magazine – it'll only take five.'

Christy weighed the bullets in his hand; they were cold and smooth. Then he pushed them into the rusted casing, and clipped it neatly into place.

After all the war films he had seen, all the times he had watched this action, he thought he could do it without thinking. But when the real thing sat solidly in his hands, with its smooth wooden stock and cold mechanism – detailed, machined, oiled – he felt foolish for thinking that he knew anything about guns. This was no toy, no Hollywood movie prop.

'What about fingerprints – on the casings?' he said, feeling scared for the first time.

'Don't worry about that right now. We'll make sure everything is cleaned down properly when we're finished,' said Mick.

'I don't mean now. What about later, when we're on our own?'

Mick looked at him with pale, doubtful eyes and Christy

regretted asking, aware that he sounded like a frightened kid. The wind lifted, and a bank of cloud crept over the rim of the hollow. A shadow fell on them.

'You'll be wearing gloves, and someone will load it before you ever get to see it. Take your shots,' said Robbie, with an irritated flick of the hand.

Putting the rifle against his right shoulder, Christy raised himself onto one knee and lowered his head to the sight. There was the target, marked by Paddy's efforts. He felt a tug of anger – at himself, his own fear. He had to show them he could do better than his friend.

He closed in on the target, blocking out everything around him: Paddy, the senior IRA men, the cold wind.

Five rapid shots rang out.

Through the sight, he watched eruptions of dust and light debris as the target shook from the blasts. He held still, drew air into his lungs and lowered the muzzle, until its tip rested on the grass before him.

'Not bad,' said Robbie. 'You'll do all right. OK, another go each, and then we're done.'

'You were good at that,' said Paddy. They were in the car again, driving back to Buncrana. 'Have you done that before?'

'Only in the street, with a stick,' said Christy. Something burnt in him, something like pride. He was a good shot. He wanted to go out and do it again and again.

And now, back in the car, he watched the men who had been training them as they talked quietly. What were their stories? What had they done in the past? What past deed prevented them returning home? Had they killed people?

The soldiers at the checkpoint on the way down – they would be his target, perhaps, the next time he held a gun.

Was it possible that he could be cold, cold enough to aim at another person the same way he had aimed at that target, to fire into them without doubt?

Peter Harkin's face, his limp body, lying awkward on the broken pavement – when he had doubts, he made himself think about that and let the anger rise in him again.

The green fields and the hedges sped past. Christy turned to the window and saw, in its reflection, a thin face, transparent and dappled in the moving light. He saw his eyes looking back – there was no joy in them. He turned away.

21

Jim gazed up at the statue of St Theresa. She cradled her rose-swathed crucifix like a babe in arms, her face blank, immobile in painted plaster.

His mother had prayed to St Theresa all her life, had a great devotion to her. St Theresa of the Roses, the Little Flower. He had seen photos of the saint and remembered her as wee and plump, with a round face and a chin that jutted out slightly – whoever had sculpted this likeness had done her a lot of favours.

The housekeeper was a small woman, with an apron over her jumper and a scarf wrapped tightly around her head, tied in a knot under the chin; a strange combination, as though she wasn't planning on staying, but couldn't decide to leave. She said very little, just smiled politely and held the door open for him to enter. Then she put him in a room.

'Wait in here,' she said, before closing the door.

The room was large, with a solid wooden desk and three sturdy chairs. And it was quiet – so quiet he could have been the only person in the building. The heavy furniture, rooted in the carpet, seemed unchanged by time or human presence. It gleamed darkly and smelled of polish and age. The longer Jim sat, the more he had the urge to leave again, but right now he needed advice, and this was what people did in circumstances like these – they went to the priest.

What would he say, when the priest finally arrived? *'My son is in the IRA and I don't know what to do?'* What if the priest told him to turn the boy in? He couldn't do that. This was a mistake.

The door opened and Father Devlin came in. He acknowledged Jim's presence with a soft, 'How are you doing?' After closing the door behind him, he moved silently across the carpet and, with a certain weariness, sat in the chair behind the desk.

'It's Mr McLaughlin, isn't it? What can I do for you?'

Jim knew the priest – he had christened both Elizabeth and Elvis Patrick. 'I'm not sure you can do anything, Father. I need some advice on a family matter,' he said.

'Is it a marital problem?' enquired the priest. 'Are we expecting your wife to join us?'

'Ah, no. She doesn't know anything about this,' said Jim. *Jesus!* 'It's my youngest boy, Father. He's gone and got himself involved, him and his friend. I don't know what to do.' Suddenly, there were tears in his eyes that he had to blink away before they had a chance to go anywhere, and a lump appeared in his throat as he spoke. Ah, Christ, this was a disaster.

The priest watched him for a moment, then got up from behind the desk, went to the door and left the room. Jim looked after him at the closed door, wondering if he should leave, but the priest was quickly back again, this time with two cups of tea in his hands. He gave one to Jim and sat down again.

'The housekeeper's finished for the night, so we're fending for ourselves,' he said, in his soft Southern brogue. They sipped their tea. Finally, the priest asked, 'Why does your wife not know about this? It's a sore burden to carry yourself, Mr McLaughlin.'

'I don't want to upset her if I can help it. I thought that I could put a stop to it before it went any further.'

Shaking his head, the priest put his cup down.

'So many young lads are caught up in it all, and it's much worse since the hunger strike has taken hold. You're not the first parent I've had sitting in that chair, in tears many's a time. I'm sorry to say that you are not likely to be the last, either.'

The old priest sounded sad.

'How do you know, for certain, that he's in the IRA? Or is it the INLA? They're on the rise, you know. I suppose there's a certain kudos in having a member martyred.'

'Somebody told me, somebody that knows,' said Jim. 'Him and his friend, Christopher Meehan; they were pals with the wee lad that died at Easter, and now they're out for revenge or something – I don't know. Do you have any pull with these boys? Can you get them thrown out or something?'

'I wish I could, but they don't listen to us – unless it suits them, of course. No, the best thing I can suggest is that you get him in here and I'll try to talk some sense into him.'

Father Devlin got to his feet and walked around the table, extending his hand. Jim took the hint and stood up to shake it.

'OK, Father,' he said. 'I'll do my best. I might have to kidnap him, though, to get him in a room with you.'

The priest was manoeuvring him towards the door. 'Bring him in and we'll see what we can do. Of course, the other alternative is to ship him out, across the water.'

He held the door open with one hand and shook Jim's with the other.

'Talk to your wife, Mr McLaughlin. A mother has a powerful influence in the family, more than me or you could ever hope to have. And she might just kill you, when she finds out that you knew all along and didn't tell her.'

'It's too late to stop that,' Jim muttered to himself, as the door closed behind him.

22

Two 'B's. Not bad, considering the past three months of sex and drink, and the idea of England. Not to mention the friends that were lost, like Peter, or damaged, like Orla. Somehow, in the middle of it all, Liz had managed to pull two passing grades like rabbits out of an unlikely top hat.

To celebrate, she was out with the girls in the class, Paula, Joanne and Ellen; they were making a night of it.

The girls were funny, ordinary, in Capri pants and sailor collars, with heavy fringes that flounced in layered curls over their eyes. She met them in a disco bar in town, where lights flashed across the walls and the dance floor, disguising the general dirt and seediness of an age that was coming to an end.

'You're a New Romantic, aren't you?' Paula was shouting across the table at Liz.

She didn't answer. She looked around her at the big hair, the off-the-shoulder frills, the daring older girls in rah-rah skirts and white heels. She was wearing a tight pencil skirt and a man's shirt, tucked in at the waist. She had pushed a beret onto the back of her head, trying her best to look like Clare Grogan. The truth was, she didn't know what she was, or what to do with herself in this place, with a pint in front of her when the others were drinking Bacardi and Coke from tall glasses, sipped through straws – and getting really drunk, really fast.

Ellen, whose shrill voice was always on the edge of a shout, leaned back in her chair and declared to the room, 'School's out – for ever!' Across the way, two men lifted their glasses and cheered back at her. Liz, Joanne and Paula saluted each other with a clash of glassware.

'Dance,' said Ellen. She was on her feet, cigarette in hand, pushing them to join her. 'Come on!' she said, pulling Liz by the arm. 'Liz, for fucksake – on your feet, girl!'

'I'm going for a pee,' shouted Liz, and she made for the door and the steep stairs that led to the girls' toilet.

Behind her, the others were on the dance floor, bathed in coloured lights, cigarettes held aloft – a trinity that needed no men. They were dancing to 'Stars on 45', smoking, shouting in each other's ears. She looked back at them. 'I'm not dancing to that shite,' she said.

Upstairs, she took her time, waiting for the song to end. The toilets predated even the brown seventies disco downstairs.

Multiple coats of brown gloss paint had, layer by layer, thickened the door beyond the dimensions of its frame and Liz struggled to close it. The brass tap on the cracked porcelain sink rasped as it turned, scraping metal on metal. A trickle of water dripped out, and the pipes above her head banged with the effort.

As the music throbbed through the floor, she criticised her reflection in the mirror.

She had found her shirt in the back of a wardrobe. It belonged to Gene, or perhaps Carl – she didn't know which. The cloth was heavy cotton, pale blue, with a button-down collar. It was too big for her but pulled in nicely at the waistband of her skirt.

'Look at her, in Ben Sherman,' called her mother when she came downstairs.

'I remember bringing that home from work, when we had the pick of the seconds.' Liz didn't ask who Ben Sherman was.

'Does it look OK, Mammy – does it look stupid?' she asked.

'You look grand. Doesn't she?' This was directed at Jim.

Her father made a point of saying nothing about anything his wife or his daughter wore. It was a trap he had fallen into more than once; he had found, to his cost, that it would inevitably earn him a night of silent rebuke, or tears, or both.

He looked at the shirt, searching for the safest response, before settling on, 'You can't go wrong with a classic.'

It earned him a smile from Bernie, and Liz didn't scowl or stomp upstairs to change, so he said no more, but retreated to his paper while the going was good.

Now Liz regretted her choice. All the other girls looked polished and new.

'I don't want their clothes,' she said aloud.

But she was out of place here, awkward and underdressed. Reluctantly, she pulled the door and left the toilet.

Downstairs, the dancing had stopped, and Joanne was at the bar, ordering drinks from their pool of cash. She returned with four glasses of cloudy liquid.

'What's this?' shouted Liz, sniffing. It smelled of liquorice.

'Pernod,' called Ellen. 'Try it – there's white lemonade in it.'

'That's lovely,' said Liz, after a sip and then another.

'Get it down you!'

The Pernod had an immediate warming effect as it blended with the lager. They drank it quickly and then threw in money for another round.

After those, the girls charged the dance floor. 'Love Action's twangy intro filled the room, and they gave it their best Human-League-backing-singer sashay. Lights flashed and swirled and the smoke machine kicked off.

Three songs later, they were still on their feet and the predators were beginning to circle; two men, moustachioed and drunk, awful dancers, wove through them, insistent on breaking into the tight group and singling out the weakest. One of them slid in front of Liz, doing the men-that-can't-dance two-step. He had to be forty – he looked old.

'Body Talk' started, creepy and suggestive. It was hot and smoky on the dance floor. The man was grinding his hips, leading with his groin as he moved towards her. She turned abruptly and walked away.

Back at the table, she lifted her Pernod and took a long drink from the glass. *No way*, she thought, watching the man making the same move on Joanne, who was much more receptive. *There isn't enough alcohol in the world.*

She looked at her surroundings. Suddenly, through the smoke and the crowds she saw Christy Meehan at the bar, buying a drink.

She called out his name but he didn't hear, so she went over and tapped him on the shoulder.

'Liz!' he said, surprised. He looked beyond her, checking who else was there.

'What are you doing here?' she shouted.

'Out with the boys from the college. Results,' he shouted back. 'What about you?'

'Same. Two "B"s – not bad, eh?' She stood back to let him admire her in all her glory, and he laughed, seeing just how drunk she was.

'Are you on your own?' he said.

'Out with the girls from my class.' She pulled a face and he laughed again. 'So, how did you do?' she asked.

'I didn't do them,' he said.

'Oh, shit, really? Why not, Christy? You would have done so well.'

'After Harkin . . . I don't know – I just sort of gave up.'

'Fuck,' said Liz, putting her arms around him. 'That's so sad. Hey, there's always next year. Do you want a drink? I'll buy you a drink.'

She stumbled back to the table to get her purse. He watched her; she looked different, out in a strange environment – out without her boyfriend. It allowed them an immediate intimacy, as though they were two fellow travellers in unknown territory. Except he had given up on the world she lived in. He might as well have been from another planet. She thought she knew him, but she didn't – not any more.

'What do you want – a pint?' She stood on tiptoe, waving a five-pound note at the barman. 'A Harp and a Pernod and white lemonade,' she said, when he finally came over.

'Since when do you drink Pernod and white?' Christy laughed.

'Since tonight,' said Liz.

'You want to watch that – they don't call it the "Leg Opener" for nothing.'

The remark bit through her drunk bravado; it was uncalled for.

'Don't be crude,' she said, turning to walk away.

'I'm sorry – it's just a saying,' he said, pulling her back by the wrist. 'Anyway, what about my pint?'

Ellen appeared by her side. 'So,' she said, eyeing Christy. 'Who's this?'

'This is Christy, a friend of my brother's,' said Liz, in a flat tone. She took the drinks from the barman and passed him the money.

'Are you coming back?' said Ellen.

'Aye,' said Liz. 'I'll see you after, Christy.'

She gave him his pint and went back to the table and the three girls.

'Who was that?' asked Joanne.

'Just a fella I know, a friend of my brother's.' Liz stirred her drink furiously. That was the problem with Christy, he pushed stuff too far. She glanced at the bar, to where they had been talking, but he was gone; back to his friends no doubt.

Outside, at closing time, they argued about what to do next. 'Chips,' said Ellen. 'We can eat them on the way.'

Paula had other plans.

'Me ma's away, but I know where she hides her vodka,' she said. She lived across the river, on the other side of town. Joanne and Ellen were up for it, via the chippy of course, but Liz couldn't walk that far. The thought of getting home was daunting enough.

She staggered backwards and leaned against the wall of the bar for support, before declaring that she was for going home. 'Now!'

'Aww, come on,' said Paula, linking her arm through Liz's.

'I'm too drunk,' Liz slurred, detaching her arm with an effort. 'I have to go home.'

She began walking, her only thought the lure of her bed and her head sinking into her pillow. Somewhere behind her, Paula called, 'Where are you going, Liz?' and the others laughed, saying, 'Leave her . . .'

With supreme effort, Liz stayed upright while the earth spun under her. *Oh, God, just get me home . . .* she begged, negotiating with the deity somewhere above.

Suddenly there was Christy, at her side and out of breath. 'I was calling you, didn't you hear?'

'I have to go home,' said Liz, pushing him out of the way.

'You are so drunk,' he said. He had seen her stoned, and they had been drunk in each other's company, but he had never seen her out of control, not like this.

She staggered. 'I'm all right – I just have to keep moving,' she insisted.

He allowed her to pass and she strode down the street a few yards, then stopped. 'Oh no,' said Christy, running to her side.

'I'm gonna be sick,' said Liz, gripping his arm as she started to heave.

Liquid splashed all over her shoes. Christy held her up as

she vomited again, standing as far back as he could. People passed them, laughing, and then a woman stopped and pulled a tissue from her bag. She handed it to Christy.

'You need to get that wee girl home, darling,' she said. 'She needs to be in her bed.'

Liz looked up and wiped her mouth on her sleeve.

'Are you all right, love?' the woman asked, leaning forward to see her. She smelled of a heady mixture of tobacco and perfume. Liz started to heave again.

'I want to sit down,' she said.

Christy was forced to hold her up by her armpits as she lowered herself. There was nothing behind her to sit on, except the pavement.

'She needs her bed,' the woman said once more, before leaving to catch up with her friends.

Christy hoisted Liz up and managed to pull her over to a low wall. She sat down, head in hands, and began to cry quietly. He looked at the crumpled tissue in his hands.

'Here, use this,' he said, handing it to her. *For fucksake*, he thought, sitting beside her.

The street was quiet. Only the occasional straggler passed them on their way home. Liz was still sitting with her head down, leaning against him for support.

He couldn't leave her. He wasn't even sure if he could get her up the hill. At least she had stopped crying.

'You shouldn't drink spirits if you're not used to them,' he said. 'That's what's happened to you.'

She lifted her head and looked at him with smeared eyes, where there had once been expertly applied make-up.

'I'm sorry,' she said.

'We've all done it,' said Christy. 'Don't worry. Are you all right now?'

He was smiling at her. She wiped her mouth with the tissue and blew her nose loudly.

'I don't feel sick any more, but my throat's sore. Thanks,' she said, showing him the tissue.

'Some woman gave me that,' he said.

'I can't go home yet – me mammy'll kill me.'

'You'll be better in a bit. I think you boked most of the drink, so you're not going to get any worse. Right.' He stood up. 'Up you get.'

Her stomach was raw, and her throat seemed swollen, but once she was standing she felt better; the world had gone from spinning to slightly woozy. She shivered with the memory of aniseed; bile rose in her throat, making her gag.

'Are you gonna vomit again?' said Christy, standing back.

'No,' she said. 'You're safe enough, I think. I've nothing left in me.'

'I warned you about the Pernod.'

'Don't talk about it, please!' said Liz.

They were quiet again as they walked, both thinking about the argument in the bar.

After a while, Liz remembered what Christy had told her.

'You didn't do your exams. You know you would have walked them, too. And I thought you were joking, when you told me you were thinking about it.'

'You offered to help me, remember?' he said. It seemed a long time ago, that day on the stairs. Christy was different now.

'Why don't we see you any more?' she said. 'You don't come out with us – is it just 'cause Peter died? But we all felt that.'

He didn't reply.

'Christy? Answer me.'

'It's nothing. You know what it's like.'

'I don't know what it's like. I wouldn't be asking if I did.' She stopped and pulled him to a halt.

'You haven't been studying, you haven't got some new job that's taking up all your time – so what is it?'

'It's just . . . stuff happened.' He started walking again.

'What stuff – what's so important?' she called. 'Oh, no – it's not a girl, is it?'

'I don't want to talk about it, Liz. Leave it, will you?' he shouted.

'Hi, you don't have to tell me anything,' she said angrily, walking fast to catch up with him. 'I just thought that when we left for England, you would come with us. I know Paddy wanted to – but he hardly talks to us any more, either.'

They were nearly at her street; her house was around the next corner. Liz stopped. She wasn't ready to go home – not yet.

They were standing at the entrance to an alleyway. She looked across at Christy. Even in the dark, she could see he was angry too.

'Do you want me to wait with you?' he said.

'Not if you're going to be like that,' she said, watching him.

'I don't want to talk about it – that's all. I don't want another argument,' he said, uncomfortable under her gaze.

She wiped the mascara from under her eyes and moved closer until she was beside him. Her hands touched the wall behind her. The rough stone felt cool, damp.

'Are you going in?' he asked.

'In a minute.' She turned to face him.

'So, you and Kev, off to England then?' he said. 'Why would you want me there?'

She answered quietly. 'I didn't say I wanted you there, did I?'

'Are you sure?' he said. He was suddenly very close.

She raised her hands to his chest but didn't push him away. His breath was on her face, her neck. Everything blurred and then they were kissing; a sweet, sour kiss that lasted a long time. His hands moved over her breasts, pulling her shirt up, undoing her zip and reaching inside to her buttocks. She struggled with herself, shocked at how much she wanted this to continue. But it couldn't.

'Christy,' she said. He groaned, feeling her pull away, knowing it was over.

'Really?' he said.

'I can't do this. I'm sorry.'

He pulled away too and stood back, in the dark, as she hurriedly righted herself, fastening her clothes.

'Thanks for looking after me – sorry,' she said, shaking her head as she walked into the open, blinking in the glare of the street lights. Then she was gone.

In the alley, Christy rolled a cigarette and lit it, watching the tip glow in the dark as he smoked.

'Shit,' he said, under his breath.

He left the lane and made for home, already feeling the hangover begin.

23

The door shook under the hammering of fists. Paddy jolted awake.

Then another three loud thuds shook the house. It was almost dawn; he lay still and listened to the growl of engines outside.

They were being raided.

It had happened once before, in the early seventies when everyone was searched. Back then, his father said, they were chosen because they had a house full of boys. Paddy remembered the army searching the attic, the bedrooms, the back yard, all over the house. Nothing was found, no one was arrested.

At Mullans' house, two doors down, the son was dragged into the street in his pyjama bottoms and taken for questioning.

'Thank God you have the sense not to get involved,' his father had said to his older brothers after the army moved on.

Now, Paddy didn't move. He wondered what he should do: should he run or go downstairs, hands up? He had been given only one piece of advice to use in this situation: whatever you say, say nothing – they don't know anything.

He heard his parents talking. 'Who is it, the army or the police?' his mother asked.

'Both,' said his father. Paddy pulled the curtains aside and looked down at the street. There were three Land Rovers, two army green and one RUC grey.

His father went downstairs. 'All right – hold on,' he said, as another series of thuds rattled the door.

There was an English voice in the hall. 'We're searching the house. Everyone down in the front room, now.'

'Bernie, get the boys and Elizabeth out of bed,' said Jim.

At the top of the stairs, Liz stood with her mother, afraid to go down on her own, to pass the soldiers and their guns. She followed Bernie into the boys' room, where Johnny and Paddy were sitting on their bunks, pulling on jeans and T-shirts.

'What is it, Mammy?' Johnny asked, swaying as he put his shoes on.

'It's the army,' whispered Bernie. 'They're searching the house. Be quiet, boys. Don't say anything to them and they'll leave us when they've had their look around.'

They sat in a row on the sofa, Bernie and Liz still in their nightwear, Jim in the vest and trousers he had opened the door in. Paddy had his head down. They were under guard.

A soldier stood by the door. A cop, a red-faced countryman with a barrel chest, waited by the window. The soldier hardly seemed real. He was listening to the activity in the rooms above: loud bumps and thuds could be heard through the ceiling.

The cop, with his dark uniform and his stillness, was the one who filled the room. He emitted an air of disregard and menace, and there was no engagement with either the family or the army.

When Jim tried to insist on accompanying the soldiers as they searched each room, it was the policeman who pushed him back down onto the sofa and told him to stay where he was.

'They'll not find anything, you know?' Bernie told him. 'Because there's nothing to find. Nobody in this house is involved in anything.'

She was answered with silence.

Upstairs, a loud crash in the boys' room made everyone jump and stare at the ceiling light as it shook from the force of the impact. Finally, the search squad came downstairs again. After some discussion, one of them entered the living room.

'Which one is Paddy?' he asked Jim.

'Why do you want to know?' said Jim, getting to his feet.

They were face to face. The soldier regarded him for a moment. The old man reminded him of his own father back home: unshaven, old, pathetic.

After two years in this town, he had grown used to searches where people shouted – the women, mainly. It was normal for things to get aggressive. This family was quiet – too polite to resist, until now.

'Which one is Paddy?' he said again.

'None of my sons has done anything,' said Jim.

With a practised touch, the soldier jammed the butt of his rifle into the old man's stomach. He doubled up in pain.

Bernie jumped to her feet. The RUC man blocked her way.

'Leave my mother alone!' shouted Johnny. Liz began to cry, and Paddy stood up.

'It's me – I'm Paddy. Leave them alone.'

Without further delay, the soldier said, 'You're coming with us.'

Two large hands grabbed him, by the arm and the back of his shirt, and he was half walked, half dragged into the hall and out the front door. He heard his mother shouting and then all the army and police, in the house and in the street, were moving with him towards their vehicles.

They put him into the back of a Land Rover and the metal door slammed shut. In the dark interior, he saw the face of a soldier in the seat opposite, watching him with seeming indifference. Paddy clung onto the edge of the seat as they pulled away at speed. He shivered, as much from fear as from the dawn cold.

★

Two nights before, he had been lying in wet grass. Christy and he were on a job together, watching distant uniformed figures patrol the checkpoint at the border. Two other men waited for them, in a car on the opposite side of the field.

'I'm not happy about this,' Paddy whispered to Christy. 'Not one bit happy. And I'll tell you another thing: your man Joe's giving me the heebie-jeebies. He's jumpy as fuck. Did you see him trying to light that fag? His hands were shaking all over the place.'

Christy rolled over to see him. 'Keep your voice down, will you?'

They were both masked; only the pale circles of Paddy's eyes showed dimly in the feeble light.

It was Sunday night and cars were lined up to be searched. Cars with parents, their children in the back seats, still sandy from the beaches of Inishowen. Cars with older couples coming home from the slot machines, a few drinks taken and a bag of chips to share between them. As the twilight dimmed, their headlamps snaked along the main road.

The checkpoint was the target. It dominated the border, dwarfing the Irish customs post on the other side. The checkpoint had been built up over the years. What had once been a hut now had a dedicated drive-through area of concrete and corrugated tin, open-ended and high enough to allow lorries and buses to enter. It glowed inside with orange light.

The hunger strike was breaking down but that hardly mattered any more. So much damage had been done, so many injured and dead. And so much ill will – it was irreparable. The strike was breaking, but it had instilled a grim energy in the movement that hadn't been felt since the early days of the seventies. And as the life of one more hunger striker reached its inevitable conclusion, the IRA were preparing to meet that end with a violent response.

'What are we looking at?' said Paddy.

'Do you not listen?' hissed Christy. 'We're supposed to get the times when they change shifts.'

Paddy was such a child; it irritated the hell out of Christy, the way he went on – too jokey when they were talking about serious subjects, not listening when he should do.

'We're to go back with a report on the time the Land Rover arrives and leaves, and what the routine is when it gets here.'

'What is it – a bomb?'

'Shut up, will ye?' said Christy.

Paddy shuffled; there was a root digging into him. He looked at the line of cars.

'There's wee wains in them cars,' he said. 'How are we supposed to do this when there's wains in the cars?'

Christy rolled over to face him again. 'Look,' he said, as quietly as he could. 'We do what we're told, right? Let the big boys make the decisions.'

It was poor propaganda to kill civilians, especially the ones from your own side; and the people in the cars were all from their own side. Right now, they were there to monitor and report back – that was all.

Paddy's jeans were soaked and the hump under him was starting to hurt.

'How long do we have to stay?' he whispered. It had only been half an hour, but it felt longer.

Christy didn't take his eyes off the road. 'Just settle yourself,' he said.

It was important to get this right – he wouldn't be the reason a big job failed. He was in charge; not that he outranked his friend, but inside, in his gut, he was. There was a determination in him. They would lie here, and they would watch. When they returned to the car, it would be with as much information as they could gather.

176

Movement was kept to an occasional shuffle, to stop cramp or a dead leg. For a long time it was quiet between them – too long for Paddy.

'Remember playing commandos in the street?' Paddy whispered, after a while. 'We're playing commandos. It's *The Guns of Navarone* – you can be Anthony Quinn and I'll be Gregory Peck.'

Winter evenings, and small boys crawling along footpaths on their stomachs, ambushing the lads from the next street as their mothers shouted at them for ruining the front of their good trousers. That's what Christy remembered: the mouthed *rat-a-tat* of a pretend machine gun, rolling over when you were pretend hit in the stomach, groaning in your imagined death throes.

'Why do I have to be Anthony Quinn?' he said.

'Because,' said Paddy, 'I'm the one with the looks.'

'No way . . . Anyway, Gregory Peck was the one with the brains, so I should be him.'

They fell silent again, watching the cars as the military waved some of them through and stopped others with a raised hand. Then Christy was aware of a low, tuneless hum. It took a while to realise that the sound was coming from Paddy. It stopped.

'That's on the single Kevin has,' said Paddy.

'What are you talking about?' said Christy. It was a bizarre change of subject.

'*The Guns of Navarone* – the Specials – we listened to it all the time last year.'

'Is that what that was? You didn't win many medals in the Feis, did you?'

'Funny,' said Paddy.

'It's an old Ska track,' said Christy, watching two army vehicles pull up on the road below them. 'Look,' he said.

Paddy pulled himself up on his elbows. 'Is this what we're waiting for?'

Men tumbled from the back of each Land Rover. There was some talk between them and those they were relieving. Christy looked at his watch; it was 11.02. He pulled a scrap of paper and a pencil from his back pocket and wrote down the time. Within five minutes, the squaddies got themselves together, climbed into the waiting jeeps and drove away, leaving their replacements behind. The night shift had taken over.

'What now?' said Paddy, ready to go.

'I don't know,' said Christy. 'Maybe we should give it another half-hour, in case anyone else turns up?'

'Them two are probably in the bar right now, having a laugh at us,' said Paddy. 'I'm going home.'

Christy looked down at the road. Less traffic meant less activity; the new shift had placed guards at various posts, but the search area was quiet, and little could be seen.

'All right,' he said. 'Let's go.'

They began to move, crawling at first, until they were sure they could not be seen from the road. Then, on their feet, they trudged over the grass and jagged weeds until they reached the place where they had left the car. Both hearts fell – it wasn't there.

'I fucking knew it,' said Paddy.

They crept along, eyes straining in the blackness.

'There it is,' said Christy. The car had pulled into a lane running off the road. There were no lights and they approached it with caution. The driver's head was slumped on his chest.

Paddy knocked lightly on the glass. The man jumped and turned with a frightened look. He had been asleep. He shook his companion awake and then indicated to the boys that the back door was open.

'So what's the score?' he asked, once they were in the back seat.

'About twenty Brits when we got there,' said Christy. 'And a few cops too. They were relieved at two minutes past eleven, by two jeeps with maybe ten soldiers. The whole switch-over took five minutes and they were driven back in the same vehicles that brought the new ones. That's it.'

'Who's down there now?' asked Joe with the shake in his hands.

'There's two on guard at the entrance and two at the exit,' said Christy. 'The rest are inside. We couldn't see them, but there's not a lot of traffic now, so they're not moving around.'

The men listened intently. 'OK, you did grand. Let's get out of here,' said Joe. The driver started the engine and slowly, without lights, the car crawled out of the lane and onto the road. Once they were sure there was no one to see, and they weren't being followed, he switched the headlights on and sped down the road towards town.

In the back of the Land Rover that was taking him to the barracks, Paddy watched the silent soldier and was pierced with fear at the thought that they were caught, and of what was ahead.

Say nothing, he told himself. *They don't know anything.*

24

'Whatever you say, say nothing' – it was a joke, right? It always seemed like a joke to him; smart-arsed, getting one over on the Brits. Not a laughing matter now though; it was all he had to hold on to.

He was in a green room; dirty, mud-coloured, military green. People in the army must think that everywhere is green, he thought. The army must have pots of the stuff in warehouses, paint factories producing British Army Green to cover their British Army Green barracks, across what was left of the British Army Green empire. But of course there were variations too – a bit of pale green on one wall, snot green on another.

He had been waiting for at least an hour on this metal chair, for someone to come and – do what? Interrogate him? Strip-search him? Hit him?

'Don't get into a conversation,' they had been told during a training session that covered being arrested and how to handle it. 'These boys are experts at getting information out of you. It's their job, their mission in life, to get you to talk.'

A door opened at one end of the room and a soldier entered. In the few seconds that the door was open, Paddy glimpsed a corridor lined with more closed doors. The soldier crossed the room to the door at the other end without acknowledging his presence. Minutes later he returned with Christy.

Christy's head was down and his Clash T-shirt was on inside out. Paddy sat up straight, thinking they would be left in the room together. Christy looked up, saw him and was about to say something, but the soldier pushed him through the door and closed it behind them.

Then Paddy was alone in the room for a long time. When the door opened again, he jumped.

'On your feet,' said the soldier.

His legs shook under him as he got up. He was gripped by the arm and forcefully led through the same door that Christy had vanished through. When they came to an open door at the end of the corridor, the soldier said, 'In here,' and pushed him.

Paddy walked into a small room which had a metal-framed window with opaque, wired glass, of the type found in the gym at school. There was a desk and two chairs. A real military type, with epaulettes and pips on his shoulder, sat behind the desk, his head bent over the beige folder he was writing in. He looked up and indicated that Paddy should sit down.

Paddy sat, hands tucked under his thighs, and watched the top of the man's head as he continued to write. His escort sat too, in a chair beside the closed door. Eventually, the military type stopped writing and looked at Paddy, pen poised in his hand.

'What's your name?' he asked, ready to write again. Paddy didn't reply. The soldier – an officer, from the look of the uniform – waited a moment before repeating, 'Your name?'

Again, Paddy said nothing, returning the officer's gaze. Not knowing where the 'say nothing' should start, he wasn't taking a chance.

Now he knew why prisoners of war were instructed to give only name, rank and serial number when they were captured and questioned. He wished he did have a rank or a serial number; the compulsion to speak was agonising. Say nothing – it would have been better to have something, anything, to repeat, over and over again.

The officer sighed. 'Look, young man. We know your name. We just want you to confirm it, OK?' He checked something on the paper in front of him, then looked up again. 'Elvis Patrick McLaughlin – is that your name?'

'Most people call me Paddy,' said Paddy, speaking cautiously in case anything else would suddenly blurt out of his mouth, unbidden.

'Age?'

'Nineteen.'

'Address?'

'Try the house you lifted me from this morning,' said Paddy. The officer sat back in his chair.

'Elvis, eh? Where did that come from?' he said.

Paddy, however, had recovered a bit of his nerve and was back to staying silent.

'It's an unusual name for Londonderry. Is someone a fan?'

Yes, his father of course, but he wouldn't tell them that. His father and that embarrassment of a name. All his life he had avoided it; calling a boy Elvis was like calling someone Hitler or Jesus or something. Why would you do it to a little baby? He hated his father for landing him with it, for using it as a weapon to wind up and embarrass his friends when they called to the front door. His father who, that same morning, had been humiliated in front of his children and their mother, showing a nerve that Paddy never knew he had.

There was no way – no way – he would allow them to mention his father now, to talk about him, or use him to soften up the atmosphere and wheedle their way into his family. The officer was smarmy and confident. Paddy felt anger revive him and with it a thick, stubborn streak. *Say fuck all*, he told himself.

'Where do you drink, Paddy – a man your age must like a pint?'

Say nothing.

'Who do you hang around with? Lads like you always have plenty of friends. Who's your best friend? Is it Christy? We have him here too, of course. Would you like to see him? Apparently he's been very chatty.'

Fuck you, you English bastard, thought Paddy, listening to this pathetic attempt at manipulation. He thought the Brits were supposed to be cleverer than this.

'We've seen you, you see. Hanging around with quite a few older men. You've been getting yourself into some strange company – what's that all about?'

There was no reply.

'We have seen you, Paddy, in a car with a man we have suspicions may be an IRA member. How did you meet someone like that?'

Silence. Paddy sat with arms folded, looking at the blurred sky. A switch had been flipped, the one that turned off the voice of authority. Access was refused.

It was the patronising tone, the one that offered support and advice, that thought it knew better, the adult voice – his father's voice at the top of the stairs. What did they know about anything? He looked at the distorted blue in the crumpled squares, graphed with wire. The voice droned. He blocked it out, knowing he could keep this up for hours.

The officer kept asking about this man.

'How do you know him, Paddy?' he said again. He slid a photo across the table. With the briefest of glances, Paddy saw a side-on photo of a car, and Joe's face at the window, looking back along the road. He, Paddy, wasn't in the car – he wasn't in the photo.

He resumed his study of the blue glass, following the lines of wires, imagining X's and O's traced on them. Nothing would get through – not the voice, not the fear. Only the practised anger that ate at him.

'This man is called Joe – we know he is an active IRA member. We know that you have been seen with him, Paddy. So how do you know him? Is there something you can tell us? What has he been up to?'

Nothing. Blue glass, X's and O's.

'If you help us, you won't be in trouble – we'll look after you. You seem like a good person, no record. You've never been picked up before. You do know, don't you, that the hunger strike is over, almost? It's all breaking down. The battle is already lost. What do you want to get involved in all this for?'

By the door, the squaddie shifted in his seat. Paddy looked at him. He was staring at the same window, with the same lack of interest. Paddy faced his questioner again.

'Is that it? Can I go now?'

The officer's face hardened. The boy thought he was smart, but this breach of the silence was the first sign of weakness, a way in.

'We know you're an active IRA member and we know you have been involved in recent actions, including hijackings.'

Paddy merely turned his gaze to the glass. If there was one thing he knew, it was this: if they had evidence, if they had anything against him, however spurious, he would have been arrested, and it would be a cop sitting behind that desk, neither reasonable nor nice, forcing him to sign something that would put him away.

The officer gave it a minute, observing. Then he began again, with a new tactic. No sympathetic tone now.

'In a car with older men – maybe it's not what we thought it is? What are you Paddy, a poof? Are you a homosexual, Paddy? Elvis? Paddy? Are you meeting these men to suck them off, Paddy? Are they paying you?'

The voice sneered. Paddy twisted in his seat, glaring at him. The officer smiled, a leery grin, his lips twisted with distaste.

'We can tell your father that – maybe he'd like to know that his son is a fag? His good Catholic son.'

Wrong thing to say – he had no faith. He wanted to reach across the table and punch the man, to shove his fist down his throat and put a stop to his sneering English superiority and contempt, his obvious tactics of empathy and insult. But he didn't. He managed to summon up enough control to turn back to his window.

'Looks like that hit a nerve, eh, Paddy? Maybe we should get your father in here with us. Is he involved as well? Should we pick him up, too? What would he tell us, I wonder?'

But the breaking point had come and gone. He would not open his mouth to this man. He was dry with thirst, hungry, exhausted. He wanted it to stop, but he would not open his mouth.

It did stop, quite suddenly, after an hour that felt like a year. There was no indication of frustration from his interrogator, no admittance of defeat, just a moment when he said to his companion at the door, 'You can take him back now.'

The change in tone took Paddy by surprise. It was such a complete switch, from disgust to bland, uninterested boredom. The officer bent his head over the beige folder, once again absorbed in his writing.

Big hands lifted him from the chair, through the door and down the corridor, to the same room he had sat in earlier. No Christy – the place was empty.

Still rattled by the abrupt end to his interrogation, Paddy was strangely peeved, full of the urge to bang the door, to insist that he be taken back to the other room and have his say. What had Christy told them? They said he was telling them loads; was he somewhere in the building, spilling his guts? The bastard.

The door opened and a soldier said, 'You can go now.'

Outside the gates, dazzled by the bright sky, he watched the traffic pass him. He started the walk home.

25

'Go and see the priest, Jim – please,' pleaded Bernie.

'What the hell do you expect him to do?' said Jim, as she forced his arm into the sleeve of his jacket.

'He can phone the barracks and find out what's going on, that's what he can do. And they'll listen to him – he's a Catholic priest.'

Maybe she had a point. He left the house and his wife to her frantic pacing. He would kill that boy when he saw him. And suddenly he was afraid he wouldn't see him again, not for a very long time.

A pain seared his guts, and it was not just from the blow. He had failed to stop the boy, when he knew what he was at.

Father Devlin was sitting down to a big fry, laid out in front of him like a sacrifice to the pagan gods. He lifted his knife and fork, and was about to cut deep into a pork sausage, when he heard the knock on the front door and his heart fell.

The other fellas were out: Father McDermott was doing the eight o'clock Mass, and Father Cusack had been called out, in the early hours, to administer the Last Rites to some dying old man, and hadn't returned yet.

He looked at his fry, already cooling on the plate. Lifting the sausage in his hand, he ate it quickly, before the inevitable tap on the door could stop him.

'Sorry, Father. There's a man here, asking to speak to one of the priests,' said the housekeeper softly.

'OK,' he sighed, rising to his feet.

The housekeeper moved to lift the plate. 'Sure, I'll put this to keep warm for you,' she said, disappearing through the door again, fry in hand.

Jim was waiting in the hall. Father Devlin remembered their conversation from weeks before; it didn't take much imagination to know what this was about. Something had happened to that stupid boy of his. He put on his concerned face.

'Hello, Mr McLaughlin. What can I do for you?'

'Sorry for disturbing you so early, Father. I need your advice about something again,' said Jim. He told the story of the early-morning raid and Paddy's incarceration.

'His mother wanted me to see if you would call the barracks – see if they're letting him out, or holding him, or something? I know you get asked to do things like this all the time – sorry.'

He did get asked to do 'things like this' all the time: calling the police, calling politicians, army officials, approaching organisations which people like the McLaughlins of this world were too scared to approach, in case information or a favour would result in some quid pro quo.

He never refused; it came with the job. He was the go-between, the one who stood between the people and authority, in all its various guises.

'Come in and sit down,' he said, opening the door across the hall to let Jim enter. They were in the office where they had last spoken. The priest took a notebook from his desk.

'What's your address?' He wrote it down as Jim leaned forward to make sure the priest got it right.

'And the boy's full name?'

Carefully, as if for the very first time, Jim said, 'Elvis . . . Patrick . . . McLaughlin.'

The priest's pen paused after 'Elvis'.

Yes, this was the one, the father who had threatened to walk out of the chapel unless his son was christened with that name. And the child had screamed his way through the entire service, he recalled. Look where he was now.

He wrote the name down and looked at it, scrawled on the page. There would be no confusion as to who he was calling about, that was for sure.

'Where do they have him?' he asked.

'I don't know,' said Jim wearily. 'It was the army – there was only one cop – so it's most likely Fort George.' He wavered between desperation and the desire to leave the room and never return, ever.

With a sigh to match Jim's despair, Father Devlin closed the notebook.

'It's fine,' he said. 'Give me a minute.'

He went to the hall, closing the door behind him. Jim strained to listen. He could hear the whirr of the phone as the dial repeated back on itself, and then the priest's mumbled words. The sound couldn't penetrate the heavy door. Jim was tempted to press his ear against it, but instead he sat down and waited. Father Devlin came back and sat behind the desk.

'Well, you were right, he's in Fort George. All they would say is that he's there. You'll have to wait and see what happens next. He'll either be moved to the police station and charged, or he'll be let out in an hour or two. Tell me,' he asked with genuine curiosity, 'did you ever tell your wife about all this?'

'I did not, Father. She can't understand why they've taken him and it's a toss-up who she kills first, me or him, when she realises that I knew and said nothing.'

Paddy arrived home at midday by the clock above the fireplace.

Bernie was already in the kitchen, putting the pan on top of the cooker for the bacon and eggs. She had watched him come down the street, after a morning tracing her own steps, from window, to door, to window. Now that he was in the house, she was afraid to look at him in case he was different, in case she stood and cried in front of him. In the end, he came to her.

'Are you all right?' she asked, once she saw that he was still her Patrick, with no marks on him. He looked so young. 'What did they want? Did they say why they took you – do you have to go back?'

'I'm all right,' said Paddy. 'Is there anything to eat?'

'I'm making you something – go in and sit down. Your daddy's upstairs.'

Fuck, thought Paddy.

His father's accusing look was the last thing he needed. Jim was already in the living room, waiting for him, and so was Liz. Only Johnny had stuck to his normal routine, relieved he hadn't been that morning's target.

Liz stared at him from the seat opposite. 'What?' said Paddy.

'Nothing,' she said. 'Are you OK? What was it like?'

'Leave him be, Elizabeth,' said Jim, before turning on him. 'What did they say, Patrick? I got the priest to call them, but they wouldn't tell him anything. They've let you out anyway – that's a good sign.'

Jesus Christ, the fucking priest. Why the hell did he have to go and talk to that oul' bastard up in the chapel?

'What did you do that for?' he said.

'We needed to know what was happening – your mother's nerves are shattered.'

'You didn't have to get the priest involved, Da – I was all right!' he shouted.

'How were we to know what you were? And don't you raise your voice to me – it's you that's got yourself here. The rest of us are having to deal with it!' said Jim, shouting back at him.

Bernie stood in the doorway, plate of food in hand.

'What's his fault?' she said. 'He's done nothing wrong – they pick young ones up these days whether they're involved or not.'

She put the plate into Paddy's hands and he started to eat, suddenly ravenous. Jim didn't answer his wife. He watched the boy shovelling the food into him.

This was a man who had to be pushed to anger. Bernie watched the rage rise in him, saw the fists tighten and his shoulders square for a fight. 'What do you mean, Jim?' she said.

'Are you going to tell your mother what you've been up to, or are you going to leave it to me?' said Jim. Paddy kept eating; it was about to kick off. In a minute, everything would change.

'I think you'd better tell me what it is that you know and I don't, Jim McLaughlin,' said his mother.

Bernie's voice was low and dangerous, but Jim wouldn't look at her. Instead, he continued to watch his son eating.

'I'll tell her, then. Tell her that you've been stupid enough to get involved with the IRA, you and that friend of yours, that Christy boy. Aye, Bernie, running around like they're big men, fighting for Ireland's cause.'

When he stopped, there was silence; for whole minutes, nothing was said. Bernie got up and walked into the kitchen. She stood at the sink and gripped the stainless-steel rim, looking out of the window to the houses behind them. No one moved. The clock ticked from the fireplace.

At last she came back, lifted the plate out of Paddy's hands and, for a second, didn't know what she was going to do with it. She wanted to throw it, at the wall or at her husband's head – she wasn't sure which.

'You knew about this and you never said one word to me – you knew. Is this the reason you two haven't been speaking? But that's weeks! Weeks, with all the tension in this house. And you,' she said to Paddy.

He ignored her.

'And you!' she said again. This time he looked up at her, afraid. There was a look of pure, dangerous fury on her face. He had never seen her look like that, not even when he was little and broke the window in the back door with a football.

'You will let them boys know that this will not be going on any longer,' she said. 'You're not to leave this house unless I say so, and I know where you are going, and who with. I don't care what kind of a cause you think you are fighting for – I am bloody sure you're not getting yourself killed, or jailed, as long as I have breath to stop it!'

'That's not going to happen, Ma,' said Paddy, trying to keep a steady voice. He had sat and listened, struck dumb by her rage, but now he had to speak. 'I've a job to do and I'm a grown man. You can't stop me.'

'Bernie . . .' said Jim. He got no further.

'I'm not speaking to you,' she said, turning on him with a cold look. And then, back to her son, 'You'll do what I say, Patrick, as long as you are under this roof.'

'What age do you think I am?' shouted Paddy. 'I don't have to listen to this shite.' He stood up, about to storm out of the room.

Bernie felt the weight of the plate in her hand, then watched as it smashed against the wall behind her youngest son's head. He ducked just in time to avoid it. The plate split down the middle and both pieces dropped on the sofa, leaving a long smear of ketchup and egg on the wallpaper.

'I'm away,' said Paddy. He ran out of the room and up the stairs. Bernie stared at the place where the plate had struck, then turned and went back to the kitchen. She closed the door behind her and sat, stiffly, on a chair.

Liz went after Paddy. Jim quietly began to lift the pieces of broken, greasy plate from the back of the sofa.

★

In his room, Paddy pulled boxes and old newspapers from the bottom of the wardrobe, searching for a bag.

'What are you doing?' said Liz, watching him scrabble through piles of shoes, toys and discarded clothes.

'I'm not staying here,' he said. He held up a black holdall, Carl's old kitbag. Shaking the dust from it, he threw it on his bed and began to fill it with whatever clothes he could find in his drawers or on the floor. All the clothes he possessed took up half of the space in the bag.

What remained was the detritus of his life: a green paisley shirt, so old it was flat and stiff, a greying vest he'd worn when he was thirteen, various socks, loose and mateless. Under it all, among the pencil shavings and dust, was a lining of faded brown newspaper, a snapshot of the past. *Twenty per cent off Suits!* declared the headline, an advertisement for a menswear store that was lost to a bomb in the seventies. The male models in the photographs stared rigidly at him, in sepia tones and strange, awkward poses. Paddy looked into the drawer as though he would fall into it.

He pulled a pair of ancient slippers from under the bed and put them in the bag too, trying to fill it. Apart from his records, this was all he had. The sum of his possessions. Exhausted, he sat on the blankets and rubbed at his eyes.

Liz hadn't moved from the door; she was afraid to go any closer. 'Where are you going?' she asked.

Surely they were wrong – what they were saying about him had to be wrong? But she remembered Christy telling her how things had taken over, things he couldn't talk about. He was so arrogant about it, so self-important.

All this time, she had thought it was her and the changes in herself that had created that distorted atmosphere. All this time she'd believed she was the one who had moved on and didn't fit any more.

None of it made sense. Her family didn't do this kind of thing – but here was Paddy, sitting on his bed, a bag packed.

'I don't want you to go,' she told him. He picked up the bag and took a coat from the hook on the wardrobe door.

'I can't stay, not after all that,' he said. He lifted Noel's copy of the *Furry Freak Brothers* and gave it to her. 'Give that back to Noel for me, will you?' he said, pulling her into a rough hug. 'See you.'

He crossed the landing and ran down the stairs. Without looking back, he opened the front door and was gone.

26

Liz heard it all, sitting on the stairs after Paddy had gone. Her mother shouting, her father trying to apologise, saying how he had tried to stop it, how he had done what he could.

'How could you not tell me?' said Bernie. 'I could have talked him out of it.'

'You couldn't, love – he wouldn't have listened. Kevin tried – he even talked to some of the boys he knew, tried to talk them out of having him. I even went to Father Devlin.'

'He's going to get himself killed, Jim.'

She sat upright. Had she heard that correctly? Her father said Kevin . . . that Kevin had tried to talk to 'the boys'? In shock, she didn't know which was worse – that he had known her brother was fucking up in a huge way and never said, or that he was talking to 'the boys'! Even she knew that meant the IRA.

Remember when Paul Weller wore a cravat on *Top of the Pops* and suddenly everyone wanted one too? Or when Pauline Black looked clean and cool in her snow-white polo shirt and it changed all you knew about how you looked and wanted to look? When those were the crucial things, along with seeing your mates on a Saturday or learning, by heart, all the words to the next 'best song ever'?

These were essential, the things that rooted you and placed you. When they were there, you knew you were there, too. You were sure that nothing would change; these essentials would remain the most important things in your life.

Then a friend dies, and somehow, among all the transitory feelings – the brief, burnt-out love affairs, the parental rows and the school work – that pain, that dreadful loss, moves on too. It rushes past as the world rushes forward, and you are untouchable again, and so is everyone around you, because you are a movement, unstoppable.

Until, one day, you turn your head and see that some people have been lost along the way. The truth of the matter is, some of you never did move forward. Some of you stopped and turned off in completely different directions. They didn't think to say that the hurt was different for them, that they couldn't move past it. And what you thought was for ever, you now know was built on very little – just a childish construction, a brief interlude before life hit.

You're not untouchable. You're not exempt from the world. You, and all the people you know, are as entwined in its complications, its tangible sordidness, as any of the poor sods you looked down on for not being you.

'When were you going to tell me about our Paddy?'

Kevin was barefoot, standing at his front door. Liz refused to come in and was shouting at him.

'Tell you what?' he said.

'About the Provos and Paddy, and Christy for that matter? Didn't I have the right to know? You never said a thing, all this time – you and me da.'

'Hold on a minute,' he said. 'What's happened?'

'You know what's happened, Kevin – how could you not say?'

Kevin had known all along that this wouldn't end well. Jim had told all, seemingly, including naming him. So much for him being in trouble for not helping.

'Your father – *your* father –' he pointed a finger in her

face – 'wanted to sort it all on the quiet, without your mother knowing what was going on. I wanted nothing to do with it, but he kept dragging me into it.'

'Oh, aye. You and your "contacts" – you kept that quiet,' she sneered.

'Stop going on like a wain, Liz,' said Kevin. 'I don't have to tell you anything, and not everything is your business. All I tried to do, was do your da a good turn, and for that I've lost two friends and have you shouting at me in the street.'

He turned and walked back into the house.

Suddenly, Liz lost her nerve. She had been full of courage, knocking on the door, and hadn't considered that he would be angry right back at her. He'd called her a child – a wain. Humiliation stung.

She peered into the dark hallway, then walked away, dizzy with adrenaline.

'Liz, hold on!' He was running after her. She kept walking until he caught up, pulling her to a halt with a hard grip on her wrist.

'Wait a minute – Jesus!' he said. 'I was only putting my shoes on. I'm sorry I didn't say, all right? What's happened?'

'Paddy was lifted out of the house this morning, and then it all came out and there was a huge row. Now he's moved out and me mammy and daddy are fighting. It's a whole big mess,' she said tearfully.

'I'm so sorry, Liz – really, I'm sorry I didn't tell you. I told Paddy to wise up, you know? He wouldn't listen to me. I swear to God, they're in some kind of Republican fantasy world.'

He tried to put his arm around her.

'One of the soldiers hit me daddy,' she said tearfully.

'Liz, me and your da did our best – bar tying him up and shipping him out of the country, there was nothing we could do.'

'Aye, well, you should have done that,' Liz said, starting to relent. She knew who to blame next, though.

Christy Meehan. This was his doing.

If they thought the interrogation was over, they were wrong. Christy and Paddy were in the army now, and a debrief was in order. They sat together this time, in front of two men neither had seen before.

Paddy had arrived at Christy's, bag in hand. The next day, they went into the town, but didn't get far before a car pulled up beside them and they were ordered in.

'Right, boys,' said the driver, twisting awkwardly in his seat. 'You were taken in – what happened?' he asked.

'I said nothing,' said Paddy, glad now that he had. 'All I did was sit there and look out the window, till the boy got fed up talking.'

'Did they ask you about anything, or mention anyone by name?' said the second man.

Paddy looked at Christy and he nodded for him to tell them.

'They had a photo of your man, Joe, in a car. But that was all,' he said. 'And they tried to make out that Christy was saying loads, but I wasn't falling for that. I said nothing, apart from my name and my age.'

Both men regarded Christy with pronounced interest.

'And you were saying loads, Christy?' said the driver.

'I didn't say anything, other than stupid stuff – I kept telling them what I'm interested in is music and getting full, that's all.'

It was true. As far as he was concerned he had said very little. They asked him where he drank, and who with, and he told them. The Cave was a blatantly non-political, dope-head hang-out and it was a good tactic to throw it in there. That's what he'd thought at the time. Now he wished he could sit there, like Paddy, and tell them he'd said nothing. What if he had let something slip?

The men obviously thought the same. They looked at him in silence, waiting for more. He searched his memory, trying to be clear, but the person who interviewed him was an expert in confusion and twisting words. He couldn't distinguish between what he had said and what the officer had repeated back to him.

'They asked me who I drank with. I only told them names that we knew before all this. None of them would be involved in anything – some of them are even Protestants. They tried to make out that I was queer, too. I've no problem with that – they can think what they want.'

'They did that to me as well,' said Paddy, jumping in a little too enthusiastically. Both the men laughed.

'You're not, are you?' said the driver.

They looked blankly at him.

'Right, you can go,' he said, still laughing. 'Say nothing about this to anyone, and I mean anyone. You did all right – this was going to happen and it's not the last time, that's for sure.'

27

The bang on the door didn't wake him; it seeped into his sleep like the resurgence of an old nightmare. When he opened his eyes, the soldier was a dark mass, filling the door frame.

'Get dressed,' he said and walked into the room.

As Kevin pulled on his jeans, he watched as the soldier, no more than twenty-five, went around the room with a curiosity that was more about what he could see than what might have been hidden there. He turned over books and inspected the posters on the walls. At the sight of the albums on the bedroom floor, he dropped to his knees and started going through them.

Cheeky bugger, thought Kevin. The squaddie selected one and was reading the cover notes – his precious Ian Dury bootleg.

'Great . . .' said his uninvited guest, taking the record out of its sleeve. When a second soldier came in, he slid the record back into the pile.

'Right, on your feet,' he said. 'You're coming with us.' Picking his rifle up from the floor where he had left it, he stood in front of Kevin.

'What's this about?' Kevin asked. He wouldn't resist, but since this hadn't happened in years, he was genuinely interested.

What could they possibly want?

'Just a few questions, mate.' The other soldier had gone, and it was just the two of them again. 'Where did you get the Blockheads bootleg?' he said.

'From an ad in the *NME*,' said Kevin, with a certain

reluctance. He wasn't sure about getting this up close and personal with a Brit.

'You've a good collection,' the soldier said, his eyes drawn again to the vinyl.

'Thanks,' said Kevin, as he was escorted out of his bedroom under armed guard.

Six hours later, at the McLaughlin house, he could barely control himself.

'Where is he?'

'Why are you shouting at me?' shouted Liz.

'I'm going to kill them, both of them!'

Christy walked past her into the front room. He was unwashed and grey-faced.

'Who are you talking about?' said Liz.

'Your brother – where is he?'

Bernie came in from the kitchen. 'What's going on?' she asked.

Kevin brushed past her and left the house.

'He looks terrible,' said Bernie.

In the hours while he waited to be questioned, in the midst of a body search in which he was told to strip to his underwear, Kevin had much time to think, but he couldn't think what had brought him there.

Neither the police nor the army had paid him attention in years.

'You've been seen with active IRA operatives, Kevin – what have you to say about that?' said the officer behind the desk.

'What operatives? I'm not involved in anything,' Kevin told him, thinking about his conversations with Rafferty. They were months ago and wouldn't have put him here.

A photograph was pushed across the table for him to see.

Kevin took a good look at a man in his thirties, with balding red hair, peering through a car window. He sat back in his seat with folded arms.

'How do you know him?' the officer asked.

'I don't,' said Kevin truthfully.

'Do you drink in a bar called the Cave?' the officer went on. And there it was.

'I do,' he said. 'Why do you ask?'

The officer ignored this and continued with his line of questioning.

'Who do you socialise with when you're there?' He had his pen ready, seemingly waiting to take down a list of names.

'Whoever's there at the time.'

'What about this man?' The officer pointed, with his pen, to the photo. Kevin started to laugh.

'You've obviously never been to the Cave,' he said. The man in the photo had a receding hairline and a moustache and looked like a relic from 1975. He was the least likely individual to be found in the Cave.

'I don't know what you're looking for, but you're looking in the wrong place. I drink there because it's as far away from people like him as it's possible to get.'

At this, the soldier relaxed back in his chair.

'So how do you know Christopher Meehan and Elvis Patrick McLaughlin?' he asked, watching for a reaction.

The stupid bastards, what had they said? Anything they could think of, no doubt.

'They're friends – or they were,' he said, suddenly much more careful. 'I haven't seen them for ages.'

The officer smiled; now he had something to go on. Kevin knew it too. He knew they had so much more to talk about now.

They kept him in the room, digging at him with questions. Why was he no longer a friend – had they had an argument?

What was that about? Ah, he didn't like you seeing his sister. But what about Meehan – why fall out with a friend? Surely there was more to it? Did he know what their politics were? What were his politics? He'd been arrested many times before. The man in the car – he did know him? Who else could he tell them about? What about the hunger strike – he was angry about that, wasn't he? What did his friends think about it all?

As he tired, Kevin struggled to keep a clear head and avoid contradicting himself, or Paddy and Christy.

'I'm not political and I'm not involved in anything,' he repeated. 'You're asking me about things I know nothin' about.'

As the hours passed, he had a feeling of time slipping away from him, of being stripped to a raw nerve.

'I had a look at your file before we brought you in,' said the officer. 'We've had quite a few chats with you, over the years.'

'I've never been involved in anything – you know that, or I'd have been inside by now,' countered Kevin.

'This is interesting.' He lifted some pages from the folder on the desk, holding them between finger and thumb.

Kevin watched the papers – there were photographs. Suddenly he was in another room, years before, and they were holding him down, pushing his head to the table, forcing him to see, up close, the obscene remains of his friend – a smashed head, a mess of broken flesh.

Panic surged through him – he couldn't go back there, not now, after so long. That was the image that had filled his nightmares – he would not look again.

Sweat broke on him. He tried to get up. A hand pushed him back down on the seat. His interrogator leaned towards him, sensing fear in the room.

'It's a report all about you. You had a friend, killed "on active service", as they like to call it. You see, we keep a careful record, lots of details – you didn't respond well to our inquiries, did you? You were a jabbering wreck.' He spread other papers across the desk, then paused.

'We can keep you here for a long time, Kevin. We can make your life a living hell. Or you can be honest with us, and we'll let you go. Come on, Kevin.'

His tone was persuasive, understanding even. 'You might not be active yourself, but you know something, don't you? I can see it in your face – you're lying.'

That was enough. Anger dispensed with fear; he was getting out of that room. Kevin leaned forward until their faces were close. His hand was flat on the varnished tabletop and, for several tense seconds, they eyed each other.

'There's a difference between then and now,' said Kevin, speaking slowly and clearly. 'I'm not some scared teenager you can terrorise. You see, you're wrong – I know nothing. You want honesty, don't you? Well, here it is. The two boys you're asking about, they're not Republicans any more than I am. I've done enough drugs with them to know. They're two wastes of space who can't keep a girlfriend, can't manage to sign on at the right time, can't get out of bed in the morning without their ma and da prising them out of it. When they're not in their pits, all they want to do is listen to music and get off their heads. They're a couple of wasters. If you think they're Provies, then you're off your head, too.'

He stood up.

'If that's all you have to ask, you can let me go now. I'm not saying another word.'

And that, apparently, was enough.

'OK, he can go,' said the officer. The interview was at an end.

*

Kevin stood outside Christy Meehan's house. The curtains were drawn. He banged on the door, then listened for a noise, but there was none, not a sound, not a movement.

They'll show their faces eventually, he told himself. And when they did, he'd be there.

28

After a hurried meeting, the local command decided the arrests weren't enough to delay a long-planned action. The questioning of the boys was a worry, but no more than that. They were small fry.

And so, on a night that was chilly and damp, more like October than late August, they waited under the branches of the trees that lined the back road, getting colder as the evening grew old. The road stretched all the way from the outskirts of the city, right down to and across the border with the Free State, not two miles away.

A few days after their debrief, Christy was pulled into the back of another car and ordered to show up at a designated corner. From there, he and Paddy would be collected by 'Jumpy' Joe, newly nicknamed by Paddy.

Jumpy Joe was in charge. That didn't stop him arriving late, however, saying he had problems getting a car – and being even jumpier than usual.

He had driven them to this road.

'I'm leaving you here,' he said. 'Get out. Someone'll be along to tell you what to do.'

'What are we doing?' asked Christy.

'You're lookouts, keeping dick for the boys down on the road,' said Joe, turning the key in the ignition.

Before they could protest he drove away, leaving them to their own devices. That was an hour ago and no one else had appeared.

'Who's supposed to be coming, do you think?' said Paddy.

'You know as much as me,' said Christy. 'I'm not one bit happy about this. It's a bit much, that your man decides to fuck off and leave us here.'

'Maybe we should go home – maybe it was called off?' said Paddy hopefully, but Christy only answered, 'Somebody'll be here.'

Waiting around wasn't rare in this line of work – waiting for patrols, for security men, for orders – but time was moving on and this action needed more precision than anything they had taken part in before. Someone would need to be here soon.

Overhead, the sky was awash with stars that were obscured under the artificial light of town. And yet they were no more than an hour's walk from their homes.

Christy looked at the stars; how still they were, clear, remote. He felt he was at the bottom of a well, looking up. Paddy was a dark shape, barely visible, only feet ahead of him.

The dark shape spoke again. 'Seriously, how long do we give it, Christy?'

He didn't answer. If it was compromised in some way, they would be the last to know, that was for sure. Suddenly, there was the whine of an engine. A beam of headlights swung through the sky, at the bend in the road.

As the car turned the corner, it pulled in beside them. The window on the driver's side rolled down and a head protruded. It was obvious the driver had been searching for them. He spoke, quick and soft, as if he was short on time.

'Where's Joe?' He was looking past them, into the darkness. Christy shrugged.

'He dropped us off here and told us to wait – for you.'

'You mean he just left you here?' he said. 'Stupid bastard.'

Something wasn't right. With an air of a decision having been made, the man spoke again.

'OK, this is going ahead as planned. Get in.'

They jumped into the back seat and the car sped up the road, stopping at a crossroads at the top of a hill.

'You two, get yourselves across that field,' he said, pointing through the window. 'Start watching the road. Make sure you have a good view, right? You let us know when you see the Brits coming down towards the checkpoint.'

He handed Paddy a walkie-talkie. 'You know how to use that?' he asked.

Paddy nodded. 'Aye, I do.'

'You press this button before you speak, OK? Don't say too much – just say, "On their way," when you see them. I'll be on the other end. Then walk away. Get yourselves back as quick as you can, into a bar or a shop – be seen. Let us know if you see or hear anything else unusual, but get yourselves away, right?' He reached under the passenger seat. 'Here. There's a short, in case you need it.'

The handgun was thrust into Christy's hand. He shoved it inside his jacket.

'Are you OK with that?' the man asked.

'We've had some training,' said Christy.

'Don't lose it,' he said, pointing to the gun in Christy's pocket. 'Take it back to the dump. Don't fuck this up.'

They got out and waited as he started the engine.

'Don't you have somewhere you need to be?' he asked, looking up at them through the window. 'Go!'

Together, they grabbed the wire fence that surrounded the field and pulled themselves over it. As they turned, they saw the headlights' beam marking the car's progress back along the road.

'Jumpy Joe's fucked up, big time,' said Paddy. 'He's done a runner.'

'Come on,' said Christy. They ran towards the lights, towards the border.

*

207

The hillside offered a clear view of the road.

Christy stood on an ancient wall, slippery with moss and clay. Above him were trees and below, the road was a strip of bright concrete. He kept a lookout while Paddy examined the walkie-talkie. He wasn't entirely lying when he had said he knew what to do with it – one of his brothers had a toy set when they were kids.

'Can you see OK?' he asked, looking up at Christy who was balancing on the wall, holding on to a branch.

'Aye – there's nothing yet.'

Christy strained to see further up the road. Cars passed, but no one was loitering, nothing was parked where it shouldn't have been.

They didn't know what was about to happen, only that it was intended to do as much harm as possible, a show of strength for the Provos. He looked down at Paddy.

'Maybe you should give that a go?' he said, meaning the walkie-talkie.

'Not until we have something to say. They scan for these things, you know,' said Paddy, meaning the army.

Almost eleven o'clock. The new shift would be on their way – the change of guard. Christy watched keenly, afraid to miss anything. They needed as much notice as possible.

Then there they were: two jeeps travelling steadily on the road below. He had a clear view of them.

'Fuck, they're here, Paddy – let them know,' said Christy. Paddy pressed the button and spoke into the device, realising he didn't know what to say.

'Hello?' he started and waited for a reply.

'Go ahead,' a voice came back, after a staticky delay.

'Two jeeps coming down the road, right now – over.'

There was silence, then, 'OK . . .'

Christy watched Paddy turn off the device and hide it in his coat.

'Let's get the fuck out of here,' he said, jumping off the wall.

They ran back the way they had come, over the fence and down along the edge of the lane. They didn't hear the hiss of the RPG, only its impact as it struck the side of the Land Rover with a crump that was amplified through the still air. The sound of it brought them to a halt.

'This place will be crawling in a minute. We need to get off the road. Paddy – off the road, now!'

There were houses up ahead. Behind these were fields, and a wall that edged the length of the road. They jumped over the wall, dropping into the field with the intention of running behind the houses. It was very dark. They could hear running water close by. Before they realised it, they were both in a shuck that cut across their path and were up to their knees in an ice-cold stream. The shock of it stopped them and they listened for sounds on the road. There was nothing.

Climbing the steep slope, up and out of the shuck, they stumbled towards the row of houses. At the last one a side door opened, and a tall man stood in yellow light, drawn to the door by the loud, distant noise of the attack. Overhead, the helicopter was already up. They ran on, keeping as straight a line as possible.

When they finally stopped, they were faced with another wall, the boundary of a derelict farm. There was distance enough behind them now, but they could still hear the roar of army vehicles tearing through the back roads, searching for those who had fired on them. Drenched in sweat and almost paralysed with fear, they didn't know what to do.

'Let's get over this wall and then we can think what way to go,' said Christy. Get back to the town, they had been told. But how? Christy leapt the wall with ease. Paddy pulled himself over heavily and landed with a thud in the empty yard behind.

They spoke, low and fast, deciding what to do next. The army would be searching farm buildings – they couldn't stay where they were.

'I think we're better off out in the open,' said Paddy. 'If we stay here, we'll be caught.'

'We should have thought this through,' said Christy. It was a far cry from the kid's bedroom where they had waited to take the oath, and the whiny doll with no knickers.

The yard fell away into darkness. Directly to their right was an outhouse butted up against the wall. Paddy pushed the door. It opened inwards, to a pitch-black interior, and he cautiously took a step inside.

Inside, the air was colder and damp; full of the sour, saliva-inducing tang of silage. Silently, Christy followed, closing the door until there was barely a strip open, just enough to see to the end of the yard beyond.

They stood in the dark and listened.

'What are we going to do?' said Paddy, his voice too loud. As their eyes adjusted to the darkness, they saw that the building was used to store pieces of farm machinery. They cast strange shapes in the blackness. Christy felt around him, until his hand rested on a flat surface, a table perhaps, dusty under his sweaty palm. Carefully, he stepped sideways to lean against it.

'We'll be OK for a bit,' he said, all the while knowing that if they were caught out here, even without evidence, they would be done. And he had a gun in his pocket; he could feel the weight of it dragging on him.

'*Don't lose it,*' the man had said. He couldn't dump it, but he couldn't get caught with it either – that meant twelve years, minimum. And his biggest fear was to find himself in a situation where he had to pull it out and use it. He'd fired at a distance, just once, as a police car passed. To be cornered, that would mean close range, right up close – he couldn't do it.

The silence broke. A roar of engines and screeching brakes came from the other side of the yard, where the wall gave way to the road. They heard footsteps, doors slamming and a voice shouting orders to the soldiers to search the buildings. There was no choice now.

Christy wrenched the door open and they ran to the wall, pulling each other over. As he hit the ground, Paddy's ankle twisted sharply. He cried out and couldn't move for several blindingly painful seconds. There were heavy boots running across the hard clay of the yard.

'Did you hear something?' said a voice. Paddy threw himself against the rough stone and ran, hunched down against its length, looking desperately for Christy, who had vanished into the surrounding darkness. More movement and shouting from behind – they were searching for the source of the noise.

There was Christy, up ahead, his figure outlined against the glow of the city in the distance. Ignoring the twisted ankle, Paddy put his head down and ran too, putting as much distance as he could between him and the bullet he was sure was coming his way. There was another shout from behind – it could have been 'Halt' – and then one burst of rapid fire from an assault rifle.

He hurled himself forward, through boggy shucks and hedges, until he caught up with Christy, grabbing him by the sleeve of his coat and dragging him along. When they saw the streets of the nearest estate, they fell behind a ridge of grass and blackthorn. There was a road and then more fields, and far away, the orange stain of civilisation reflected on the overcast sky.

In miles, it wasn't far, but in the dark every stone was a

hazard, as the ground rose and fell beneath them. They lay under the blackthorn hedge and waited.

It began to get light, and a helicopter droned above them, circling out of sight. They huddled behind the mound of soil, too afraid to move further. All night, they had kept themselves hidden in the undergrowth, listening to traffic, distinguishing the everyday cars from the harsh acceleration of the army and the police.

They were not followed – not over the fields anyway – or somehow they had succeeded in evading the searchers from the farm.

But now as day broke around them, it seemed more likely that a decision had been taken not to track them in the dark; better to wait for them to emerge from the fields, back onto the concrete roads and pavements that were their only way home.

'What are we going to do?' whined Paddy, miserable as he held his swollen ankle between his hands. 'We need to make a move some way, 'cause if we sit here much longer, they're gonna just walk up and find us. And you've got that fuckin' thing in your pocket.'

'I know,' said Christy. Paddy had kept up a consistent stream of complaint through the long hours, without coming up with a single helpful suggestion of his own. 'It's not my job to get us out of this. You tell *me* what to do, for once,' he said.

'This whole bloody thing was your idea,' said Paddy. 'I knew it was a bad one, right from the start.' He took his hand away from his damp sock, to point an accusing finger at Christy. 'You talked me into it.'

With that, he slumped back into the bushes again. He was cold, tired, hungry and scared. More than anything, he wished he was home, in his own bed. If he'd had the sense, he would have listened to Kevin Thompson that day, when they came to blows in the Strand Road. Too late now, though.

'Hi, Christy?' he said.

'What?' said Christy, refusing to look at him.

'Kevin lives around here.'

'Where?' said Christy. He had never been to Kevin's house. Twisting onto his stomach, he looked through the thick trunks of blackthorn. 'Do you know his house?'

Paddy was a frequent visitor at one time. Now, he tried to get his bearings in this strange countryside, to think where they were and where, exactly, Thompson's house was from here.

'Away over there, it is – I think.' He waved his arm vaguely towards the houses. 'A good bit away, but we could keep to the back lanes. It's worth a try.'

'He won't want to help,' said Christy sourly.

'If we turn up at his door, he won't turn us away, will he? And I don't think we have a choice.'

Paddy got unsteadily to his feet. 'We definitely can't stay here.'

They clambered out from the hedge and moved fast, running across open ground, all the time exposed, in the broad expanse of waste that lay between the farmland and the cluster of council houses up ahead. The whirr of overhead surveillance ebbed faintly in the air – it was far away, for now, circling the site of the attack.

The council estates they were approaching were built between the Foyle and the border with the South. Families, uprooted from the gerrymandered slums around the base of the walled city, swelled into the fresh air of nearby country-side, glad of the room. But care had been taken with the new town planning.

Viewed from above, this stretch of modern housing was an archipelago, a cluster of island estates in a sea of green. Long, straight roads cut through broad, flat swathes of grass, open to harsh winds and flooding. The paths and walkways were narrow and meandering, connecting each group of houses, allowing residents to come and go. But there would be no barricades built here, no streets to seal off and keep the State out.

The boys ran to the first flank of houses. Pain spiked in Paddy's ankle with every thud of his foot on the sods, but he kept going, keeping pace with Christy. They ran between two gable ends, and stopped in the cover of the houses. There was still a long way to go.

'Where now?' asked Christy, bent double and breathing heavily.

'Right through and out the other side,' said Paddy. 'Give us a minute – this hurts like fuck.'

'We can walk from here – it'll look weird if we're running.'

Trying to move with an easy gait, just two stop-outs coming home from an all-nighter, Christy walked, and Paddy limped, sadly, across the car park and into another alley on the other side. It led them to the next wide stretch of grass. They could skirt along the houses to where the grass narrowed, leaving only a few yards to cross.

It was still too early for most people and they ran across, unseen, to another huddle of houses.

Everything, each street, was interchangeable: brick, stone and gravelled ground in hues of grey, a warren of lanes and paths, grim, hard and empty. They kept moving, sore-footed and starving. If the drone from the sky buzzed above them, they pulled themselves close to the walls of the houses and pressed into the brick, wishing they could merge with it.

Once the noise had passed, they moved with greater urgency until sore legs and exhaustion slowed them down again.

One lane led to another; the sameness of it all left them disoriented.

'Are we going in circles?' asked Christy.

Before Paddy could answer, the unmistakable whine of an army jeep brought them to a stop between two rows of houses.

They were out of sight of the road. Christy pulled Paddy into a recess, where there was a gated entry to a back garden. He stuck his hand in through the semicircle opening in the gate, reaching for the bolt on the inside, and pulled it out again, fast.

A deep, snarling growl came from behind the gate. He looked up to see a huge black body rise on hind legs, and a massive head, dark-eyed and furious, watching him over the top of the gate.

They both jumped back in alarm, and the dog snarled again, dangerously baring its teeth. It began to bark viciously. Saliva drooled from its jaws.

Sure that they were caught, sure the army would be there in minutes, Paddy tried shushing the beast. He was at eye level with it.

'All right, boy,' he said. 'We don't want in your house.'

He reached out his hand to touch its snout but pulled it back when the dog snapped fiercely at it. Its dark eyes rolled in its head. In a frenzy of madness, it began scraping and pawing at the trembling gate, jumping down, circling round and then back up again, slamming against the shaking wood with the full force of its muscular bulk.

A man appeared at the window above, naked from the waist up and shouting. Christy grabbed Paddy and pulled him away.

'Let's go, for Christsake!' he shouted, dragging him down the lane again, away from the house.

'Get away t'fuck, ya wee thieving bastards!' the man shouted after them as they ran.

They made it back to a block of flats at the other end of the lane, and then up some steps to the first floor. Still they could hear the dog barking wildly, and its owner telling it to 'Shut the fuck up.'

'Listen to the bastard,' said Christy. 'It's a monster! I'm not going down that way again.'

Paddy looked at the path below. 'We won't be able to stay here. But if we go the other way, we'll walk right out in front of them.'

'Did I say to stay? Did I?' said Christy, shaken.

'I never said you did – stop having a go at me.'

They started down the steps again. Christy trudged wearily behind the limping Paddy. 'I don't think you know where we're going,' he muttered, watching Paddy's hunched shoulders. They ran past the garden that contained the dog; the man was gone but the dog paced inside.

Paddy knew that Kevin lived close to the tunnel, an underpass beneath the main road that cut right through the area. He had always arrived at Kevin's from the opposite direction; this way, he was acting on utter guesswork. He figured that by going through the estates they would eventually arrive at the road, one way or another.

Pangs of starvation cramped his stomach; adding that to the aching in his legs, the pain in his ankle – his head spun. If it wasn't for the fear of capture, he would have sat down, right there in the road, and refused to move. The brick-shaped walkie-talkie felt heavy in his pocket.

'Hi, Christy?' he said.

'What now?' said Christy, from behind.

'Do you think I should try contacting somebody on the

walkie-talkie?' The sheer idiocy of the question brought Christy to a halt.

'Who?' he said, trying not to shout again. 'Who are you going to contact, Paddy? It's not like there's a fucking base somewhere, we're not in a fucking war film, you know? That thing only works within a certain range, you dickhead!'

'Jesus, it was only a thought – there's no need to go off on one! What should I do with it then – sling it?'

Christy started walking again. 'I don't know,' he said, as his hand came up to touch the gun in his own pocket.

There was the tunnel, about fifty yards away. They had stolen two pints of milk from the back of a milk van, and now they stood drinking it, watching the entrance and the road above it, where a heavily guarded police roadblock was doing a stop-and-search on the morning traffic.

The milk van was parked invitingly while the milkman got out to do his rounds. The lure of it was too much to resist; they ran to the idling vehicle. Warmed by fumes from the engine, each pocketed a bottle. It tasted like school milk, sitting in the heat of a sunny classroom; creamy and sweet, it coated their empty stomachs.

'How do we get past that?' asked Christy.

The tunnel entrance was squat, square and dark in the distance, like a Second World War German bunker. The lights inside had been vandalised, and the entrance to the tunnel grinned at them in the early morning; a blackened, toothless, gaping mouth, functional and without design.

Above it, police lined the road, guarding the officer on the white line as he bent to question the drivers. Beyond him, on the far side, they watched an army patrol drive slowly past the houses and then turn back towards the middle of the estate, out of sight.

'Maybe we can brass it out and walk straight down there. They might take no notice of us,' replied Paddy, emboldened by the milk in his stomach.

All of Christy's thoughts were on the gun. 'Do you want to risk it?' he said. 'If we're stopped with this, it's all over.'

Behind them, there was a vulgar laugh. Three women, drunk and in their twenties, came stumbling along the path towards the two of them. In their short skirts and white heels, big earrings and bigger hair, they lurched together, arm in arm, on their way home from a party.

'Look at these three,' said Paddy, as they tottered closer.

Christy was already looking and this time he had an idea. He didn't see women, he saw camouflage. They were almost level with them. He leaned against the wall and turned on the charm.

'Hi, gorgeous, where are you going?' he said as they passed. The nearest one turned a smudged eye to him but kept walking.

'Ooh, Linda – looks like he fancies you,' said her friend. They all laughed.

'Hi, Linda – is that your name?' he called after her. 'Come over and talk to me. Come on, girls – you three are the nicest thing I've seen all night.'

The girl on the inside looked back at him. She was in no hurry to get home, and he was cute.

'Hey, do you think so?' she said, as she pulled the others to a halt and swaggered over to him. They were in.

'Aileen, I want to go home,' called Linda, but Aileen wasn't taking her on. She tottered up to the grinning boy, close enough for him to smell the stale drink on her breath and the remnants of cheap perfume that clung to her clothes.

'Where are you going, and can we come too?' said Christy.

She leaned against him. The other two waited, watching and laughing.

'Aww, they're just wains,' said Aileen. Still though, she didn't take her eyes off him. Young or not, she was up for it.

Her warm alcoholic breath almost snatched the air from Christy's lungs as he was suddenly the victim of a deep, moist kiss. Aileen's tongue stuck far into his mouth. With effort he responded and then realised he was getting hard in spite of himself. Aileen felt it too and moaned as she pressed against him. He pushed her away and looked at Paddy, sitting with a reluctant expression on the steps.

'These ladies need an escort home,' he said. 'There's bad'uns about.' He nodded to him to get involved.

Paddy pulled himself up and lumbered forward, an embarrassed smile on his face. He hadn't the required charm of Christy.

'What happened to you?' said Linda.

'Nothing – just a war wound,' Paddy laughed, putting an awkward arm around her waist. But she wasn't as keen as Aileen. She pulled away, wrinkling her nose as if he smelled. *In fairness*, he thought, *I do.*

The cop turned his attention from the road to the slope of grass, the row of houses, the dishevelled bunch of drunks staggering and laughing as they came down the hill. He heard them shouting to each other.

They're some rough dolls, he thought, as they got closer. The redhead was fairly going for it with that lad. *These people have no breeding.*

They had been on patrol since four a.m., and there were still five hours to go before he would be in his own house again. He yawned.

Look at your woman, full-on kissing that wee boy, with no shame at all.

On the path below, Paddy tried his best, but Linda wouldn't take him on.

It wouldn't matter soon – they were almost there. They disappeared into the black tunnel, past a shopping trolley full of smouldering carpet, and he looked up.

Above him, the police officer looked down, his cap rigid and dark against the pale sky – his face a picture of contempt.

29

The tunnel echoed with heels and laughter. Aileen made full use of the dim lighting to have another go at Christy, pinning him to the wall with a hard kiss. Paddy looked at Linda and was relieved to see the undisguised disgust on her face.

'Christsake, Aileen,' she said, beneath her breath. She folded her arms and tapped her foot, waiting for her friend. For Margaret, however, this was enough.

Margaret was the third girl; small and fine, with a flick of heavily sprayed hair and large hooped earrings. She had been both ignored and silent, until now.

'For fucksake, Aileen – I'm fucking tired and I want to go home.'

Her thin voice bounced off the walls, its volume shocking – she looked like nothing. But the vodka was rapidly wearing off; she was starting to shake in the cold. Aileen ignored her and continued to grind against Christy.

'Fuck this,' Margaret said, picking her way through the rubble and brick towards the light at the other end.

'Wait for me, Margaret,' said Linda. She went over to Aileen, who had Christy plastered against the wall, grabbed her by both shoulders and physically pulled her off him. Christy emerged, shocked, from under her.

'Would you get a grip?' she said. 'We need to get home.'

She held Aileen by the tops of her arms, and marched her, half supporting, half pushing, to the end of the tunnel, where Margaret waited. All three disappeared up the path.

'Fair play to you, mate,' said Paddy. 'And I thought dying for Ireland would be the problem.'

At the exit, they waited in a square patch of sunlight and watched people begin their day. Women opened doors and windows, chased kids out into the bright morning; people who had jobs left their homes to do them. The army patrol swung around the corner again, into the street above; the boys pulled back at the sight of it.

They were prowling with intent, monitoring the area for movement. When they reached the hill above the tunnel, they stopped.

'Do you think they're looking for us?' said Paddy, sounding genuinely scared. They were trapped, unable to go back or leave the tunnel and go on.

'I don't know,' said Christy, looking out at the street above them. His body ached and he was hunched over with exhaustion.

He thought seriously about dropping the gun there, in the tunnel, and walking out into the sun. He could pretend he was coming from a mate's house, like the girls they had used as cover. He wanted to fling it away and run for it.

Paddy sat on the ground across from him; tired, dirty Paddy with his twisted ankle, his 'war wound', who'd had enough – Christy could see it in his face. All they could do was wait for a chance, for the army to move.

There were footsteps. A woman was coming through the tunnel, pushing a pram. She was young and slight, pretty in her light dress and cardigan. A toddler danced along beside her. He held tightly to the handle of the pram with one hand and watched his mother's face as he tripped along. She didn't return his gaze. She wanted to get through the passage, past the dirt and the urine stench, as fast as she could.

When she saw the two figures at the exit, she hesitated;

Christy saw it, her reluctance, as she came closer to them in the semi-darkness where they stood sinister against the light. She was frightened – they frightened her. She quickened her step as she got near and stiffened her back. And he knew that, to her, they were a threat; it made him incredibly sad.

Paddy struggled to his feet. They nodded, but she walked briskly past, avoiding eye contact. The little boy looked away from his mother and turned his steady gaze to Christy, who tried to smile, but the muscles in his face felt stiff and awkward. He didn't want to be scary. The boy's face fell into a frown and he gripped the handle of the pram with both hands, searching his mother's face again.

'I don't like it in there, Mammy,' he heard him say.

When they looked again, the army had gone. 'Please tell me you know where to go from here,' said Christy, wearier than he had felt in his entire life.

Kevin's house was close, that was certain. Paddy closed his eyes and tried to retrace the steps he had last taken months ago; Kevin's house, turn right, down a path, turn right again, there was the grass and the tunnel on their left, and the mobile shop where Kevin bought his fags was straight ahead.

'This way,' he said, moving quickly and following the dip and curve of the grass with a clumsy gait. He covered the ground fast, now that he knew where they were.

Whether it was chance or not, the helicopter drone closed in above them, buzzing loud in their ears as they ran, spurring them to keep moving.

It was there, their goal, just around the corner. Blades stuttered as the helicopter banked through the air. When they reached the top of the hill, they stopped running and walked rapidly past gated yards. Paddy stopped.

'This is his house,' he said. He looked through the gate. 'This is Kevin's.'

The house was locked up. The blinds in the kitchen window were down, and those of the bedroom above. Along the row, all the houses looked the same. 'Are you sure?' asked Christy.

'It's his house – that's his room.' He pointed to the window above the door. 'He's probably in bed.'

Looking around his feet, he picked up a stone and threw it at the glass and missed.

Christy put his hand through and opened the gate.

'Just wait a minute,' Paddy said. The helicopter stuttered again in the clear sky. He frantically searched for another stone and threw it. This time the glass shook, and the sound of the impact echoed off the houses behind them.

For a breathless minute, they watched. The curtains moved, and a bleary Kevin looked out at them. He opened the window an inch.

'Did you throw a stone at my window?' he said.

'Come down and let us in, will you?' said Paddy.

'You two fuckers are some craic coming here – get away to fuck,' he said, closing the window and letting the curtain drop.

Paddy threw another stone, less carefully this time. It bounced off and landed back at his feet. Kevin pushed the window open again.

'You nearly broke the glass!' he shouted.

'Kevin, please . . . come down and let us in,' said Christy. He flinched under the noise of blades, sure it was above them.

Kevin had heard on the radio about the attack. He couldn't believe they had shown up like this – up all night, by the looks of them, and obviously in trouble.

'Stay there,' he said. They heard the key in the lock and the door opened. Kevin stood barefoot. 'Come in,' he said, as they ran past him and into the kitchen.

★

'What do you want?'

'We need your help,' said Paddy.

Kevin sat at the kitchen table and looked at them. They were filthy.

'Do you know I was lifted because of you? That I was questioned for six fucking hours?'

His parents were in bed and he kept his voice low. 'You have some nerve, landing at my door for help. Was that you two, last night?'

'We can't talk about that,' said Christy. At this, Kevin stood up.

'Are you serious?' he whispered. He wanted to reach for him. 'Don't you dare pull that fucking IRA crap in my house.'

He opened the back door again.

'Get out,' he said.

Neither moved.

'Get – to fuck – out of my house,' he said again, this time grabbing Christy and hauling him to the door. Paddy tried to get between them. The noise of the helicopter filled his head until it was all he could hear.

'Please, Kevin,' he begged, but Kevin shoved him away and he fell, hitting his back on the kitchen cupboard. He slid to the floor and sat there, his head in his hands. Both Kevin and Christy stopped to look at him.

Kevin closed the door again and released his grip on Christy.

'I tried to tell you, Paddy,' he said, sitting down on the chair so that he faced him.

Christy didn't move from the door.

'Why can't you just go home – what are you doing here?' he asked them.

'The whole area is crawling. You were the closest place we could get to from the back roads,' said Christy. He wasn't pretending any more. No more 'IRA crap'.

'So it was you – the checkpoint. Did anybody actually see you?'

Christy shook his head. 'Only in the dark and from a distance. We were lucky – they took a shot at us.'

Then Christy pulled the gun out. 'We couldn't risk getting stopped.'

The weapon lay flat across his open palm. He held it out like an offering. Kevin jumped to his feet.

'You brought that into my house?' he said, unable to take his eyes from it.

'I didn't know what to do,' said Christy.

Paddy lifted his head. Christy still had his hand out, hoping Kevin would relieve him of the weight of it, but Kevin was pacing the floor and each time he turned, he looked at the gun again.

'Everyone in this house will do time if that's found here,' he said, pointing in horror at the weapon. 'Why do you still have it?'

'I couldn't throw it in a field,' said Christy.

'You put it in a dump!' said Kevin. 'You'd better come upstairs, before me da gets up. Put that thing away, for Godsake.'

They followed him through the house, and upstairs to his room. Paddy threw himself on the unmade bed and lay there, already asleep. Christy sat by his feet at the end of the bed.

'That has to go as soon as possible,' said Kevin, pointing at the gun.

'I don't know anywhere – not round here,' said Christy. He wanted to explain that this wasn't supposed to happen, about Jumpy Joe and the change of plan, but Kevin put his hand up.

'Tell me nothin',' he said. 'I don't want to know.'

What he did know was the importance the 'RA placed on their weapons, more even than on their volunteers – and they would be looking for this one. He started to dress, pulling on his boots, stripping off the T-shirt he had slept in and reaching for a clean one from a drawer.

Christy sat in silence, watching him.

'Are you going out?' he finally asked.

'Aye,' said Kevin. 'Stay in here and stay quiet.'

He pulled on his coat.

Before he left the room, Christy tried once more to explain.

'We thought it was the right thing to do, Kevin. I thought it was the right thing. I know you're not interested, so you don't get it – but they shot Pete. Were we supposed to do nothing, like it didn't matter that they got away with murder?'

With his back to him, Kevin answered.

'He's still dead though.'

He turned to face him, his grip tight on the door handle. 'Do you feel like you won anything, Christy? Is this better? I don't care what you do – you can take out every Brit in town and I wouldn't cry over one of them – but I could cry for him,' he said, looking at Paddy sleeping soundly on his bed. He left the room.

Christy lay on the bed. There wasn't much room; Paddy's bulk took up most of it. But he squeezed his aching body into the space between Paddy's legs and the wall. Pulling his knees to his chest, he closed his eyes, then opened them as someone entered the room.

Kevin put two mugs of tea and a plate of toast on the table by the bed, and left without a word.

Across town, in the room with the Holly Hobbie bed sheets, three ranking officers were discussing the events of the previous night – specifically, the mysterious disappearance of Joe.

'It's really not on,' said one. 'He left them two lads in the lurch.'

'He's been hitting the bottle way too much. That's him, vulnerable. He's a liability,' said another.

'Has anybody been to the house?'

'I'll get somebody to drop by later, nice and casual, see if he's there. Get the eyes open on the street – I want to know when he surfaces. Did the boys get across the border?'

'They called in early this morning – sitting pretty in Letterkenny, eating a fry.'

'I want Joe found,' said the officer in command. 'And I want him back here – he has questions to answer.'

30

Of course, the gun had to go.

Meehan and McLaughlin might not be the subject of a man hunt, but they were in the loop. And that meant a sweep of the area that could bring the Brits, or the police, to his door again very soon.

Kevin knocked on Brendan Rafferty's door.

There was no answer. He knocked again. There were noises and movement behind the opaque glass, and a small figure in pyjamas toddled along the hall to the door. The little girl reached up and pulled on the door handle and the handgrip on the outside moved as she tried it. It was locked. She shouted into the letter box.

'Mammy's in bed . . . are you the postman?' Her chubby fingers wriggled through the opening.

'No, I'm looking for your daddy. Is he in bed, too?'

The child laughed at his silly question. 'Aye,' she shouted, skipping from the door and singing aloud, '*Row, row, row your boat, gently down the streeeaaam . . .*'

He knocked again. This time, a larger figure appeared behind the glass.

'Get in there,' he said to the girl, before coming to the door. Without opening it, he asked, 'Who is it?'

'It's Kevin Thompson. I need to talk to you.'

After a delay, Brendan opened the door an inch and looked past Kevin to the street.

'There's nobody with me,' said Kevin.

'What do you want?' Brendan looked like a man who hadn't had much sleep.

'There's something in my house that needs to be gone, quick,' Kevin said.

Brendan rubbed a hand over his face and looked at him, bemused. With a sigh, Kevin started to explain.

'Remember them two from a while back – the two I was talking to you about? They only turned up at my back door this morning, shit scared. They're holed up in my room, and that's all right, apart from the short they're carrying. I don't want it in my house, Brendan. What do they do with it?'

'They need to get it to a dump.' Brendan looked increasingly uncomfortable.

'You don't have to tell me that,' said Kevin. 'But where? They can hardly walk through the streets with it – is there somewhere close, somewhere around here?'

'It's not our weapon – it belongs to another section,' said Brendan. He started to close the door, but Kevin put his hand to it and pushed it open again.

'Look,' he said. 'It's better with your lot than in his pocket when they stop him – and they will.'

Brendan pushed his hand away, but the door stayed open. He had to think.

'Wait here,' he said.

Kevin watched the street. The sky was blue; it was going to be a great day – sunny. Two boys sat on their bikes, blatantly watching him. He turned his face to the door again.

Somewhere inside the house, Brendan was talking on the phone. It was a low, urgent conversation, but he couldn't hear what was said. Brendan hung up and came back to the door.

'The back of Shantallow shops at eleven o'clock. There'll be a gold-coloured Astra – the boot'll be open. Drop it in there,' he said, and promptly closed the door.

Back in his own house, Kevin was met by his father.

'You're out early,' he said.

'Had to go and get fags,' said Kevin, running up the stairs.

The curtains were still closed, and Paddy and Christy were asleep. It was nine-thirty. An hour and a half to wait, less in fact – it would take fifteen minutes to get there. He closed the door quietly, sat on the floor.

The nicotine from the first cigarette made him dizzy. Nerves put a stop to any hunger he felt. He smoked and watched the hands creep, inevitably, towards the hour. They reached ten o'clock and passed on, and the boys slept, breathing softly.

10.15 . . . 10.25 . . . He wouldn't wake them yet – less chance of noise. 10.35. He reached over.

'Meehan, wake up,' he said, shaking him hard. 'Christy!'

There was a knock at the front door and Kevin froze. Christy opened his eyes but didn't move. They both waited, listening.

Another knock, and then the turn of the latch; there were voices, but not police, not army.

Kevin's mother sounded friendly, her tone one of recognition. They heard light feet on the stairs, and Liz came into the darkened room. It took a second for her eyes to adjust to the light: Kevin and Christy's frightened faces looked back at her. Then Paddy sat up on the bed and yawned.

'What's going on?' he asked.

'Close the door,' said Kevin sharply.

'Where have you been?' she said to Paddy, ignoring Kevin.

'Liz, for Godsake, close the fucking door,' said Kevin again.

She did as she was told and sat on the bed, nudging Paddy to move over.

'Mammy's livid with you,' she said. 'What are you all doing?'

Kevin turned to Christy.

'There will be a gold-coloured car at the back of the shops, in behind the bookie's in Shanty. That's the dump.'

231

He looked around the room. 'Where is it?' he said.

Christy gripped the pocket of his coat.

'Put it in the boot, Christy. The car will be there at eleven, so you have to leave now.'

'Who owns the car, Kevin? What if I'm asked who has it and I can't tell them?'

'It's sorted, Christy. A gold Astra and the boot'll be open. Just dump the fucker and walk away.'

The butt of the gun had worked its way through the lining of his pocket. Christy pulled it out; there was a loud rip as the lining tore.

'You do it,' he said, shoving the gun at Kevin.

'Fuck no.' Kevin backed off with raised hands. 'I've done more than enough for you. Now get that thing out of here, and don't you think about coming back.'

When she saw the gun Liz moved away, crawling further onto the bed. 'Patrick, what's going on?' she asked.

He didn't answer, because he didn't know. The night before was like a bad dream, and he had woken up in the middle of a detective show. Christy was terrified, Kevin was beyond angry – grim, taut – ordering Christy to dump the gun. It was quarter to the hour.

Kevin had his hand on the door handle. 'You have to go now,' he said again.

Christy got to his feet. He stuck the gun into the waistband of his jeans and zipped his coat over it.

'A gold Astra, is that right?' he asked.

'That's right,' said Kevin. 'Dump it and walk away. Nobody knows you're carrying it but you.'

Paddy shrugged when Christy turned to him. Kevin opened the door and Christy left, stepping quietly down the stairs. From the landing Kevin watched him open the door and slip out.

Back in the room, Paddy and Liz sat side by side on the bed. For the first time he saw the resemblance between them in the strained, worried eyes, enlarged with fear, and the set of the jaw.

He knew that expression. He had seen it on their father's face; the worried McLaughlins. He'd had enough of that look to last him a lifetime.

Sitting on the floor with his back to the wall, he lit another cigarette. There was no guarantee that Christy wouldn't be stopped. Then it would be over for all of them. One arrest would lead to more. He traced the lines on the carpet, his eyes down.

'Are you coming home, Paddy?' Liz asked.

'Aye,' said her brother, watching Kevin. 'I think so.'

31

Christy stopped at the edge of the kerb, watching the police drive past. Then he ran across the road and over the green. He regained his casual gait as he slipped behind the row of flat-roofed shops.

A few vans were parked there, and a gold-coloured Astra as promised. It wasn't the gleaming vehicle he had imagined. The paint was dull in the shadow of the buildings.

From a distance, the boot appeared to be shut. Christy walked over and tried it; it lifted in his hand. He pulled out the gun and threw it in, then slammed the boot closed and walked on. It was over in seconds. He didn't look back. The driver would be waiting, making sure he wasn't followed before driving it away.

When he left Kevin's house he was thrown to the wolves, or so it seemed. Now that the gun was someone else's problem, that fear left him, to be followed by sweeping exhaustion and something else.

They had come through, unscathed. It had been terrifying and exhilarating and they had proved themselves, avoided arrest, got the gun out of harm's way.

His friendship with Kevin – that was a small sacrifice in the end. They were soldiers. They did what they had to do. Now all he wanted was to go home and sleep.

Bernie walked from shop to shop in a kind of daze. The tenth hunger striker, a lad from Derry, had passed away in the night.

There had been that attack, bad enough according to the

news, and some rioting in the early hours, but in general the death had been accepted, acknowledged, and then ignored by most.

Someone spoke. 'Are you OK, love?'

She looked up from the can of beans in her hand. The girl in the beige overall was blurred by tears. 'Are you OK?' she asked again.

'I'm fine – sorry,' said Bernie. She put the can back on the shelf and left the shop.

All her thoughts had been for his mother, for her grief that morning, the gut pain that she would be feeling. The emotion rose like a wave, filling her up. Where was Patrick?

Her anger at Jim had not cooled; it was hard to forgive him. And now he refused to look for the boy. He said it was on his own head, whatever happened now.

Was it like this for the others? The other mothers whose sons were involved? The ones she saw in graveside photos, half collapsed in grief? Or had those mothers offered their support, hidden them, washed their clothes and fed them, as they acted the part of the soldier? Did they have them at home with them until they died, and then waked them from their bedrooms? Did they walk the streets consumed with fear, waiting for the word that their children were arrested or dead?

She went home with an empty shopping bag. It was three weeks since he had stormed out. But he was still signing on – his giro came through the letter box last week. She sat it on the fireboard.

Every time she dusted, she looked at his name. That giro was the only influence she had now, her last means of control. It was up to him to come home and collect it, or go without. There it remained, behind the candlestick. Stubborn.

Music blasted from the open window as she put her key in the door. She threw her bag on the sofa. The grease mark was

235

still there, staining the wall; they would have to repaper eventually. Her eyes went to the fire and the envelope. Or to the empty space where it had once been.

'Elizabeth?'

Had it gone into the fire? She poked the embers – there was nothing to show for it.

'Elizabeth!'

Liz leaned over the banister. 'What?'

'Where's Paddy's giro?'

Crap, thought Liz. 'Nowhere,' she called, coming downstairs. Bernie's hand rested accusingly on the spot where the letter had been for a week.

'Paddy's taken it to the post office, to cash it,' said Liz.

'He was here, and you let him go?' said Bernie.

'It's all right, Mammy.'

The front door opened and closed and there he was, limping through the living room to the kitchen, taking his coat off like nothing had happened.

It hadn't been a hard choice, to come home. Having Liz there made it easier. Perhaps he should have gone with Christy to complete the mission? He had abandoned him. It was personally disloyal and probably against IRA rules, but Paddy didn't care.

'So you've decided to come back, have you?' said his mother.

Her relief lasted seconds and was quickly overtaken by hurt and anger; she heard the contempt in her own voice and hated herself for it.

Paddy came in and sat down.

'Did you hear me?' she shouted. 'Where were you?'

'I'm home, all right?' he shouted back.

'I hope you're done with that carry-on. When was the last time you even washed yourself, young fella?'

Stupid, hollow words and too angry, but he was thin and

grubby. And limping. All her instinct was to fuss, to bully him back into her care. But she couldn't trust herself not to kill him if he opened his cheeky mouth to her again.

Liz sat between them.

'I'm going to bed,' he said to her. 'Are you going out tonight? I've got money.'

She nodded.

'Wake me,' he said.

'I'll wake you when your father gets in,' said his mother, as his back disappeared through the door. 'And don't think you're leaving this house again today.'

The glass in the window shuddered as the door slammed behind him.

That night, with a pint in front of him, it shocked Paddy how relieved he felt. Not because he had overcome great odds and was still 'at large', so to speak; on the contrary, it was as if he had emerged from a strange madness. As if the previous months had happened to another Paddy, one who was lying in a ditch somewhere, still hunted, still trying to get home.

This new Paddy had woken up realising that it was all, in fact, bollocks, that he had been swept into an alien world, and he could hardly believe that he had done those things. He had no sense of guilt or regret, no desire to pretend it hadn't happened. It was just that right now, sitting here, he knew he was done.

Liz sat with him, her own pint in front of her. They didn't talk. Her presence was a show of solidarity.

He had slept for hours and, when his father came home, she was sent to wake him. He was still in the same clothes, and dirt, as that morning. She looked down at him curled around his pillow, a trickle of saliva running down his cheek and onto a damp patch on the pillowcase.

'Paddy – your dinner's out,' she said.

Her mother had been silent, brooding. She had spent the weeks of his absence scrubbing the house. When she had cleaned everything that could be cleaned, she stared at the television, or left the house, telling no one where she was going.

Her father had manoeuvred around his wife's bad temper like a whipped dog. That giro had sat like an accusation – no one could touch it.

Well, they were drinking the value of it now.

'They'll calm down,' Liz said. 'You know she's happy you're back, really; she just can't say it. And me daddy only shouted at you because he thinks he has to, to get back in the good books. She cleaned that house until we couldn't even sit down; throwing stuff out – even the hot press got a going-over. That's definitely a sign of a nervous breakdown.' She raised her drink to her lips. 'I think you're her favourite,' she said, after a sip.

'Really?' said Paddy.

He took a big drink and lit another cigarette. 'Anything else happen? How's Orla?'

'Huh – you remember her, do you?' said Liz. 'Your friend who's grieving for her boyfriend?'

That hit home. The person who had been most hurt by Peter Harkin's death, and she had become an afterthought. Some heroes they'd turned out to be.

'She's fine, actually. A lot better than she was – we might see her tonight. Are you staying out?'

Paddy stared into the amber depths of his drink and flicked the growth of ash on his fag into a tin ashtray. There was a warmth in the bar that had nothing to do with the weather. He would gladly stay there for ever.

'You know something, Elizabeth? I think my contribution to the struggle is complete,' he said and, lifting his pint, he chinned it.

★

Orla and Sinéad arrived in a haze of hairspray, full-on New Romantic, with sculpted cheekbones and overdone lips.

Sinéad's ornate red dress, made mostly of frills and elastic, required constant adjustment – up or down, at either end.

Orla wore purple velvet knickerbockers. Her heavily laced cuffs were in the way of everything – the ashtray, her drink, the pools of spillage that covered the table. The world had moved on during Paddy's revolutionary hiatus.

In the toilet, he supported himself at the urinal on one steadying arm. The door opened behind him.

'McLaughlin!'

Noel slapped him heartily between the shoulder blades.

'All right, Baxter,' said Paddy. He straightened up and fixed his fly.

Noel was thinner than the last time he had seen him, and that was saying something. He was gaunt, hollow-eyed. His worn T-shirt sagged on shoulders built to carry more muscle.

But it was the movement of his friend's head, an angular, unconscious jerk and a clenching and unclenching of his hands, that made Paddy wonder.

'What are you on?' he asked, though the wide eyes and pin-prick pupils gave him away.

'Just a wee bit of speed,' said Noel. 'It's good to see you, mate.'

'Have you any left?' said Paddy.

'Ah, no. Your man upstairs gave me a line, that's all.'

If Noel had to pee, he'd forgotten. They walked out to the bar together. Paddy bought them both a drink.

'All right, "War is Hell",' said Noel, passing the joint he was smoking. 'Where's Meehan?'

'Don't know,' said Paddy.

His attention had moved on to Sinéad, who sat across the table from them, adjusting her frills. She was laughing.

'What's funny?' he asked.

'None of your business,' said Sinéad, smiling.

He leaned over until his mouth was close to her ear. 'I like your dress,' he slurred. 'I wouldn't mind taking it off.'

'Is that right?' said Sinéad, their faces almost touching. Then his tongue was in her mouth.

32

Jumpy Joe was missing.

'What did he say to you?' said the men who were debriefing Christy.

'He said he had to go and then he left,' said Christy. What else could he say?

'Let us know if he gets in touch. And find out where your pal is – he was supposed to be here too,' they said, before dismissing him. They were playing it down, but there was a distinct air of fear in the questioning.

He had done well. Staying free and alive was a bonus in this racket; it led to status and respect. While the attack hadn't killed anyone, several Brits were hospitalised, and a Land Rover was put well out of action. It was considered a coup for the brigade.

Christy knew where Paddy was. He had called to his house the day before, to tell him they had been summoned. Liz greeted him with a frosty contempt and kept him on the garden path, looking up at her.

'Is he in?' he had asked, standing firm under the glare of her anger.

'No,' she said. There was silence.

'Tell him I'm looking for him,' said Christy.

Liz closed the door before the words left his mouth. When Paddy didn't show up that night or the next day, he knew he was out.

Christy wasn't out. He went alone to meet the two IRA

men; their approval reinforced his decision. But something was wrong. A word came into his head.

Tout.

Jumpy Joe had been seen in the back of a jeep as it drove through town. He was pointing people out and naming names.

As the days passed, the rumours were more elaborate.

A person 'in the know' had seen him at the barracks, along with two Special Branch. They were smoking fags and drinking tea. It was him for sure – definitely.

Joe's wife received a visit.

'It's bad enough he's left me with four children. Now I've you lot questioning me – like he ever told me anything,' she said to the heavies in her living room.

'It'll go better for you if you tell us where he is,' they said.

She dabbed her eyes with a tea cloth and pulled on her cigarette.

'He cleared me out, you know? Before this latest vanishing act. The money I had for the wains' Christmas, all gone. I wish someone would tell *me* where he is.'

She pulled on the cigarette again. The youngest child climbed down, off her knee.

33

Bernie found the letter when she was tidying and 'accidently' opened the drawer in Liz's bedside table. There it was, in its torn envelope, enticingly tucked within the pages of her diary.

The diary didn't interest Bernie; she'd thumbed through that already. This wasn't her first covert search for contraceptives.

University of Manchester: it was printed across the envelope. With a look towards the door, she lifted the letter out and read it.

'Miss McLaughlin,' it started. 'We recently wrote to you with a conditional offer of a place on English Literature Full Time, course 901E.'

She read that three times, before she got the gist of what it meant.

'We are pleased to say that you have met all the academic requirements. The commencement date for the course is 28th September.'

Bernie let the page drop to her knees. Oh, this was worse, so much worse, than the pill.

It was terrible, and wonderful. Her daughter was going to university, the first in the family. She always knew she was bright.

Lifting the letter, she read it again. It was dated two weeks earlier, so she must have received it last week. And Elizabeth had said nothing.

But why?

Perhaps she wasn't going? Oh, but she had to go, of course she had to.

'And sure, why would she tell me, the way I've been?' she

said. The letter shook in her hand as the tears started: Patrick was only back and now it was Elizabeth's turn. The house would never be the same.

A door slammed shut downstairs and she jumped off the bed, hurriedly stuffing the letter back into the drawer.

'Who's that?' she called, waiting for an answer. None came, then Jim's heavy tread was on the stairs.

'Jim, come in here,' she said, sitting on the bed again.

His head appeared around the door. 'What?'

'Look at this, will you?' She slid the drawer open and handed him the envelope.

'You shouldn't be going through her things,' he said, turning the envelope over in his hands. 'What's this?'

'Read it,' said Bernie. 'You might change your mind about that.'

He pulled his glasses from his trouser pocket and put them on. Then, holding the letter to the light of the window, he read it closely.

It took a minute for it to sink in. He looked down at Bernie, on the bed.

'She's got into a university – how did that happen? Did you know about this?' For some reason, his tone was accusing.

'Of course I didn't bloody know!' said Bernie, pulling the letter out of his hand. 'What are we going to do?'

'Well, she's going – I can tell you that. If I have to lift her, bodily, and put her on the boat myself – she's going.'

'I don't think she wants to go, Jim – she didn't tell us,' said Bernie, a quiver in her voice.

Jim sat beside her on the bed. 'She was always a smart girl, too smart to turn down a chance like this.' He took the letter back and read it again.

'I don't know if I want her to go,' said Bernie. Jim put his arm around her.

'We've always wanted the best for them, love, haven't we? This will be good for her.'

He took her hand in his.

'And, sure, we'll always have Johnny.'

'Oh, Christ!' she said, pushing him away with a laugh.

'You were going through my stuff?'

It seemed a matter of little importance to Bernie and Jim, who were waiting for her when she came home later that afternoon.

As soon as she was in the living room, they were on her. Her mother waved the letter at her like a flag, and her father sat in his chair expectantly; he was happier than she had seen him in months.

'You're going to university. In England,' said Bernie.

'You were in my room – going through my things,' said Liz. Her mother brushed that aside.

'Yes, I was in your room. Who do you think changes your bed – the fairies?' She wasn't going to apologise or make excuses. Her actions were those of a caring and responsible parent and she would not be criticised for them. She had rehearsed this response for the day when she would finally get her hands on the contraceptives she knew were stowed in there somewhere.

'This is just the best news,' her father was saying. 'Why did you leave it till now to tell us?'

Liz looked at him in disbelief. 'I didn't tell you – you went through my stuff!' she repeated.

Jesus, what else had they found? Her mother wouldn't be in there without having a good root around. Liz ran up the stairs, two at a time.

They had all learned, early on, that privacy was sought after in their house, and so were hiding places. If you were to hold on to anything of value, you had to be inventive.

She knew about Paddy's tin under the bed, where he saved his money and hid his dope from Johnny. He never seemed to notice the tiny nuggets of cannabis she nibbled off occasionally – she made sure to smooth the raw edge with her finger, so the little brown ball stayed round and worn.

As she was the only girl, she was lucky, having a room of her own. Sinéad's sister stole eyeshadow from her make-up bag, tights from her drawer. Liz only had her mother to worry about.

But she had taken her eye off the ball with the letter.

In the room, the tidy bed was the only sign that Bernie had been in that day. Everything was the same squalid mess it always was: each surface lightly dusted with face powder; lip gloss and foundation smeared across the dressing table, clothes everywhere.

A life-sized Jim Morrison was pinned to the wallpaper above her bed. Reaching up, her hand caressed his bare chest, across the taut frame stretched cruciform. She came to his right shoulder and felt the outline of the slim packet, still there, which she had pinned in place. Once again, Liz congratulated herself on her ingenuity. Her mother was rigorous, but not even Bernie would think to look behind a poster.

Downstairs, she faced her delighted father and less delighted mother once more. There were a million questions.

'I don't know whether I want to go,' she said. 'I can't decide what to do.'

Jim would have none of that. 'Of course you're going,' he said.

'But Daddy, I haven't applied for a grant and I've nowhere to live. It's probably too late.'

'Here – get yourself on that phone, and find out what you have to do,' said Jim. He pushed the letter at her, pointing to the number at the top of the page – 'Helpline', it said. Helpline, indeed.

She had wanted this for so long – two years, planning for a future. Now she could happily run away from the whole thing. She dialled the number and a man answered. His name was Trevor.

In his kind English voice, he explained where to apply for money and how a room in 'halls' would be kept for her, once she said for certain that she was accepting the place. His enthusiasm for her success reignited the desire in her and she heard herself tell him that, yes, she was accepting it.

'Well done, you!' he gushed. 'We look forward to meeting you – you'll have a great time,' he said, before she hung up. His happiness for her made her feel important.

Back in the room, Bernie and Jim were already discussing the Credit Union. 'He said that I can stay in "halls" for the first year,' she told them.

'Halls,' said Bernie. 'And where's that – somewhere in Manchester?'

'They're rooms, Mammy – rooms that the school keeps for their students, where we all live together,' said Liz.

She had said 'we' as though she was already there.

34

Christy knew what it was before his father had shuffled across the landing and down the stairs, before the bang on the door below. By the time the police arrived to take him in, he was already dressed.

At the McLaughlins', Bernie was in the kitchen. The thud on the door made her jump. She heard the growl of engines outside.

Paddy had come in three hours earlier, drunk and stoned. He woke in a sweat. They were lifting him out of his bunk before he could register that he was being arrested again. Johnny stood by his own bed, shivering, watching silently. There were voices throughout the house, in every room.

At the top of the stairs Paddy saw his father and their eyes met; he was pinned to the wall by a soldier, his face full of contempt for his son as he passed, followed by the rest of the raiding party.

There was no point waiting for Kevin to get in touch, not now when all plans with him were off. It was Manchester now, not London. On her own, not with him. Right?

His mother answered the door with a smile. 'He's upstairs,' she said. 'Kevin!' she called. The door upstairs opened, and Liz watched him descend. He didn't smile, didn't speak. Sensing trouble, his mother went inside, leaving them to it.

'I wanted to talk to you about something,' said Liz.

He didn't come close; he didn't even seem interested in what she had to say. She ignored this show of indifference.

'I got an offer from Manchester, and I've accepted it.'

'Right,' he said. 'When are you going?'

'The classes start on the twenty-eighth. I have to be there a week before.'

With his hands behind him, he leaned against the door frame, refusing to look at her. Instead, he bit his bottom lip and looked to the ceiling.

'Right,' he said again. 'So, is that us done? Are we finished?'

It seemed impossible that they had got here, to this huge gulf between them; he was cold beyond words. She didn't answer – his question answered itself.

'Our Paddy's been lifted again – three days he's been in. Me daddy's been at the police station all day yesterday, and this morning. They told him to go home.'

'Right,' said Kevin.

'Stop saying "right", will you? Don't you care that I'm going?'

Her eyes filled and, for the briefest of seconds, it seemed that he would come towards her, but he stopped himself. She reached up to open the front door, but Kevin wouldn't move out of the way.

'Excuse me,' she said, pulling the door hard and forcing him to give ground. Then she left without another word.

He'd considered himself lucky she would look at him – had planned to stay with her for as long as she would have him. Now Kevin was cold-shouldering her, because it was too hard to deal with the trouble that came with her.

He couldn't go back to night raids and fear.

Paddy had five brothers; where had they been all this time? Certainly not sitting in cars with their father.

They weren't being woken up, forced to offer refuge. No one was bringing a gun into their houses, like it was OK, like it was expected.

McLaughlin, in a cell; he wondered where? Getting a hard time, no doubt. Paddy, the fool who thought that everything was a big laugh.

You won't be laughing now, eh, Elvis?

They would use that, to goad him, humiliate him. What was his father thinking, giving him an enemy for a name?

35

Paddy stared at the flies as they circled the fluorescent strip on the ceiling, landing, then taking off and landing again. He shivered; they had given him a blanket that smelled of mould and shit; it lay unused in the furthest corner, as far away as he could throw it.

He could no longer tell if it was day or night, or how many days had passed since they brought him in. He had been processed, stripped, fingerprinted and put in this cell.

They took him down for questioning a few times a day, but mostly he lay like this, passing long hours under the glare of the light and listening to the constant noise of the building: doors banging, water running through pipes, footsteps and then silence – long stretches of nothing, not a voice, not a creak.

At some point in what he assumed was the early hours, the silence had been shattered by shouts, scuffles and the crunch of metal on metal, as a door slammed and keys rattled. In a nearby cell someone roared incoherently, raging against the police, demanding to be let out. No one came.

Eventually he went quiet or passed out.

The cops were harder than the army, much more direct in what they wanted from him.

They knew he was involved and they wanted names. Did he know Sean; did he know Danny? Who was in charge? Did he know Joe?

Had Joe been in touch – had Joe recruited him? What about the Buncrana Road attack – that was a bit daring? Who gave him the orders that night?

Paddy said nothing, but there was no bravado this time. They knew so much he began to think the rumours were true, that he was in very real danger. When they pulled him up the corridor and into the room, he sat with his head down and waited for it to be over.

There were always two: one asking the questions, the other pacing behind him. He threatened him with nudges, shoves, pulled his hair when he didn't respond. Paddy never saw his face but he feared him, flinching when he felt him close behind.

'Tell us who your contact was on the twentieth,' said the cop behind the table. When he refused to speak, the room swung sideways as he was felled by a fist, slammed into the side of his head.

He lay on the floor, stunned, until big hands lifted him and sat him on the chair again. The questioner continued as if nothing had happened, hardly missing a beat. Paddy had his head down again, hiding the tears.

Once more, the same questions were thrown at him and he felt the presence behind him, the heat on the back of his neck, and he tensed for a blow that didn't come.

'What about Meehan – is it him we should be talking to?' This was the first time Christy's name had been mentioned. Paddy looked up.

Bam! His face slammed against the tiled floor. Through the table legs he saw a pair of brown lace-ups and he hoped they would leave him there, on the floor. When they lifted him, he couldn't sit and started to tip sideways, falling off the chair again. Each time he was pulled vertical.

At last he was carried back to the cell where he lay, dazed, on bare boards.

Was anyone out there, he wondered, waiting for him, asking about him?

He imagined them sitting in bright light, his father somewhere in the same building but far away. And what if there was no one, if all his family were in their beds, his mother and father lying together, close and warm? Johnny turning over onto his side, looking at the empty bunk and turning back again.

The light went off in the cell and he was in darkness, so complete, so thick he was sure he could touch it; he held his hand out, waved it where he thought his face was, feeling the cold air against his skin as he touched his cheek, disembodied, blind. He followed the contours of his head to where the soft, swollen lump moved under his fingers as he prodded behind his ear.

His skull ached, and he lay still, to contain the room as it spun. Why didn't the flies buzz, he thought? The light buzzed, but the flies lifted and alighted, with quick movements and no sound. Vomit rose in him again and he crawled to the end of the bench and brought up a bitter bile, all that remained in his stomach.

Christy's father had begged the police to let his son out. Granny Christine was in hospital and they knew she was close to the end. He contacted a solicitor to intervene on their behalf and finally, late on the second day, he was released without charge.

His father waited outside with his older brother. Christy's dad was sober and unshaven, Martin red-eyed. When Christy saw them, he laughed; never in his life had they shown this much concern. But when his father put his arms around him, he knew something terrible had happened – something worse than two days in the cop shop.

'Your granny passed away this morning, Christopher,' said his father. That was all.

They went back to the house; not their own, but hers. There was a wake to get ready. Someone sat Christy down in front of a plate of food, but he couldn't eat. He went to a room at the back of the house, wanting peace, to be left alone. The house wasn't full yet, but old relatives began to gather, paying their respects and asking about the arrangements. It was a taste of what the next two days would bring.

Mrs Cullen, the woman from next door, sat beside him.

'She was telling us all about you last week. Her wee grandson that had brains to burn. She was that proud of you.' He said nothing as she squeezed his hand before going back to the kitchen.

'Did she say anything before she died?' he asked his father.

'She was too far gone, Christopher. Mrs Cullen found her on the floor of the kitchen. She didn't come round again. They had her all connected up to machines, but there was nothin' they could do. She was just old.'

He remembered the last time he had seen her. He was with Paddy, of course. She stopped him in the street, gave him a couple of pounds, slipped into his palm with a conspiratorial wink as she squeezed his hand. She looked after him and he never thanked her; wasn't there to say goodbye.

The men of the family brought her from the morgue the following day, and the house filled with people and didn't empty. He waited for someone to come for him, to shake his hand and say they were sorry for his loss: Liz, Paddy, Noel. But no one did.

A few Provos turned up, some of the younger boys, lads he had done jobs with. They shuffled through the crowd to the coffin in the sitting room and looked down at his granny, laid out with the Sacred Heart pinned to her chest and a veil covering her face.

After a respectable length of time they shuffled out again, to stand awkwardly, holding cups of tea outside the house. They were full of information; most of the senior staff had taken a short holiday over the border, out of the way, while the rumours remained strong about Joe.

'He's a dead man,' they said, drinking their tea and solemnly smoking their fags as people passed them on their way in.

Bernie sat up through the night, smoking. She passed the Rosary through her fingers without saying a word of a prayer. She drank tea, gave the grate a clean-out and polished the fire surround until it shone. Jim came downstairs, ready for work, at six thirty and she rose from her seat at the window to make him breakfast.

'They're going to let him out today,' she said.

'They'll either let him out or charge him,' said Jim, sipping his tea.

'Don't go to work,' she said.

He shook his head. 'I can't miss another day, love.'

He had sat in the lobby of the station for five hours the previous day. It was a busy place; people buzzing themselves through doors, the officer at the desk answering calls, phones ringing constantly.

'He's in custody – you're not going to see him. Go home, sir,' said the desk sergeant in his hard-edged country accent.

Today he had no choice. Come what may, he couldn't afford to lose another day's pay.

The key turned in the door. Paddy's mother had him in her arms before he could close it again. Her scent, her warmth, covered him.

'I'm all right, Mammy,' he said.

An hour earlier, blinding light had flooded the cell, and keys rattled as the lock was turned. When the door opened, a policeman entered.

'Up you get,' he said. Paddy sat up slowly, but the cop hadn't time to be patient. 'Come on,' he said, lifting him by the arm.

They went to the desk, where he was given his belongings and put out into the pale morning.

'What time is it?' asked Paddy. The desk sergeant pointed to the clock on the wall. It was six a.m. He walked unsteadily down the steps. The steel door buzzed, and he was out in the street. No one waited for him.

His mother looked at the bruise on the side of his face and ran her thumb across it.

'I'm sorry, Da,' he said.

Jim had stayed by the fire, pulling on his work boots. 'They haven't charged you, then,' he said.

Paddy shook his head.

'I'm going to work. You be home when I get back – we're having a big talk, you and me.'

Bernie followed Jim to the door. 'What are you going to say to him?' she whispered.

'I'm going to be late,' he said and left. When she went back, Paddy was asleep, curled up in the armchair. Those bruises on her child's face; she brought a blanket down from her bed and laid it over him.

Five hours later, he woke.

The fire blazed and the TV was on. He stayed under the blanket, watching George and Zippy arguing over a watering can and a pot of fake flowers. After a few minutes, he looked over his shoulder. Liz was on the sofa, reading the newspaper.

'Do you want tea?' she asked. He wiped the saliva from his face and sat up.

'Where's me ma?'

She handed him a mug and a buttered bap. 'Out – you're not allowed to move until she comes back.'

He ate the bap and drank his tea, and did not move. On the television, someone had zipped Zippy's mouth shut.

'Anything interesting happening?' he asked.

'Me and Kevin are finished,' she said. She seemed very matter of fact about it. 'And Christy's granny died. The funeral's tomorrow.'

'He loved his granny – she bought him his leather jacket,' said Paddy. Poor Christy. 'Was he lifted too?'

'I have no idea,' said Liz. 'I read it in the paper – that's how I know about the funeral.'

'What happened between you and Kevin?' he said, laying his head back on the armrest.

'Nothing,' she said. But he was sleeping again.

'Patrick, your dinner's ready.' Someone shook him, and he sat up in the seat; the television was still on.

Now everyone was in the room, all his family. Children sprawled on the carpet, eating dinner. Carl's youngest ran a toy car along imaginary roads in the woven pattern. Liz stepped over him, with her dinner in her hand.

'Bring the wain out here, Carl – he can eat with me at the table,' his mother called, from the kitchen. Carl picked the child up by the waist and carried him out, coming back with a plate of his own.

'You're some craic,' he said, as he sat down.

'What?' said Paddy.

'Putting me ma and da through hell – dickhead.' He tucked into his dinner, forking piles of mash into his mouth.

'Leave it,' said Gene, from the other side of the room. He bit into a sausage. 'From the looks of him, the cops did a better job than you could have.'

Paddy went to the kitchen and sat between Jerry and the boy, at the table. A plate was put down for him.

The child rolled his car between glasses of milk and the salt cellar. Every few minutes, Bernie reached over with a spoonful of mush and he opened his pink mouth obligingly, tilting his head back like a bird in the nest. 'Good boy, Conor,' she said after each mouthful.

Jerry, the eldest brother, waited until their mother was out of earshot.

'You need to tell us if they have anything on you,' he said quietly.

'I'm done with all that,' said Paddy. 'I don't know why I let myself get involved in the first place.'

'Did you say that to the cops?'

'I said nothing at all, not even when they hit me – don't tell the parents that. No, if they had anything, I wouldn't be sitting here now.'

Jerry went back to his dinner. 'They're talking about sending you away, you know? To Aunt Patsy's in Liverpool.'

Paddy put his fork down. 'For Godsake,' he sighed. 'I can take care of myself.'

His father got home and Liz was ordered off her seat, to let him sit. She came to the kitchen and took his dinner out of the oven.

'I'm not going to Patsy's,' he said to her. 'We were supposed to be going away together, you and me.'

'You'll go where I tell you!' shouted Jim, from next door. Liz brought him his plate, holding it carefully in a tea towel.

'Why can't he come to Manchester, if I'm going anyway?' she said.

'Because he's an idiot and he needs to be watched,' said Carl helpfully.

'I'll be there on my own – no one'll be watching what I do,' said Liz.

'What, is the big love affair over?' said Johnny. His mother took the tea towel and swiped him across the head with it.

'Fuck off, Johnny,' said Liz.

'Hey . . . language, miss,' said her mother, aiming another swing at the back of her legs where she stood.

'I'm not going and that's the end of it,' insisted Paddy.

There was a knock at the door. 'Get that, Róisín,' Bernie ordered, and one of the older girls went to answer it. The adults sat in silence, as Jim finished his dinner and drained a glass of milk.

'There's someone for Elizabeth,' said Róisín, closing the door to the hall behind her. She slumped on the floor by the television again.

Liz went out, expecting Sinéad; it was Kevin who waited.

'What do you want?' she said. An unexpected feeling of warmth surged through her.

'Is Paddy out?' he said.

'Aye, he's in there,' she said.

'That's good.'

They stood in silence.

It wasn't over; she knew it as soon as she saw him. Still, he had something to say to her, something she needed to hear. She waited.

There were the beginnings of a plan brewing in the back of her head, maybe one that would suit everyone. But first Kevin had to tell her they had a future. She was giving him a chance, if he was prepared to take it.

'Liz,' he said at last. 'I am really, really sorry. Are we over? It's not what I want.'

That was enough for her. 'You haven't spent the money, have you?' she said.

'Some of it – why? Do you need it to go away?'

'No, but you might. Come here.'

She pulled him into the house and for the first time, Kevin saw all of the McLaughlins in one room. A row of faces, all a variety of blended Bernies and Jims, looked back at him. He was acutely aware of his unwashed and hungover appearance.

'What if Kevin comes too?' Liz said to her father. 'What if he comes to Manchester with us? Then he and Paddy can get a place to live together.'

Counting on Jim's regard for Kevin was a long shot. Most decisions could be overruled with a word from her mother.

She kept going. 'They could get work, Daddy, and Kevin is older. He can make sure Paddy's OK, right?' At this, she looked at Kevin for support.

'Aye,' he shrugged, trying to keep up. 'I suppose so.'

'You're not going over there to live in sin, young woman,' said Bernie.

'Mammy, I won't be – I'll be living in halls, with a crowd of girls,' said Liz.

It was perfect.

'If Kevin's willing, then I'm happy with that,' said Jim, silencing Bernie with a raised hand.

'I thought you two were finished?' said Johnny.

'Aye – well, we're not,' said Liz, smiling at Kevin.

36

Father Devlin walked around the coffin, the censer swaying in his hand, and the heavy, sweet scent of comforting incense drifted over and around it, blessing the body, asking for redemption and forgiveness.

Christy couldn't cry. As the priest intoned the final words, he hated himself. He had taken for granted the woman who held the last tenuous threads to his mother. He was a fraud, unable to mourn because he had let her down.

His father and brother moved into the aisle. His father beckoned to him. Together with two uncles, they lifted the coffin on their shoulders. His brother's arm draped over his, forming a bridge between them. His cheek pressed against the wood; the resinous scent clung to it. He felt the weight of the body shift inside, as they moved through the church and then outside.

In the sunshine, the coffin was taken from them and placed in the hearse. Christy waited by it, watching relatives and friends shake hands. His father, in a suit and tie, was thanking people for coming. Everyone wanted to talk about Christy's mother.

'Your Ann was a lovely girl,' they said fondly, shaking Christy's father by the hand.

'I know,' he replied. 'It broke her mother's heart when she died. She's been missed every day.'

It was strange to hear his father talk about her, to hear her name mentioned. Ann.

There was a hand on his shoulder. He turned around.

Before he realised it, someone was hugging him. It turned out to be Liz, and then Orla and Sinéad, in turns. The three of them had obviously cried their way through the service and were red-eyed, their faces streaked, dabbing fresh tears away with damp tissues. Behind them, Kevin reached out and shook his hand.

'Sorry about your granny, Christy,' said Paddy. 'We couldn't get to the wake. Me ma wouldn't let me out of the house.'

'That's OK – thanks for coming. Some craic though, all this?' He hadn't believed they would come, any of them.

'She would have liked it that you wore the jacket she got you,' said Liz.

Christy looked down at the scuffed leather, immediately blurry and choked with emotion, and found he couldn't speak.

'You're all right, mate,' said Kevin, embarrassed. 'Paddy, give him a fag, for Godsake.'

37

They were leaving in a week, earlier than Liz needed to. A friend with contacts in England had set them up with a bedsit.

The timing suited Jim and Bernie; the sooner Paddy was out of harm's way the better. Liz told them the university had let her move in early.

'They do it all the time, Mammy.' They didn't need to know that halls wouldn't be ready for at least two weeks.

Paddy had taken to staying over at Christy's, sleeping on the floor.

One night, from nowhere, he said, 'I wonder what happened to Jumpy Joe – have you heard from anybody since?'

It was the first time he had raised the subject; he didn't want to risk it all kicking off again.

It was hard to remember that there was still a hunger strike going on, in a prison somewhere near Belfast. It dropped down the news agenda, overtaken by the tabloid fascination with newly-wed Royals and New Romantics. The families remembered their own importance, that they had some control over events. They refused to comply with the wishes of their starving sons, denying them a martyr's death and ordering the doctors to intervene as each lapsed into coma. Outside the prison, all but the hardened few had long realised it was over, before it was.

'No,' said Christy.

He wasn't going to England, and had been subdued since the funeral. He, too, was reluctant to talk about it, to stir the anger and shame he was carrying.

And now, as his friends were beginning a new life, he was left to contemplate Derry, alone and abandoned. There was no prospect of him uprooting immediately and leaving with them – no one was hitting the CU for a wee loan for him.

At that moment, neither of them wanted to recall how, for a while, they were soldiers, commandos, Fianna.

'Hey,' said Paddy finally, lying with one arm behind his head and a smile on his face. 'We learned new skills.'

The night before his friends were to leave, Christy was at home with his father.

Since the funeral, he had looked at his father differently. He was the man who had failed them, the waster who drank whatever they had. And Christy had been an angry and unforgiving child. But at the side of the hearse he had seen a man in pain, whose worst sin was his inability to cope with the death of his wife when he hadn't been much older than Christy was now.

His father rustled the paper in his hands; a bottle of stout sat on the floor beside him. He needed a shave, as always.

'Your beard is getting grey, Da,' he said. His father smiled and rubbed his hand across the bristles. He looked older than his forty years, damaged by drink and the effort to stay alive.

There was a knock at the door. When his father didn't stir, Christy opened it to a man in his late teens.

He didn't know him. The lad had been given his address and was there with orders, to be in a certain place at a certain time. The message was abrupt, the assumption was that nothing had changed. Of course, the change had happened only in his head. No superior in the brigade knew that he had already left. Christy closed the door in the messenger's face.

Inside, his father was still reading, his glasses dropping to the end of his nose.

264

'Who was that?' he said, when Christy returned to his seat.

'Nobody,' said Christy. He felt his father's eyes on him.

'Is that you done with all that?' he said. It was the first and only time he had ever addressed his son's involvement, asked him about it, or even made it known that he knew of it.

'Aye,' said Christy.

His father put the paper on the floor beside the beer bottle and left the room. A few minutes later, he returned with an envelope. He held it out to his son.

'You'll be wanting this,' he said.

Christy took it from him; his name was written on the front and it was sliced open at the top. There was money inside.

'It's not from me,' said his father. 'We found it in your granny's, when we were sorting through her things. She meant that for you, Christy. I think she was saving, to give you something when you went away to university. Anyway, it's yours.'

He had little time to get ready, get a bag, get clothes. He would have to do with what he had, which wasn't much. But first, he had to let them know he would be coming with them, if that was all right.

Liz's entire wardrobe was laid out, ready to be packed. Paddy had shoved his belongings into a holdall, roughly what he had taken that morning when he ran away to war. There was new underwear, of course, and socks and pyjamas from his mother.

They felt her agitation; it shivered through the walls of the house.

'You two be good,' she had told them, at least five times that day. 'You're a reflection of this house and you remember that.' Like they could forget.

Each had packed the Novena she forced into their hands. Paddy wondered what he was expected to do with it.

'Just take it and say nothing,' said Liz, before he could open his mouth.

Christy told them his news, brimming with excitement. Jim looked doubtful when he heard he too was going.

'Maybe it's the chance the boy needs, to grow up?' said Bernie.

He would meet them at the bus stop in the morning.

'Don't leave without me,' he said.

Jumpy Joe, jumpy as fuck, but he hadn't squealed. He had lost his bottle.

He had emptied the money jar hidden on top of the kitchen cabinet, and put himself on a bus going west into deepest Donegal.

As the rumours tore through the organisation in Derry, Joe was to be found nursing pints of stout, in an old man's pub in the wilds of Gweedore; tapping fags and living off war stories in return for more pints. He wasn't going home to her and the wains – not until the money was gone, anyway.

The real tout was a cleverer man by far; impeccable in his credentials, trusted by all. He recruited, facilitated, organised. No one knew that he had been compromised, threatened with annihilation, unless he gave generously and frequently of his valuable inside knowledge.

It wasn't hard to convince him; his handlers were experts in their craft. They had evidence, enough to send him down for twenty years. And if he didn't comply, it was easy to put a gun to his head and finish him, then denounce him as a tout anyway.

Even a martyred brother couldn't stem the liquid fear they set coursing through him. He had no loyalty to the man who had survived when Ciaran had died, no care for the friends who were too stupid to look after themselves. And a gun, abandoned – that would cause minimal harm.

He had waited in the shadows when the gun was dumped in that gold-coloured car; it was he who drove it away, the stolen car reported by no one.

He had scooped the gun in a blanket and dropped it inside a barrel, sunk in the earth, beneath a hedge on the edge of town. With a single phone call, he was off the hook for at least three months; it was enough time to plan an end to this nightmare.

When it was examined and analysed, there were fingerprints all over it, one set from the boy who forgot to wipe it down in his rush to get rid of it.

Kevin, Paddy and Liz carried their bags through the town, filled with a nervous charge that gave everything around them a shimmering, rare quality.

Christy's father waved to him as he left the house with his bag full of books and clothes. He had time for a detour.

The flowers from the funeral were withered and the clay had yet to settle. He read the gold lettering on the headstone:

'In Memory of Ann Meehan'

A wooden cross had been stuck into the soft clay, a temporary marker, with his grandmother's name scorched into it: Christine Donnelly.

'Thank you,' he said aloud, looking at the cross and feeling foolish now that he was there. He looked at the rows of headstones that climbed up the steep hill, trying to remember the place where, somewhere, Peter Harkin lay. Then he turned, picked up his bag, and walked into town.

He almost made it.

He got as far as the crossing at the bottom of William Street before they picked him up, pulling him into the black interior of the police jeep.

★

They tried to make the driver wait, but there was a schedule to keep. As the bus pulled away, Paddy watched from the window, at the buildings and streets as they passed, at the grey surface of the river as it rippled and churned under the touch of a breeze.

They followed the Foyle until they came to the bridge and crossed over, leaving the city behind.

1996

In her kitchen, in the morning, she put on Captain Beefheart and laid the newspaper across the table, so that it filled the entire surface. Then, with a mug of tea in one hand and a slice of toast in the other, she began reading.

Things hadn't changed so much. There was always a football or darts team, and a priest handing them a trophy, smiling, black-coated.

There were two pages devoted to wedding photos: brides and grooms, buttonholes and flowers. There was the line-up for a charity run, and a report on campaigning for the elections to the city council.

She read about the search for Miss Derry, and found herself appraising the teenage girls surrounding the lucky winner as she balanced her crown on top of her perm, delighted with herself. Miss Creggan was better-looking by far.

Her mother still sent her the local paper. It arrived with a thud on the doormat at the beginning of each month, rolled in a fine paper cover. The address was printed in her mother's hand, in thin blue ink. She never asked for it – it was her mother's way of keeping her home.

She avoided the page where the death notices were, until there it was, as her mother had told her it would be. Seeing it in print didn't help make it any more real. Her friend was gone.

She ran her finger down the long column of names and traced his – Christopher Pius Meehan – and the three lines that said nothing of how he had died, only the arrangements and the names of the bereaved. She stared at it for a long time.

Captain Beefheart jangled from the CD player.

The first time she heard the Captain she was sitting on the floor in Christy's house. Kevin and Paddy were there, and maybe Sinéad, although she couldn't be sure.

It was Christy's latest buy, and she remembered how Kevin sat with the cover in his hands, how he read every note and turned it over and over, so obviously envious that it was Christy's and not his.

They were all very stoned. Paddy lay on the floor, mocking the rough voice and howling like a dog along to 'Dachau Blues'.

She made no comment, but her teenage ear had not been prepared for the chaos, the lack of melody or the growling lyric.

They didn't often go to Christy's house – it was always too cold. Where her home was comfortable, and full to the point of suffocation, his was empty, the furnishings dead, neglected, unwarmed.

They sat in his bedroom where his bed was unmade, and his walls lined, like everyone's back then, with pictures cut from the music papers. What she remembered now were the books he had, neatly piled beneath the window: school textbooks, comics and novels, mostly stolen. The tattered paperbacks were thoroughly read, and she had lifted *Slaughterhouse-Five* from the top of the stack, to leaf through it.

'Do you want to borrow it?' he had asked her.

They were a gang back then, Sinéad and her and Orla – best friends. And the boys; their friends, brothers, lovers, a self-contained unit, until everything changed.

She saw him last summer, when she and Kevin took the boys home for a visit. Heavy drops of rain were bouncing off the cover of the buggy as she pushed James up the hill to her parents' house. And there he was, coming towards her with his familiar walk, hands in pockets. She stopped to speak, and he stopped too, and she felt his reluctance immediately.

But it was unthinkable to pass him without saying hello, so she made some remark about the rain, asked how he was. He wouldn't look at her. This had never happened before. All the while, as he was speaking, he was moving away from her, there under sufferance as though it pained him. And they had always been friends, comfortable with each other, comfortable enough to fight and forgive, never needing a reason, never needing an act.

In those few minutes in the street, as the child lay sleeping in the buggy, and the rain started to come down heavy – even as it happened, she observed the absence between them. *He won't look at me, he won't look in my eyes.*

She had blamed herself, of course, no longer believing that she was interesting enough for him. When they parted and she walked away, it never occurred to her that he was hurt, too – that he was in danger.

She looked down at the paper where her hand lingered. Her fingertip smudged his name as she moved it away. Captain Beefheart was still playing and Liz rose from the table.

She turned the music up.

Acknowledgements

There are a few people I would like to thank for all their support and encouragement in bringing this book to life.

Firstly, Áine McCarron, my first and best reader; if you weren't so nice I would have given up on the whole writing carry-on years ago. And Siobhán Curley, who sent me the link to the WriteNow project and changed my life. Thank you both.

To Juliet Annan at Fig Tree, who found this story among all the WriteNow applications and loved it almost as much as me. She is the best and I am very lucky to have her as my editor. And, of course, Cathryn Summerhayes at Curtis Brown. I can't express my gratitude to these great women.

To Siena Parker, who has coordinated the WriteNow programme since its inception. She has been an advocate and a friend. And, of course, my eleven fellow mentees: Benjamin G. Wilson, Nazneen Ahmed, Emma Jane Smith-Barton, Katie Hale, Rebecca Pizzey, Elizabeth Jane Burnett, Nelson Abbey, Charlene Allcott, Emma Morgan, Chris Brougham and Manjeet Mann. The Class of 2016! I have so much respect and love for these wonderful people and wish them all the success in the world.

There are so many people in Penguin Random House to thank: the very classy Assallah Tahir at Fig Tree; Mary Chamberlain, who made copy-editing fun; Natalie Wall, with whom I shared a macaroon; Louisa Burden-Garabedian and Ithaka Cordia, from the WriteNow team, who took great care of the writers when we met. And everyone else who has done their very best for me.

I want to thank Joe England for approaching Mr Linton Kwesi Johnson on my behalf. I am honoured to have his lyrics reproduced within these pages.

Working on this novel was a bit like time travel, back to a misspent youth in the company of the best people and the Cave, where, essentially, I grew up. They are the inspiration for this story. They know who they are.

Finally, and most importantly, thank you, John, for taking care of me while I worked long shifts and wrote on my days off. Without your help and understanding, and your extensive musical knowledge, none of this would have happened. It's as much your book as it is mine.

And Damian, Kathleen and Maeve, our children. The best thing we ever achieved.